This Ain't That

by

Michelle D. Dartis

Dedication

This book is dedicated to my one and only progeny and first inspiration, Kelli Noel, my one and only grandchild Trinity Na'Kayla Michelle, my parents, Alfred and Evelyn, my sisters Pamela and Gina, and my longtime homie Monique.

Acknowledgements

There have been many hands, minds, thoughts, and feedback at play in the development of "This Ain't That" (TAT) over the years and I am truly grateful for all of them. I want to thank my first professional editor based in Atlanta, Georgia, Grace Wynter. Her expertise, candor, and due diligence really helped me fine-tune my story, even when we didn't always see eye-to-eye. I am forever in her debt and appreciate her in every way.

Shoutout to Mr. Jamie Martindale! Jamie was my high school psychology teacher and later became my unofficial editor, friend, and champion. I have always appreciated his easy-going demeanor, kindness, open-mindedness, and expertise (he's a writer, too!).

My bestie Monique Holland is another contributor to TAT. We met our freshman year at North Central High School and went through A LOT together over the years, had our ups and downs, but she has proven herself to be a guiding light, a super friend who is also gracious, giving, and selfless. Thanks for always having my back through the good, the bad, and the ugly.

All respect and appreciation to my book cover designer, Gabrielle Prendergast of Loudspring Digital/CYD Designs. Thank you so much for helping me bring my idea to fruition. Your input and know-how were invaluable.

To all those cheering me on from the sidelines, providing financial support along the way, and accepting my request for TAT's Facebook page, I appreciate you all! Thanks for hanging in there with me and for your understanding as I juggled finishing TAT, pursuing my doctoral degree, caring for my elderly father, and teaching college courses.

Inshallah,

Michelle

About the Author

Michelle's passion for writing was noticed at an early age when she found herself writing on just about any and everything including bed sheets, walls, and furniture. She began keeping a journal at eleven years old and continued this practice well into adulthood—and she still has all of them!

As with writing, Michelle has always enjoyed reading. Some of her favorite authors include Audre Lorde, Alice Walker, E. Lynn Harris, and Terry McMillan. Though she is an adept academic writer, she gets much more pleasure from exploring creative writing where her bawdy thoughts, schemes, and mindlessness can freely run rampant.

She teaches in higher education and is a freelance writer and independent historian. Some of her past work can be viewed on BlackPast.org, *The Indianapolis Star*, and the American Library Association's Rainbow Round Table Book and Media Reviews. Michelle holds a bachelor's degree in social work and three distinct graduate degrees in library science, higher education with a specialization in leadership for student success, and human and social services. Presently, Michelle is in the dissertation stage of her doctoral program in Human and Social Services.

Michelle is the recipient of various awards, including the Indiana Librarians Leading in Diversity MLS Fellowship Project and the American Library Association/Spectrum Institute REACH 21 Scholarship Initiative. She has over twenty-five years of professional experience in mental health, developmental disabilities, sexual assault counseling, case management, and teaching.

She is the mother of one adult daughter, Kelli, and is the proud and doting MiMi to 4-year-old granddaughter Trinity. She resides in her hometown of Indianapolis, Indiana with her two cats, brothers, Cairo and Tanis. A self-proclaimed Daddy's girl, she is also the primary caregiver to her 83-year-old father.

In her spare time, Michelle delights in spending time with family and friends, watching her favorite shows such as *Queen Sugar, The Daily Show, Ozark, The View, First Wives Club, Insecure, L Word: Generation Q*, and *Godfather of Harlem*, reading, writing, discovering new adventures, watching or playing tennis, dancing, swimming, working out (at least sometimes), attending cultural and musical events, and traveling (something she definitely wants to do more of!).

*UPDATE: 11/13/2022: After publishing my novel last year, I was initially very excited for 2022 to begin as I had plans to promote my novel in as many ways as possible and finish my doctoral program by the end of summer. Sadly, life had other plans. I encountered a total of six deaths since January 2022. The passings started with a first cousin, then my mother a few weeks later in early February. The next one broke me, my dearly beloved father took his last breath on April 18, 2022. A good friend I met at church years ago succumbed to cancer a few weeks later. My granddaughter's paternal grandmother was called HOME in May at just 51 years old. My half-brother was the last one in June. My world got turned upside down and inside out. I was absolutely devastated, and everything came to a jolting STOP. I was mourning the losses and had zero energy to do much of anything for several weeks. As of today, I am on my healing journey and have done the work to get there. I am back on track with my dissertation and promoting TAT. I'm looking forward to what 2023 has in store for me and everyone else in the world!

Author's Reflection

Writing has been a passion of mine for as long as I can remember. I was the kid that wrote on any and everything, including sheets, furniture, walls, etc. My mother used to quip, "If you stand still long enough, Michelle will even write on you!" That wasn't far from the truth. My very first published article, "Former teen mom wants to buck up others in same boat" was published on April 6, 1997, in the *Indianapolis Star*. My article described my journey with becoming a teenage mom and was directed at other young women who found themselves pregnant at an early age. Becoming a mother early does not mean their life was over before it had even started…that we as young moms still could dream, plan, and go after what we wanted in life. This opportunity also solidified my passion and interest in writing for years to come. "This Ain't That" (TAT) is a story I began writing off-the-cuff back in the early 1990s. My inner voice spoke to me and said, *Michelle go over to your computer and write.* So that is exactly what I did. That first attempt resulted in about eight pages of what I would later title, "This Ain't That." For more than twenty years, I picked it up and put it down for myriad reasons, including my academic pursuits and raising my daughter as a single parent.

The one thing that was always clear to me, though, was the realization I would eventually complete my story. I believe in never giving up on a dream and I believe everyone has a story to tell. I am very pleased to share mine with the world and it is my hope you as the reader enjoy my story and writing style.

Disclaimer, Copyrights, Book Cover Design Credits

Disclaimer

Though very loosely based on the author's life experiences, this novel's story and most of the characters are fictitious. Certain long-standing institutions, incidents, events, agencies, and public offices, venues, and spaces are mentioned, but most of the characters involved are wholly imaginary.

Book cover Design - Gabrielle Prendergast, Loudspring Digital/CYD Designs.

Leave A Mark
PRESS

ISBN: 978-0-578-30364-2

Prologue

Milk-chocolate complected and standing at 5′8 and around 160 lbs., Cleo Stinson is thicker than a Snicker in all the right places, 44-years-old and single. Like a lot of women, she has the innate desire to have the quintessential lifestyle that includes a loving and faithful husband, the white picket fence, a dog, and 2.5 children. However, as her life unfolds, she experiences a transformation that sends her on an unexpected and life-changing journey…

Set in 2016 in Indianapolis, Indiana, Cleo begins to experience a sexual attraction to a colleague. It comes as a complete surprise, and not just because her colleague is married with children. The object of Cleo's desire is smart, sophisticated, and intelligent. And she's also a woman. When an incident at work confirms the attraction is mutual, Cleo sets out on a journey of self-discovery, uncovering desires she didn't know she had. Along the way she must navigate romantic entanglements with the opposite gender, keeping her secret from family and her best friend, Shelby James, all while fighting to keep the job she loves. But when Cleo's quick temper threatens to reveal her secret, will her world tumble, and will she lose the love she thinks she's just found?

Unique Terminology

Earth disturber or E.D. - Someone who is always on game, a troublemaker, drama queen, enjoys stirring up chaos and confusion. Source: urbandictionary.com.

KAO - Kisses all over.

LYLAS - Love you like a sister.

LZ - Landing zone, as in you are crowding me or you are crowding my space. Source: urbandictionary.com.

Wusband - Wusband is a word comprised of *wife* and *husband* that describes a masculine-of-center female (stud or butch) who is in a committed relationship or marriage with another female.

⚢ 1 ⚥

"Good morning, Cleo. Are you ready to get this party started this bright, sunny Monday morning?" asked the always chipper Pepper O'Brien, Exodus's longtime receptionist.

Cleo playfully glowered at her. "How is it that you're always in such a good mood?" She glanced at the black-and-white clock hanging on the wall, directly above Pepper's head. It was just past seven o'clock in the morning. "I'm just amazed. How do you do it, girl?"

Pepper ran a freckled hand through her thick, frizzy, fire-engine-red hair. "Oh, Cleo, you are something else! Now, you know I've just always been blessed, and I'm so happy to be here on God's green Earth for another day."

"Yep, indeed. You never waver from that line, or some variation of it, so long as it contains *God*." She threw her hands in the air and shook her head.

"Well, the best I can muster is an 'I'm here and that's as good as it gets'."

"All right now, I'll take that. Oh, yeah, how did things go with Javon last night?" Pepper took off her matching, red-framed eyeglasses and handed Cleo a few messages.

"Ugh." Cleo rolled her eyes in distaste. "Pepper, he is really getting on my nerves. I don't know why I continue to deal with him after all these years."

"Yeah, but did he come through like he said he would?"

Cleo watched Pepper lean forward on her thin freckled forearms on her desk, eagerly waiting.

Despite her obvious annoyance, Cleo found herself smiling. "I mean, yeah, he did make it over …"

"Oh really? Do tell," Pepper implored.

Cleo shifted her feet. "OK, well, not to give away the juicy details, but, yeah, he put it down as he always does and we had a good time, but, well … it's just not enough for me anymore."

Shaking her head, Pepper gave Cleo a reassuring look. "I get it, Cleo. I know he has disappointed you countless times."

Both of their eyes were drawn to the office telephone switchboard as it lit up.

"I know you gotta take that, but thanks, Pepper. That means a lot, it really does. Enjoy your day, dear."

"Thanks, you too," she said just before answering the incoming call.

A tidal wave of emotions engulfed her when it came to Javon. There were moments when she loved him deeply, fiercely, only for him to go and fuck up by cheating or disappearing on her. This kind of behavior went on at various times in their tumultuous relationship that had been going on for more than eight years, and she was at her wit's end.

Cleo walked down the narrow, dimly lit hallway. Despite the early hour, seeing Pepper sitting at her receptionist desk was comforting, like a warm, fluffy blanket: familiar and inviting. Every morning, when Cleo walked through the door at the Exodus Resource Center for Mothers and Babies, Pepper was there with a bright smile to greet her. Cleo adjusted her work bag on her shoulder, then rounded the corner and headed toward the elevator, happening upon Mister Sexy himself.

"You're looking absolutely ravishing, Ms. Stinson," Reese Maxwell said in his velvety voice. The old, rickety elevator made a rattling noise when it stopped at the first floor, and, ever the gentleman, Reese stood to the side. "Ladies first."

Cleo smoothed out a wrinkle in her pleated black skirt and smiled. "Why thank you, Mr. Maxwell. You aren't looking too shabby yourself." She stepped onto the elevator, and he followed closely behind her.

"I love the color of your blouse, Cleo. Isn't that what you women call 'cobalt blue'?"

Cleo grinned. "Why, yes, it is cobalt blue," she said, nudging him in his well-chiseled upper arm. "Look at you, knowing your colors."

Reese shrugged. "Well, what can I say? I grew up with four sisters, so …"

"It's no wonder, then." Cleo shifted her feet, batting her eyelashes at him.

Reese held her gaze for a long moment, and she wondered if he was having the same kinds of thoughts she was. Cleo had finally made up her mind to speak when the elevator screeched to a halt on the second floor, erasing all other thoughts from her head.

"As always, it was nice chatting with you." Reese took a step back. "After you," he said, inviting Cleo to walk out of the elevator.

"Thanks, Reese. Enjoy your day!"

"You too," he responded, heading in the opposite direction.

Suddenly, Cleo felt a slight tug in her belly. *Is he watching me from behind?* She pretended to accidentally drop her rain jacket onto the worn green hallway carpet just so she could stop, bend over and look toward him. *Hmmm, yeah, just like I thought, he's got those puppy dog eyes glued on this round ass of mine sitting up in this A-line black skirt.*

"Oops," Cleo said. Slowly, methodically, she reached down to retrieve her jacket, all while keeping her eyes locked on his. She could see Reese standing just past the men's bathroom door, staring in her direction, arms folded with a toothy grin.

Cleo batted her long, dark eyelashes and waved. *Yeah, that nigga wants some more of this.* She laid her rain jacket over her right forearm and readjusted her skirt. She decided to stop in the break room for a refill of coffee when she happened upon her secret crush, a female colleague by the name of Kennedy St. Martin.

"Good morning, Kennedy."

"Morning, Cleo. How are you doing?" Kennedy had just finished filling her cup.

Cleo was hypnotized by Kennedy's striking good looks.

"Are you alright?" Kennedy asked, laying a thin, manicured hand on her shoulder.

My God, why is this woman so damn fine? "Yes, yes, I'm okay," she said breathlessly.

Kennedy flashed a smile. "Came in for a refill, huh?" she said, nodding toward Cleo's empty coffee mug, before looking into Cleo's eyes and holding her gaze for several seconds.

Cleo looked away. She wasn't sure what to make of it, but this wasn't the first time she'd been on the receiving end of Kennedy's penetrating gaze.

Was it possible Kennedy recognized something that was forbidden or taboo like the forbidden fruit Eve indulged in thousands of years ago?

"As long as you're okay."

Before Cleo could reply, a few others walked into the room.

"Yes, I promise, I'm okay." She gathered her composure and made a beeline toward the coffee pot.

"Good. I hope you have a nice day."

"Thank you. You do the same."

An overwhelming feeling washed over Cleo whenever Kennedy was close; her lingering gaze enveloped her whenever they made eye contact. But it wasn't the feeling that was so astonishing. It was the fervor that shot down her spine and landed somewhere between her legs. It was the fact that she was, for the first time in her life, experiencing *that* feeling for another woman.

****

Coffee in hand, Cleo made her way down the hall to her office, which was abuzz with the chitchat of the charming, new fiscal department head, Cole Crawford. Much of the commotion had gone right over Cleo's head until she saw him stroll out of the executive director's office. He was truly the sexiest man who had ever walked through that office—and that included Reese Maxwell.

There's going to be a catfight over that handsome hunk of a man, Cleo thought, rummaging in her purse for the key to her office door. She imagined a few of her coworkers—Tuesday, Reginald, better known as Regène and since her transition last year—dressed in silky boxer shorts, tight tank tops and red-brick-colored boxing gloves going at it vigorously until the last man, or in this case, the last woman fell.

Aw, damn! I meant to take out the key while I was on the elevator, she said to herself, forgetting all about the interaction she'd had with Mr. Maxwell. She slid the key into the doorknob, then heard a cheerful roar down the hall from her.

"Hey girl, are we still on for tonight?" Cleo turned toward the sound of her colleague and best friend's voice. Shelby James walked toward her, statuesque as ever, her clear complexion glistening like honey. Her auburn ringlets bounced as she walked, grazing the shoulders of her heather-gray pantsuit.

The women walked into Cleo's office and were greeted with a warm hue of lavender on the walls and newly laid carpet in a light shade of rose dust.

"Girl, you know we gonna do that tonight." Cleo opened the left desk drawer and placed her purse inside, then planted her rear in her leather office chair that was beginning to show signs of age.

"I'm still mad that I had to cancel last week due to having to finish up those reports."

"I hear ya," Shelby responded while stretching her long, sleek body across the weathered leather sofa across the room from Cleo's desk.

Cleo powered up her desktop computer, then picked up the messages Pepper had given her earlier. Moments later, Cleo's cell phone rang.

"Damn. Hold that thought, Shell. It's Javon."

Shelby shook her head and continued wiping away her tears.

"What do you want, Javon?"

"Why you answer the phone like dat? You soundin' all mean and shit! You wasn't actin' like that last night when I had them sexy-ass legs up in the air and my face buried in that phat pussy of yours."

Cleo squirmed in her seat. "Um, anyway, what do you want?

"Well, I know you're at work 'n' all, but I just wanted to take a few minutes to let ya know how much I enjoyed you last night. That nighttime snack was great! My compliments to the chef."

"Well, you're welcome. Look, I'll get back to you later, okay?"

"All right, baby. Have a good day an' I'll be thinkin' 'boutcha."

"Okay, bye." Cleo hung up.

"What did he want?" Shelby asked.

Cleo didn't feel like going into detail about why she'd been with him last night. Shelby couldn't stand Javon, ever since the first time he'd broken Cleo's heart just over seven years ago.

Cleo began thumbing through client folders stacked in front of her. "Oh, nothing really."

"Shit, you already know how I feel about his ass, anyway." Shelby rose from the couch, walked over to the mirror hanging on the wall and checked her makeup. "You need to drop him like a bad habit."

"Oh, now, don't you start." Cleo took off her reading glasses and placed them on the folders. "I know full well how you feel about him, but he's unimportant right now. Let's talk about what is important: lunch. How does Culver's sound?"

Shelby smoothed out a wrinkle in her top and touched up her muted chestnut lipstick. "All right, girlie. I'll check ya later alligator!" Shelby replied as she headed for the door.

Cleo giggled. "In a while, crocodile."

****

After Shelby left, Cleo's mind wandered to the carefree, happy days of their childhood. She and Shelby were thirteen when they met in 1983. They spent many summer days just hanging out at Shelby's because her home was THE PLACE to hang. She and her brothers had everything. They were the first to get cable, and Atari, too. You name it, they were the first ones to get it. They were pretty well off for a black family back in the day. Just as she was about to get back to reviewing her staffing hours report, she heard rapping on her office door.

"Come in," she replied.

"I'm in need of a midday snack, please," Reese said, licking his full and tantalizing lips.

Cleo took off her reading glasses, smiled and said, "Oh, are you now?"

"Yeah, I'm hungry," Reese replied, shutting the door and locking it behind him.

This wouldn't be the first time they did something naughty at their workplace, but that only added to the forbidden adventure.

Cleo felt the heat rising between her thighs as she rose from her chair. "Well, okay, then, let me see about accommodating you," she said, unbuttoning her trousers and walking toward the sofa on the opposite side of her office. Reese was already on his knees waiting and anticipating.

Cleo bent down and faced him, staring into his yearning eyes. She thought about the last time he'd eaten her pussy. His long, slim but mighty tongue went to town, taking her on a whirlwind voyage filled with alluring erotic thrills and shrills while he licked and tongued her down the nape of her neck and dipped his tongue in and out of her crevices. She was not one to turn down a good tongue thrashing, uh-uh, no siree!

Reese helped her finish undressing from the waist down, all the while still using his wet tongue in every way imaginable, spreading her legs open wide and diving into her now very moist pussy, her womanly scent wafting in the air, engulfing them both.

"Damn, girl, you are so fucking intoxicating, " he exclaimed in between slurping up her juices. Cleo sat halfway on the sofa, braced herself with her forearms and giggled.

"Yeah, I know, my scent is very intoxicating." She breathed in her own seductive myrrh. Her aroma always did make her hot as well. "Ummmmm, ahhhhhh, ohhhhh," she managed to let out in low, soft grunts, serving up her vagina like a smorgasbord for one.

This escapade went on for close to half an hour when Reese finally came up for air, panting feverishly. "Thank you," he mumbled, eventually rising from his knees.

Cleo was spent, having explored the galaxies on her eighth climax … at least she believed it was, but she lost count after her fifth. She sprawled her body onto the sofa, writhing from all those climaxes, looking on as Reese pulled himself together, then went and grabbed disposable towelettes from her desk drawer. Cleo always made sure she had some. Reese winked at her while he slowly licked all her remaining cum juices from around his happy mouth. After completing his mission, he strode over to Cleo and landed a big wet kiss on her lips. "Can't wait to do that again," he said vivaciously.

Cleo sat up from the sofa and began putting her disregarded clothing items back on. "Shit, me too, sugar."

"I'll see you later, Miss Stinson," he said, his hand on the doorknob.

"Yes, sir, you surely will." After he left, Cleo's mind began to wander, as it often did. *Damn, there's just something about that man that gets me going, at least sexually, but I really can't see it being any more than that. I mean, he's cool and all and he can eat the hell out of my pussy, but I don't see anything real coming out of us hooking up from time to time, even though he's expressed numerous times that he wants more from me. And then there's the question about my own sexuality.*

I can't lie to myself. Lately, I'm finding certain women sexually attractive. But where is all this coming from? Kennedy is most definitely on my radar … I wonder if she's feeling the same way. Those looks she gives me may be an indication, but I just can't be sure, at least not yet.

Cleo sighed, staring down at the paperwork lying in front of her. Well, I guess like everything else in this world, time would tell.

****

As one of the department managers at the Exodus Resource Center for Mothers and Babies, many of Cleo's duties were tedious at best, which included disseminating information for her monthly report, finalizing staffing hours for payroll, reviewing new case files, notifying the Department of Children's Services and the courts about any changes with clients, and summarizing her department's affairs. Cleo had spent much of the morning on the monthly report, and before she knew it, it was time for lunch. Sifting through the heap of staff schedules, client data sheets and lead coordinator checklists on her desk, Cleo uncovered the phone and dialed Shelby's extension. "Hey, sister-friend, what's on your mind for lunch? I'm starvin' like Marvin."

Giggling, Shelby responded, "Meet me in the lobby."

⚢ 2 ⚥

They arrived at Culver's at a quarter past twelve. The parking lot was so crowded they had a hard time finding a place to park. After circling the parking lot several times, they came upon a souped-up hunter-green Mustang pulling out of a parking space. Curious, Cleo sneaked a peek at the driver, a beautiful woman with a butterscotch complexion, long, sweeping locks and eyes so mesmerizing, Cleo felt as though she could see straight into her mind and all the secret desires stowed away deep inside.

It seemed an eternity went by as they checked each other out. Suddenly, Cleo's heart skipped a couple of beats. *Wait just a damn minute, is that my clit jumping?* She clenched her thighs together in a feeble attempt to settle down the clitoris that was now pulsating in the same way it did when Javon gave her head. *What in the hell is going on here?* She rummaged through her handbag in search of something to wipe the droplets of sweat that had formed on her forehead. Why was this woman looking at her *like that*? Even more importantly, why was *she* giving this strikingly attractive woman the eye? Cleo wasn't so sure she wanted to know.

"Hey, could you hurry it up, please! I need to park!" Shelby yelled, jerking Cleo back to the present.

She felt almost ashamed of the naughty thoughts that ran through her mind in those fleeting seconds. And, like a bat out of hell, the sexy feline and her sharp-ass chromed-out hunter-green Mustang sped out of the parking lot.

"Uh, why was that woman staring at you *like that*? Do you know her or something?" Shelby asked, a perplexed look on her face.

Regaining her composure and damn glad Shelby didn't ask her why she was staring back, Cleo responded, "Naw, girl. I've never seen her before in my life. I don't know what that was all about. Maybe she thought I was someone else. You already know how often people approach me thinking I'm their cousin, long-lost friend or something."

Cleo prayed Shelby bought her explanation because she was not ready to delve into that cloaked part of her fantasies, even though she was now having them on a regular basis. But what would she say to her lifelong best friend, the one person she'd never hesitated to talk to about anything? How could she explain she was finding herself more and more attracted to the same sex, or more specifically, alluring, vibrant black women? She'd never realized just how becoming they really were. Still, the thought seemed so outrageous.

"I don't know what I have a taste for now. Are you still gonna get a chicken salad, Shelby?" asked Cleo.

Shelby was scanning the order board; it wasn't long before her gaze became transfixed on the Butterburger Value Basket Meal.

"You know, seeing that picture of that juicy-looking burger just changed my mind. Girl, forget that chicken salad, I'm going to order a number two with cheese and a Diet Pepsi. Yum, I can taste it now! Culver's has the bomb burgers. Besides, we're going to work out tonight. First, I'ma jog a few laps around the track, then I'll cool down on the roll-master."

"Well, I'm not in the mood for a burger. I'm gonna go with a roasted chicken sandwich, medium fries and a sweet tea."

Waiting patiently for their lunch, their eyes wandered around the restaurant as customers bustled in and out of the chaos. Cleo took notice of a very pregnant Hispanic young woman with almond-shaped eyes that alluded to the fact she was dog-tired. Her stomach was protruding so much Cleo felt sure she was going to give birth at any moment. Four children loudly talking and laughing were in tow behind her.

"Mommy, I have to go to the restroom 'cause I cain't hold it!" said the cute, pig-tailed little girl with skin as smooth as butterscotch pudding. She looked like a burst of sunshine in her plain saffron-colored sundress.

"Yeah, Momma, I gotta go too, before I pee on myself!" exclaimed another child who looked to be about seven. His complexion reminded Cleo of the Toll House semi-sweet chocolate morsels her mom used back in the day to make homemade chocolate chip cookies.

"Didn't I tell y'all to go to the bathroom before we left home?!" the mother yelled. "Now, y'all can see how crowded it is in here. It's gonna take forever to get back in line!" She huffed loudly as she trotted to the bathroom, with her kids in tow doing their I-gotta-pee-really-bad dance.

Even though she had yelled loudly enough to be heard in China, no one paid attention. Instead, they were all too busy gobbling down their lunch, yapping on their cell phones or chatting up the customer next to them. It always was amazing to Cleo how people caught up in their own lives were seemingly oblivious to their surroundings or other people.

"Did you hear what I said, CeeCee?"

"Huh? I'm sorry, girl. That mother yelling at her kids distracted me. Now, what did you say?"

"Our food is ready for pickup at the other end of the counter."

"Oh, okay." They walked through the thick crowd to get to the other side.

"Excuse me, sir." Cleo was growing agitated by being so close to other people, especially the two homeless men who were standing by the server with their food orders.

"Orders for numbers eighty-eight and eighty-nine?" asked the fresh-faced server.

"Yes," Cleo and Shelby said in unison as they retrieved their bags. "Thank you."

They threaded back through the crowd.

"Ma'am, do you have some spare change?" It was one of the homeless men.

"No, sorry," Cleo responded as she did not break her tread.

Luck was on their side when they came upon a table that was just vacated by a white elderly couple. It was close to one o'clock. Though the restaurant was still quite full, dozens of people began filing outside, undoubtedly in a race to get back to work.

Cleo shook her head as she began eating her sandwich. "The nerve of that homeless man, and he smelled awful," she exclaimed.

Shelby settled in the seat across from her and opened her entrée. "Don't go there—we don't know what the man's circumstances were that got him to this situation, Cleo," she reprimanded.

Cleo turned her nose up. "Oh, uh, okay. Excuse me, miss thang, but you know how I feel about those people."

"Those people? Are you for real, Cleo?" Shelby said with disdain. "Okay, we're gonna end that convo right here." She took a bite of her fries. "So, what do ya think of the new fiscal head?"

Looking perplexed, Cleo thought for a moment.

"Well, I did get a pretty good look at him earlier today. Hmmmm, I must say he is fine as wine, girl. Those sexy-ass dimples and hazel-grey eyes had me thinkin' naughty thoughts. You know pretty-eyed men always made me melt like butter. And let's not even go down there," Cleo said, looking down toward her crotch with a wicked smile.

"Girl, whatchu talkin' about?" Shelby's almond-shaped eyes grew wide with anticipation. "Oh, wait just a damn minute, don't tell me he made your panties wet, too!" They both broke into a cackle, sounding like two old, nosey hens carrying on about the new man in the office.

Cleo leaned forward. "Hey, let me tell you. I saw him walking out of Jim's office. Girl, he is a fine one; a tall glass of water, about six-four, broad shoulders, neatly manicured mustache, bald, and his complexion reminds me of Denzel's. It was obvious why he got so much attention from the ladies in the office this morning."

Shelby's eyes began to glisten. "Owwwee! I know them witches were checking out my future husband. They need to step off 'cause I got first dibs on that piece of ass! I heard he moved here from Atlanta, and he got his master's degree from Kush University, he's never been married and—"

"Well, damn! At first you made it sound like you didn't know much about him and now you runnin' off the man's bio to me!"

Shelby laughed and said, "Girl, I know. Well, you can probably guess who gave me the scoop ..."

"And who might that be?" Cleo asked, barely able to contain herself from busting out laughing because she already knew the answer.

"It was Katrina Williams in the human resources department. You know it don't take much to get information from her."

Cleo nodded. Over lunch, Shelby rambled off the rest of Cole's personal business. Not only did she have a lot of it memorized, but she'd also written down all the important details. Though Cleo thought she'd gone overboard with getting all up in the man's business, she kept quiet. She knew it would lead to an unnecessary argument, and frankly, she was not in the mood. Through the years, they'd had numerous squabbles, especially about Shelby's choices in men.

⚢ 3 ⚥

They arrived at StarWing Health Club around six-thirty. Shelby was clad in a deep purple jumpsuit. Her bouncing ringlets were now gently pulled into a loose ponytail. Cleo decided to sport a pair of simple lime green workout shorts and a top.

StarWing opened just a few months earlier. The hype had been that once it was completed, it was going to be the latest state-of-the-art health club facility in town, complete with an indoor and outdoor Olympic-sized pool, three saunas and four jacuzzis. It was hard for everyone to contain their excitement about StarWing and what it had to offer.

Upon the grand opening, it was apparent it was all that and then some. The main entrance was magnificently crafted with cathedral ceilings and the walls were painted in a muted but soothing shade of green. The entryway contained compelling artwork by local artists Leanna Conway and Austin Timberland.

"Let's start out taking a few laps around the outside track, okay?" Cleo asked.

"Okay, sounds good to me," Shelby responded.

"All right, the last one out the door is a rotten egg," Shelby shouted as she ran out.

Fast on her tail, Cleo shouted, "Aw, hell no! No, you didn't just do me like that! Okay, you wanna get all ugly and thangs, that is A-OK with me. You're gonna pay for that trick!"

"LYLAS! LYLAS! Girl, you know I'm just messing with ya," Shelby giggled as they took off around the track.

The track was almost empty. But after about twenty minutes, two rather nice-looking men joined them. Suddenly, one of them hollered, "Cleo! Cleo! Is that really you?"

Craig Brown's swaggering voice was unmistakable. Cleo jerked her head around. There he stood: six-foot-seven, cocoa brown complexion, deliciously thick frame, complete with broad, manly shoulders. And the two exclamation points: captivating tiger eyes and one of the most exquisite dicks she'd ever laid eyes on, or her mouth, for that matter.

Instantly, Cleo drifted back to the night they first met. It was a hotter-than-July night out at Picadilly's. Even though they all were under twenty-one, Cleo, Shelby and Janice 'Jai' Daniels had all been able to obtain fake IDs. They were so over the young, inexperienced BOYS, that they agreed they were mature enough and ready to hang out with grown men. To get their freak on, dance on and anything else on, the place to be was Picadilly's.

****

There she was, dressed in her favorite come-fuck-me outfit, sauntering across the floor, on the prowl for her next unsuspecting victim.

"Hey, hey, wait up a minute!" A voice called out from the crowd over Zapp's 'Computer Love' blaring from the surround-sound speakers.

"Hey, didn't you hear me? I'm talking to you!"

Looking back, Cleo eyed the sexiest man she'd ever seen in her life. Gasping for her next breath, in a high-pitched voice, she asked, "Are you talking to me?"

"Well, yes, ma'am. Didn't you see me waving at you?" asked the dubious gentleman.

Cleo shrugged her shoulders, a look of innocence plastered on her face. "I am so sorry. I didn't hear you over the music. How can I help you, er… what's your name?"

"The name is Craig Brown. I am very pleased to make your acquaintance. And what, may I ask, is your name?"

Blushing, Cleo whispered, "Cleo. Cleo Stinson. So, is this your first time coming to Picadilly's? I don't think I've ever seen you here before."

"As a matter of fact, this is actually my second time coming to this club. I visited Naptown about a month ago, mainly to hang out with my frat brother from college and to check out some job prospects. I must say, I was pleasantly surprised to discover your city has a lot to offer and the cost of living, well, let's just say it is one of the most affordable cities I have ever visited. I absolutely love downtown.

There are so many venues, clubs and restaurants, and most of them are within a few blocks of each other. One of my favorites is a cozy place called Rick's Boatyard on the west side. Have you been there before?"

"Yes, as a matter of fact, it's also one of my favorite places. Their dinner bread is the truth!"

The twosome spent the rest of the night staring into each other's eyes, immersed in their own little world. It captivated Cleo that they had so much in common. He loved to read and write. So did she. He grew up playing tennis. So did she. They vowed to get together the next day for a game. It was so rare to come across a black man who not only played tennis in the neighborhood where he grew up, but the mere fact that he still enjoyed playing made Cleo even more interested. Who knows? This man could possibly be my future husband, my baby daddy, Cleo thought to herself.

It was a whirlwind affair. He was the honey to her buttered bread. She fell so hard for him. They tried their damnedest to spend just about every waking moment together. Already, a month had gone by, and yet, they still had not had sex. However, they'd done just about everything else, from penetrating tongue kisses to the oh-so-sensuous suckling of her breasts to the tantalizing feeling she got every time he entered her with his skillful fingers. Cleo's body was yearning to feel every single inch of his enormous dick. The way he so effortlessly fingered her sexy, erect nipples made her screech with ecstasy.

Already, a month had gone by, and yet, they And, oh, the first time they made love … words simply couldn't describe the intensity of this man's lovemaking. We're talking mind-blowin', got-me-so-sprung-I-can't-see-straight, toe-curlin', make-ya-wanna-slap-yo-momma and all that shit …

****

"My, my, my. It has been a long time, Mr. Brown. How have you been?" Cleo asked while accepting his embrace. As she stepped back to look at Craig, she noted that he was dressed in a blue and white Adidas sweat suit and matching running shoes, sporting something totally different from what she remembered: a bald head and goatee. When they were an item, he had a full head of hair and she spent many a day washing and braiding. He was not afraid to try different braided styles, just like his favorite basketball player, Allen Iverson. They'd spent countless nights watching Iverson take on all those other players who were much bigger than him, though you would have never know it the way he played. Craig used to always say Iverson had heart, that he played ball for the love of the game and not just for the paycheck.

"I've been missing you. Wow! Let me take a look at you. Some things never change, stunning as always. We've let too much time get away," he said, eyeing her up and down.

"Well, something has changed with you," Cleo said as she reached out and touched the top of his head.

"Oh, yeah," Craig laughed as he nudged her on her side. "Well, you know how it goes with us men. I started balding at the top and I was not about to be like some of them other cats out here tryin' to hold onto the little hair they have or combing it forward or sideways in a feeble attempt to escape the inevitable."

"I know that's right," said the shorter gentleman with a black-as-coal complexion, dimples and a thousand-watt smile.

"Oh, my bad, man. Cleo, I would like you to meet James Connor."

Cleo accepted his handshake. "Hello, Cleo. It's nice to meet you."

"Likewise, James."

"Hey everybody," chided Shelby.

"Well, hello, beautiful. It is a pleasure to meet you, Shelby," James said as he gazed upon her shapely body.

"Thank you, James, so sweet of you to say," Shelby said, blushing.

After the introductions, they decided to walk a few miles on the track together. Cleo observed how Shelby and James were getting well acquainted with one another during their stroll. She hoped Shelby would think about the mantra from the old days when Judge Ephriam presided over *Divorce Court*:

"Look deep before you leap." Shelby had always been too quick to jump into relationships, and Cleo really didn't want to have to come to her rescue once again.

"So, it looks like a love connection has been made, huh?" Craig suggested.

Cleo shook her head. "Um, well, I guess so …" She looked at the twosome several steps ahead of them.

Craig jumped in front of her. "Uh oh, I know that look. What's up, what, you ain't feelin' my boy, already?" He defensively folded his arms.

"Naw, it's not that, Craig … it's just that, well …"

Boy, this just got awkward, she thought.

"Come on, spill it, CeeCee, what's the problem? I mean, I don't know James that well, but I believe he's a good cat."

Cleo rubbed her forehead. "Look, I'm not saying I have any reservations about James because I don't know him, but I do know my BFF and she tends to, let's say, jump head-first into relationships without thinking. So, I'm just a little concerned, is all."

"Ah, I see. The protector, I get it," Craig lamented. "But, eh, they're grown and you gotta trust that she'll be alright, OK, boo?"

Cleo noticed him eyeing her once again, causing her knees to buckle a little. She mustered up a weak grin and winked at him.

"Okay, enough about them. What's up with you? Got a man or fuck buddy?"

Cleo laughed out loud. "Wow, getting straight to the point, huh?"

"Hey, might as well not beat around the bush, right?"

Cleo noticed something gleaming for the first time. "Is that gold I see in your mouth, Mr. Brown?" It was his turn to giggle. "Why, yes, Miss Stinson, it is," he said, then began fingering the shiny tooth. "I was wondering how long it was going to take for you to notice it."

About a year ago, I lost my real tooth playing basketball, got elbowed in my jaw when I darted for the ball that was going out of bounds."

"Oh, wow, bet that hurt like hell, huh?" she asked, fingering the same tooth in her mouth that he lost.

"Yeah, it did, but it ain't no biggie," he responded while he rubbed the sandy-coated textured hairs on his chin. He draped his arm around her shoulder. "Now, let's get to the real deal, about when you gonna let me taste them sweet juices again?"

Cleo batted her eyelashes, unsure of how to respond. "Oh, wow, that came out of nowhere."

Craig leaned in and whispered in her ear. "Baby, I know I made some mistakes and wasn't the man you needed or the one you deserved back then. I think about you all the time, and if you're willing to work with me … give me another chance to show you I've changed, I would be so grateful." He gently kissed her neck.

Cleo pushed him away. "I just don't know about all that, Craig … I mean, well, you know what happened, what you —"

He shushed her with his thick, index finger against her glossy lips. Cleo took notice that he'd recently paid a visit to their favorite nail salon, Monicure Palace.

"Saw Monica recently, huh?" Cleo asked, nodding toward his immaculate hands.

Craig grinned. "Yes baby, I did. She's still the bomb-diggity with the nails. But back to what you were saying, honey, let's not go there, okay? We're turning over a new leaf. Beginning anew." He threw his arms into the air.

Cleo contemplated for several seconds. *Well, I ain't never been one to turn down some head, so ... but no. I'm gonna have to pass this one up.*

"Look Craig, for now, we can just exchange numbers. You good with that?" Cleo watched his shoulders slump.

"Okay, okay. I hear you. I ain't happy about it, but I get it and I respect it."

"Good. It has been a while since we last saw one another. It'd be great to catch up."

Cleo observed a smile spreading across his handsome face. "Agreed, that sounds wonderful."

She looked deep into his twinkling eyes, remembering the good times they had together so long ago and how they came close to jumping the broom as young lovers.

⚢ 4 ⚥

"Can we please focus on the real issue here?" Cleo asked.

"And what do you think the real issue is, Cleo?" Cleo's new boss, Samantha Merriweather, asked as she crossed her arms and settled into the tattered, gray office chair.

Holding back the urge to roll her eyes, Cleo swallowed hard and took five deep breaths (as her mother had instructed her to do whenever she was feeling the urge to say something inappropriate) before answering, "Well, from reading the case notes, I noticed immediately that Ms. Tennyson is feeling very overwhelmed with everything she's going through right now, and it doesn't appear she has any help from family or friends."

"OK, we already got that much. Now, what's your solution? How can we help this mother and her four small children and inform the courts of any new changes or updates?"

Coughing could be heard from the opposite end of the table. "Excuse me, but may I interject something here?" Shelby asked as she leaned forward so everyone could see her face.

No one said a word but instead nodded their heads.

"Samantha, you may recall that I, along with our new intern, Caitlyn, visited Ms. Tennyson just a few days ago," Shelby said.

"Yeah, and?" Samantha asked.

Giving her one of those *looks*, Shelby continued.

"Anyway, as I was saying, Ms. Tennyson seemed very distraught when we arrived. I don't think she remembered we had scheduled a home visit. But once we put her at ease, she seemed to be more receptive to conversing with us. The children appeared to be well behaved and were clean and neatly dressed. Turns out she has an aunt in Kentucky, and they have been in contact recently. The aunt is thinking about moving here, at least temporarily, to help Ms. Tennyson get on her feet. I've been so busy with my other cases that I have not had the opportunity to update her case file."

Looking dumbfounded, Samantha replied, "Oh, I see. Well, keep us posted when you learn of anything new with her. It appears we'll be able to close this case sooner than what we initially thought."

Uh oh, do I detect the remnants of a smile on her face? Cleo watched Samantha as she stood up and gathered the remaining agendas. *Well, I'll be damned, it is. The ol' bat actually permitted her thin lips to curl into a version of a smile.*

"That's good news. I have a stack of new cases from DCS to assign on my desk as we speak. Expect an email from me in the next few hours. Dismissed."

****

"Damn! Why does she have to be such a bitch all the fuckin' time?" Cleo said as they stepped into Shelby's office. It was more of a statement than a question.

"Girl, I know. Did you see all their faces?" Shelby closed the door. "Nobody likes her anymore. She's become more of a bitch than ever since she got the promotion." Shelby dropped her notebook and several files onto her desk and plopped down in her chair. "She acts like she got a stick up her ass. Or perhaps her husband ain't hittin' it right. And, of course, she waltzes into the office every day like she's all high and mighty now, too. She needs to stop for real 'cause it ain't that deep."

Leaning back into her worn black leather chair, Shelby said, "Girl, I still can't believe they passed you over for that coveted position. You deserved it way more than that snob."

Cleo sighed. "I really thought I had it in the bag. But as the saying goes, everything happens for a reason, so I ain't gon' trip on it. Besides, I've been thinking about starting a job search or maybe pursuing that doctorate I've been putting off. I've been here so long and after being passed over again, I don't think I can continue to work for this agency much longer. There was a time when I thought I would retire from Exodus.

But lately, I've been thinking more and more about pursuing something else, especially with all the changes and new forms DCS and the courts are demanding from us."

"I know, right? Every time we turn around, they've changed something on the paperwork. It's so fucking annoying. I can't blame you for wanting to leave at this point. Maybe it's time for both of us to move on, see what else is out there. You know, to change the subject, I didn't get the chance to tell you about what's going on with James and me," Shelby said with a sly grin.

"Oh, yeah, but hold that thought. I'ma get back to my office and finish up 'cause I'm tryin' to get out of here on time today. Hey, what do ya say you come over for dinner tonight so we can have a for-real girl talk about James, men in general, life, family?"

A slow smile spread on Shelby's face. "That sounds good to me. Guess I'll just follow you home after we get off then. Now that I think about it, it has been a while since we engaged in *girl talk*. It's way overdue."

As she headed for the door, Cleo said, "Yeah, you're right. Just come down to my office at four-thirty. I should be good to go by then.

"Okay. See ya then."

****

Hearing a knock on her office door, Cleo raised her head from the report she was reviewing.

"Shelby, why are you knocking on the door? Girl, you are so silly sometimes, get your ass in here."

"Um, no, Cleo. It's Kennedy. May I come in?"

Cleo felt the tiny hairs rise on the back of her neck. After hearing her unexpected yet enticing voice, Cleo quickly whipped out a convenient hand-held mirror from the top left drawer of her desk and feverishly checked her hair and make-up.

OK, Cleo. Snap out of it. Just because you've fantasized about her tonguing you down don't mean a thing since it never really happened. The woman is married with children.

"Oh, please come right in, Kennedy. What can I help you with?"

Kennedy turned the rickety doorknob and walked into Cleo's office. She had the kind of chiseled beauty that made her the envy of all the ladies in the office. Standing at six feet tall, raw sexiness danced in her dreamy oyster grey eyes, a body reminiscent of Foxy Brown—the original one—and long, edible-looking smooth caramel legs were a testament to her undeniable yet reserved comeliness. Without even trying, she commanded attention when she walked into a room. Indeed, not only did she turn the heads of her male colleagues, but also the women.

Cleo had long admired her easy nature, open smile, and willingness to help her colleagues. Hell, it wouldn't have surprised Cleo at all if other so-called straight women that fantasized about Kennedy lickin' them up and down, too.

"Well, um, I, I was wondering what you thought about Samantha's antics earlier today."

No. There was something else going on in her mind. Cleo could tell by the way that she looked when she first walked in.

"Hmmm, now that is an interesting question, Kennedy. But you already know I don't care about engaging in gossip at work. The walls are paper thin and you just never know who may be listening in on our conversation."

"I know … I know you don't get caught up in all that tomfoolery, Cleo." Kennedy shifted uneasily in her chair. "But it's just that I was really taken aback by her behavior and the things she said and the *way* she said them. It made me wonder how it made you feel since everyone knows that position should have gone to you anyway. You deserved it. She didn't."

"I appreciate the vote of confidence, Kennedy. I really do. But the decision has been made and I have accepted it and moved on." Cleo found herself almost squirming in her chair.

Despite herself, she turned her attention toward her window. Sashaying towards the small retention pond was a family of geese. Cleo could see one of the babies was having a hard time keeping up with the rest of the crew. It reminded her how sometimes she felt like that lone duckling in life, the feeling of being left behind. Unimportant. Insignificant.

"I kind of figured that would be your response because that's just the kind of person you are." Kennedy leaned forward and opened her mouth to go on, but nothing came out.

"Seems as though you have something else on your mind, Kennedy." Cleo diverted her eyes back to her. "Is there something else I can do for you?"

This time, there was no mistaking it. Kennedy got up from her chair and sauntered over. Before Cleo could utter another word, she felt Kennedy's oh-so-soft lips press against hers, followed by her hungry tongue sliding into her mouth. Instinctively, she opened wide to receive Kennedy's long, lustful tongue, and for what seemed like an eternity, their tongues delighted in a carnal dance. They relished in their private dance, fondling mountains of heaving breasts, winding freeways of thick thighs, and sumptuous hills of prime derriere. Cleo was alarmed and amazed. Sharing in their intimate moments of pleasure seemed as natural as sliding into a pair of jeans. Neither of them gave thought to the possibility of getting caught while frolicking in Cleo's office where at any time ANYBODY could walk right in on them.

After a while, Cleo ruefully withdrew from Kennedy's embrace and took a gasp of air. The sweet aroma of Kennedy's perfume tickled the wee hairs in her nose as they stared longingly into each other's eyes. Just as they finished adjusting their clothes and wiping mocha crème and red alarm lipstick off their faces and necks, Shelby came bouncing in the door laughing hysterically.

They both looked like a deer caught in headlights, but luckily, Shelby was oblivious, she was too enthralled in whatever it was that had her laughing so.

"What's so funny, girl?" Cleo wanted to make sure Shelby hadn't taken notice of what had just taken place before she walked in. She was damn glad she withdrew from Kennedy when she did. She shuddered with fear thinking how she would've explained to Shelby what was going on with her and Kennedy St. Martin.

"Girl, you wouldn't believe the joke Reese just told me and Pepper. That man is not only fine as hell, he's also full of some funny-ass jokes! Oh, hey there Kennedy."

Shelby was so busy laughing that she hadn't noticed Kennedy standing a few feet away from Cleo.

"Hey, Shelby," Kennedy replied or, rather, whispered, as she nervously smoothed out a wrinkle on her peach-colored blouse.

Shelby's curious amber eyes dodged back and forth between Cleo and Kennedy a few times, which made Cleo's heart race a hundred miles an hour.

Oh, God! Oh, God! Please, please Shelby, don't ask any probing questions with your nosey ass.

"Was I interrupting something, ladies?"

"No, goofy ass," Cleo said quickly. "Kennedy came by to see how I was doing after that fiasco earlier this morning with Samantha's high and mighty ass."

That's my story and I'm sticking to it, dammit. Well, it was partly true. I mean, she did inquire about how I was feeling.

Cleo let go a sigh of relief as she saw calmness blanket her best friend's face. Thankfully, rigidity gave way to a relaxed posture.

"Oh, I see. I really can't stand that bitch either, Kennedy. She gets on my last nerve, too. And I'm fed up with that uppity attitude she's been carrying around ever since they gave her that position she didn't deserve."

"Okay, okay. Please don't get her started. I had to listen to her earlier ranting and raving about Samantha. I ain't tryin' to go down that road again." Reluctantly, Cleo eased away from Kennedy and took her seat in her tattered chair. Secretly, Cleo marveled at Kennedy's arresting beauty and the stolen intimate moment they shared a short time ago.

"Well, ladies, if you're anything like me, you're ready to get out of here for the day."

As she stepped toward the door, she took her well-manicured hand and brushed a few golden-hued strands from her exquisite oval-shaped face.

"All right, Kennedy," Cleo said as she slowly came out of her trance. "Have a good night and see ya tomorrow."

"Yeah, see ya tomorrow. And don't forget about our strategy meeting at two o'clock with Jim, okay?" Shelby asked.

"Oh, yes. I have it penciled in my calendar. Thanks for the reminder, though. Good night."

"What's up with Kennedy? She seemed shaken when I came in here." Shelby hopped up on Cleo's desk instead of sitting her ample backside in a chair. Cleo looked on as Shelby's ears appeared to perk up like a feline, eyes bulging as if she were waiting for a treat. "What were you two talking about? Did she confide in you about something? Have you heard the rumors going around about her? Oh, God. I hope they're not true."

"What are you talking about?" Cleo found herself getting defensive but wasn't sure why.

"Well, you didn't hear this from me, but you know Katrina in HR, right?" Shelby was obviously enjoying herself. But, then again, she always did love being all up in someone else's business.

"Yes."

"Well, her cousin Bam Bam's girlfriend said that her sister Ari, who's gay, by the way, saw Kennedy at that lesbian club over on Emerson about two months ago. Now, she was by herself, sittin' at the bar staring down into her drink. There was all kinds of studs and femmes tryin' to step to her 'cause she was fresh meat, but she wasn't givin' them chicks no play."

Cleo shook her head in disbelief. "Fresh meat?"

"Oh, come on, CeeCee. You know what I mean. Fresh meat … a newcomer … pretty face and the body to match."

Cleo's nostrils flared. "Are you serious? I don't believe it. And listen to you … all that second, third-hand information. You of all people know you can't trust what that damn Katrina spits out anyway. Damn! That chick is such a hater and always spreadin' business around like she ain't got nothin' else to do."

"Uh, excuse me. What makes you think it ain't possible for Miss Kennedy St. Martin to be all up in the Dikes-R-Us den? It don't matter that she's married. Shit, from what I hear, a lot of them married freaks are into gettin' their groove on with other women from time to time."

Cleo gave her a strange look, a mixture of surprise, disgust, and concern. "Look, Shell. I'm just saying." Before continuing, she shifted in her chair and coughed a few times to clear her throat. "You just can't believe everything that comes out of Katrina's mouth. Hey, I know we made a date to hook up later tonight, but I'm kinda pooped and just wanna go home and chill. Raincheck, okay?"

"That's cool. I'm a bit worn out, too. I'll try to give you a call this evening to reschedule, but before we go, hear me out for one sec, okay? About Kennedy and Katrina, I agree for the most part. Sometimes her gossip can be overly colorful.

I mean, she can sho' put a spin on things when she wants to, but I digress. Anyway, enough about her. She ain't nobody no way. You ready to go? Let's bounce," Shelby said as she jumped down from Cleo's desk.

All Cleo could do was shake her head and say, "Yeah, let's bounce."

⚢ 5 ⚥

After arriving home, she laid her purse and keys on the foyer table, slowly walked into her spacious living room and laid down on the brown leather sofa her parents had purchased for her birthday a few months ago. Euphoric visions of the fleeting moments she engaged in with Kennedy earlier floated through her mind like an old projector home movie. She almost couldn't believe it had happened and even pinched herself once she was alone in her ride to make sure she wasn't in la-la land.

Wow. Ms. Kennedy St. Martin came on to me. Me, of all people. All of a sudden, a light bulb went off in her head. *Hold on just one damn minute! But at the same time, she also went to the club ... does that really mean anything, though?* Now alarmed with the revelation settling in her head, Cleo quickly sat up and yelled out loud, "Why did she pick me out of all these women floatin' around, why me?"

How many times had she been to the club and what was she doing there?

Is she just playing me, tryna get me caught up in her web?

These questions plagued Cleo. *Damn, maybe I should just call and ask her if it's true and see if she'll be honest with me.*

Well, it ain't like we a couple or anything. She ain't gotta explain how she spends her time or where she decides to go out. OK, Cleo, you really need to slow your roll. I'm really in my feelings, so I'm just gonna let this ride tonight. Hell, I may not say anything at all 'cause in the end, it ain't none of my business, anyway.

The phone rang, interrupting her thoughts. Reese Maxwell's name appeared on the Caller ID. "Oh, shit. I forgot all about my date with him tonight!" It rang a few more times before she decided to answer it. "Hello, Reese. What's up?" Cleo asked, twirling an auburn-hued strand of hair that had fallen in her face.

"Hey there, lil' lady, with your fine self. I was calling to make sure we're still on tonight. I was thinking about swoopin' you up in an hour or so. How does that sound to you?"

While Reese was tryin' to get his rap on, Cleo found herself absentmindedly massaging her clit, which was still slightly excited from her secret encounter earlier. She couldn't shake it. Kennedy had first invaded her personal space at work, and now, she was invading her mind. What was a girl to do?

"Hello, CeeCee? Are you there?" a perplexed Reese asked in his deep baritone voice.

"Oh, yes. I'm here, Reese. Something caught my attention on TV," she lied, still rubbing her clit.

"Oh, okay. I thought I'd lost you. So, what do you think about what I said?"

Cleo was no longer listening. Instead, she was too busy pleasuring herself and thinking about Kennedy. "I'm sorry, Reese, but something has come up and I'm gonna have to cancel tonight. I promise I'll make it up to you next weekend." By now, she was close to orgasm.

"Oh, wow. It's like that?" stated Reese, sounding like a wounded hound. "We've been planning this for a while now. As a matter of fact, the last time we were supposed to hook up, you backed out on me. Okay, just be real with me. Do you wanna go out with me? Does my breath stank or something? You know I'm really feelin' you, but now I'm starting to get the feelin' you ain't trying to give a brotha a chance ..."

Annoyed with his begging, Cleo reluctantly put her nut on hold. "Look, I'm sorry, Reese, and not that it's any of your business, but something really important has come up with one of my family members and I need to be there. In fact, I'm about to head out the door. So, as I already said, I'll make it up to you next weekend. I'll see you at work tomorrow."

"Okay, I understand. Sorry for goin' off like that. I didn't mean nothing by it, just wanted to spend some time with you, that's all." His baritone voice dropped an octave. She almost felt bad for him. Almost.

“Hey, it's all good. See ya, Reese,” Cleo said, springing off the sofa and sprinting to her bedroom to finish what she'd already started. She quickly undressed, swung the white linen comforter back, pulled out her pocket rocket, which she'd lovingly nicknamed Orbit, and eased into bed. She knew it wasn't going to take long because she was already on edge while talking to Reese. Lying on her back, she opened her chocolaty-smooth thighs and with Orbit in her left hand, she turned him on and placed the three gold-pronged gadget against her clit.

Pulses spiraled in and around her erotic zone, sending chills up and down her spine, her whole body in rhythm like a symphony skillfully playing her favorite song. Moving Orbit around lightly on her plump pussy lips and deep inside her kitty-kat sent her into orbit. Her orgasm cascaded down and settled nicely between her legs. "Ohhhhhhhhhhh, shit!" screamed Cleo she yanked Orbit out of her snatch and panted like a puppy dog. After coming back down from the stratosphere, Cleo rolled over on her stomach, curled up into a ball and went fast to sleep.

⚢ 6 ⚥

Cleo woke up in a very chipper mood, still ridin' off her climax from her rendezvous with Orbit. Peeping outside her bedroom window, she looked for the neighborhood's favorite cat R.K. (for roadkill), but he was nowhere to be found. One of her neighbors blessed him with that name because he'd been hit at least twice by speeding cars but miraculously survived. Crisp morning air mixed with the scent of fresh-cut grass filled her lungs as she breathed in deeply. After getting herself together for work, she grabbed her keys and headed out the door, bounced into her ride, slid the key into the ignition, cranked up the engine and pushed the power button. The sound of Rickey Smiley's booming voice filled up her truck's interior. He was commenting on Juicy's report about the splitsville rumors of the merry-go-round of celebrity couples. Suddenly, "I'm Workin'! Workin' up a black sweat" filled the truck's interior; her BFF was calling.

She clicked the talk button on her steering wheel. Singing along with The Purple One, she answered, "Hey Ma, what's up? I'm workin' up a black sweat, workin', eh, workin' up a black sweat!"

"Uh, excuse me, I mean I know you are Prince's number one fan-for-life, but sorry, honey, Mariah Carey, you ain't!" Shelby said.

"Ah, don't hate, you know I can out-sing you. Must I take you back to the North Central talent show when I belted out 'Sweet Love' and took the winning prize home? Shit, them flunkies had no idea a girl like me had them kind of pipes. Remember how those who couldn't see who was singin' thought it was the real Anita? I'll never forget that glorious night. All them hoes was all on my tip," Cleo gloated.

"Now, see, why you gotta go there? Always gotta bring up old shit!" Shelby shot back.

Cleo giggled. "Girl, you about to make me have a wreck on my way to my nine to five. Anyway, I was calling to remind you of our girls' night out with Donnieka and Crimson at Club Isis. Did you forget about it?"

"No, I didn't forget. I know this is our Friday to hang out with the girls, Shell," Cleo replied as she glanced to her left and saw the huge *Golden M* calling her name. "Hey, I'ma stop and get me an egg McMuffin. Do you want anything?"

"Naw, I'm tryin' to watch my girlish figure this week. Besides, I gotta be able to squeeze into my hoochie outfit tonight. You know how we single girls do it. Tonight, I'm on the prowl for some new booty, are you with me, boo?"

As she pulled into the McDonald's drive-thru, Cleo asked, "What about James? I thought you two were all into each other, but then again, you haven't mentioned him in a minute."

"Ugh! Just the sound of his name irks the hell out of me. Girl, that nigga ain't shit just like all the rest of these punk-ass bitches who call themselves real men. But we ain't got enough time right now to go all into that crap. I'll tell ya all about it tonight at the club, and girl, you gon' be trippin' after I tell you what that lil' shrimp of a man did to me. Boy, I sho' can pick 'em, cain't I?"

Knowingly, Cleo responded, "Yeah, Shell, you sho' know how to pick 'em. I'll see ya at the office shortly. Bye."

"Bye, girl," Shelby said in a hushed tone.

Cleo knew exactly what that hushed tone was all about. She'd heard her best friend go into that voice whenever she was dealing with a man who don't know how to keep his hands off a woman, the kind of man Cleo despised. A decade ago, she'd almost had one of Shelby's exes killed for beating the shit out of her, leaving Cleo to rush her to the hospital with a blackened eye, a broken rib and a swift kick to her protruding stomach, which caused her to miscarry *their* baby. It took Shelby almost three years to come out of her dead-to-the-world state after the loss of her child. After that brutal attack, Shelby was never able to carry a child to full term again after trying multiple times. Though Joshua's severe beating—which left him with a permanent walking handicap—was a deed Cleo was not exactly proud of, she'd do it again if she had to.

Nobody fucked with the people she loved, and if they did, they had hell to pay. Shit, just ask Joshua. That fucker knew all about the vengeance she (and a few of her buffed male friends) brought down on his ass back in the day.

****

Cleo was well on her way to exploding into orbit (or in this case, Craig's mouth) with her fifth or sixth orgasm, but who was counting? All she knew was that she was feeling mighty good and didn't have a care in the world at that moment.

Sweat beads trickled down Craig's flushed forehead as he eagerly lapped up her sweet juices flowing freely from her pussy.

"Oh, yes. Oh yes, oh yes, yes, yesssss!" Cleo screeched as she grabbed a fistful of soft curls atop his head.

"Oh yeah baby, you taste so damn good, girl!"

His long, ardent tongue was gently perusing back and forth over her rock-hard clit when the phone rang, interrupting their sexcapade.

"Ah, hell naw! Who the hell's callin' me this time of the mornin'?" Cleo hissed as she reached for her cell phone. The caller ID flashed Shelby's name.

Pushing Craig away from her snatch, she quickly sat up in bed, back firmly pressed up against her black leather headboard. A call in the middle of the night from her best friend could only mean one thing: something awful had happened.

Craig raised his head, looking dazed. He must have known something serious had gone down by the terror-stricken look on her face. The ambrosial scent of her honeyed nectar tickled the wee hairs in his nose as he licked her cum off his thick, luscious lips and chin.

Shuddering, she picked up the receiver. "Hey, what's wrong, Shell?"

Shelby was sobbing uncontrollably. "CeeCee! CeeCee! He – he – he …"

"What did he do? What has that fool Joshua gone and done now?" Cleo demanded. Her beating heart was racing so fast, it felt like it might explode.

"Oh, Cleo, I'm in so much pain! Oh! It hurts so much!"

"What hurts?" Impatience had set in and she felt herself becoming more and more agitated. "What's goin' on, dammit?" she screamed.

"Josh … he … he ... I think he killed our baby, CeeCee. Oh! There's so much blood. It's everywhere! I even got some on our new carpet! I tried gettin' it up, but the pain, oh the pain just made me double over. Please come take me to the hospital. Hurry!"

Cleo first felt that she was in the middle of a nightmare. Is this real? Am I dreaming?

Suddenly, everything went black. Cleo had fainted.

****

"Get a gurney quick! She needs a doctor now!" Craig yelled. Dressed in a sleek pair of black slacks and hunter-green Sean John shirt, he looked delicious, like a sweet piece of nugget inside a three musketeer.

"Cleo, Cleo, can you hear me? Please talk to me, baby! Please!" He was frantically waving his large, veined hand back and forth in front of her flushed face. Her big, brown eyes glazed over as she stared blankly straight ahead. No flinching or batting of the eye.

"Where am I?" Cleo asked herself as she slowly came out of her trance.

Dreary sea-green walls. The stark scent of old urine mixed with some kind of sterile cleaning agent and bright fluorescent ceiling lights beaming into her bloodshot eyes. People with embroidered white jackets wrapped around their bodies.

Still in her own world, she whispered silently, "I'm at the hospital." The realization jerked every bone in her body. The memory of her conversation with Shelby came rushing to her mind as she tried to make sense of everything.

"Cleo?" said Craig. His deep voice cracked, and tears welled up in his penetrating blue-green eyes.

"Ma'am are you all right?" asked the young, beautiful nurse. 'M. Carrington' was printed on her name tag. Miss Carrington's bright ice blue eyes stared deeply into hers as she held Cleo's trembling hand with her right hand, and in her left, she held a stethoscope, apparently trying to see what Cleo's vitals were doing.

"Where is Shelby? How's her baby?" Cleo wailed as she struggled to stand up.

"She's in the operating room right now. The doctors are tryin' to save her baby's life. They didn't get a heartbeat when we first got here, and to be honest, Cleo, it doesn't look too good for the little one."

Waves of anger and disbelief bolted through her trembling body, almost causing her knees to buckle. But, luckily, her tall, strong man was there to keep her from teetering forward.

"What? Are you serious? I'm goin' to kill that nigga, I swear if it's the last thing I do!" Cleo hissed.

"All right, all right, Ms. Stinson. Please calm down. You've been through enough tonight and your energy should be used for your friend and her baby right now. Let the police handle him," Ms. Carrington said.

Cleo's first thought was to tell Ms. Carrington to shut the fuck up and that she didn't know what the hell she was talking about. But there was something about the cool, almost serene look in her twinkling eyes. If she was at all uncomfortable, she sure didn't let it show. After staring into the nurse's eyes for a few minutes, Cleo felt her body relax, and the pounding in her head came to a halt. The emergency room was abuzz with activity. One young man perched in a corner was sweating profusely. He was holding his pale, bluish-looking left hand across his chest and his clothes were filthy as if he'd been in a recent fight that ended with a trip to the hospital. Another gentleman was gently rubbing his wife's forehead while colossal tears trickled down her burning ruby-red cheeks.

Aides, doctors and nurses of various ages and body types were walking about. Cleo was amazed at her new, eerie environment that continuously unfolded into organized chaos.

"Damn, you're right. Please take me to Shelby. I've got to see her, gotta let her know I'm here for her!" Cleo cried as her eyes darted around the room, trying to identify which door to run through to find her friend.

Ever-so-gently, Craig took her by the arm and led her to a shiny black leather chair. It contrasted with the rest of the room's decorations, which appeared to be straight out of the 1970s, complete with burnt-orange and sage-green low-slung upholstered chairs and rickety wooden tables placed throughout the room.

"Craig, what are you doing? I need to be with my best friend right now. She needs me," pleaded Cleo.

"CeeCee, chill, okay? Shelby is being well taken care of," he said, taking a seat next to her.

The strain from the night's events was beginning to take its toll on him as evidenced by the huge, bulging blue-green veins in his face and neck. His sparkling eyes now bore dark circles around them, reminding her of an owl. Anguish and sleeplessness encircled him like damp, somber evening rain.

Inside, she knew that tonight Craig had gone above and beyond for both her and Shelby. Her instincts dictated that she do as he said, for they all had indeed been through enough this unforgettable night that would remain etched in her memory forever.

⚢ 7 ⚥

"Hey, good morning, Cleo!" Cleo heard Pepper yell out after stepping into the Exodus' foyer.

"Good morning sunshine. How's everything?" Cleo implored, looking around for any sign of Kennedy.

"All is well, my dear. Is that McDonald's I see in your hands?" Cleo looked on as Pepper's piercing blue-green eyes lit up.

"Haha! You already know I didn't forget about you. Here's your favorite," she responded, handing over a bag filled with a breakfast burrito and piping hot hash brown.

"Ooh la la! Thanks, friend."

Cleo winked at her. "I know how much you love their burritos, and you're welcome. Hey, have you seen Kennedy yet?"

Pepper took a big bite of her burrito. "Um, she has a few home visits and a court hearing this morning and will be in this afternoon. Do you want me to tell her to stop by your office when she gets in?"

Cleo thought for a minute. "Yes, please. I need to follow up with her about a case. Have a good day, Pepper," she said, then headed for the elevator.

"Okay you too, and I'll let her know."

Cleo's emotions were all over the place. She was unsure of how to handle what had transpired between her and Kennedy. A million questions flooded her mind, and she was very anxious to speak with her and find out where exactly her mind was. Cleo went about her day as usual while eagerly waiting for Kennedy to arrive, but the moment never came. She would learn when Pepper called to inform her that after her last visit, Kennedy would be picking one of her sick sons up from school.

Their tête-à-tête would have to wait.

****

Electric green strapless top and black miniskirt: too sexy. Her favorite burgundy silk wide-legged pants and vanilla crème camisole: too dressy for Club Isis. Cleo shuffled and discarded several outfits before finally settling on her basic black halter dress, one of many variations of "the basic black dresses" she owned. Whenever she couldn't decide on an ensemble, she always defaulted to one of her black dresses.

As she slid her lovely, full hips into the dress, the realization of Shelby bawling her out if she backed out on their monthly girls' night out came tumbling down from the stratosphere, and the memory of the last time they fell out over this very same thing still haunted her.

Well, fuck it. Kennedy's a very married woman—with kids—and ain't got the time for me no way. I mean for real, it ain't like she gonna leave her family and run off into the sunset with me and shit. I may as well give these niggas a try ... see if their game has improved since the last time I was at Club Isis. Besides, I'm still looking for my sweet, charming beau to whisk me off my feet and ride me into the sunset on his two-horse chariot—

Yeah, right.

****

One of DJ Khalid's latest jams rang out from the club speakers as the ladies strolled into Club Isis for what promised to be yet another humdrum night of wannabe's, has-beens, gold-diggers and self-described playas. "Damn! Look who's here, y'all," said Crimson, who was neatly dressed in dark slacks and a provocative indigo-hued blouse made by Prada, her favorite designer. Her long, flowing, lavender-hued hair was pulled up in a sexy ponytail, showcasing the well-chiseled cheekbones she was so graciously blessed with by her attractive mother, who was also a well-paid runway model back in the day. Simultaneously, Cleo, Shelby and Donnieka turned their heads in the direction Crimson gestured to.

Cleo squinted for a better glimpse. Like most clubs in Nap, it was extremely dim, damn near pitch black, in fact. Buffed Mandingo brothas, slim cats, chubby hoochie mamas, and hot girls lined the walls of the club. Then she spotted their old pal Janice 'J'ai' Daniels from their Picadilly's Nightclub days. Always the fashion upstager, Janice had a *unique* approach to her attire. Indeed, she was never one to follow suit with the rest of the world. She was always proud to tell anyone who asked that she marched to the sound of her own drum. The number she selected for tonight was no exception. Miss Daniels sported a skin-tight leopard print mini dress, gold fishnet stockings and matching leopard print chunky-heeled sandals.

Donnieka's mouth fell wide open. "What the fuck does she have on?"

But she was one to talk. For some ungodly reason, she chose a blinding yellow form-fitting top she undoubtedly picked up from Dots, along with a thigh-high blue jean skirt that was two sizes too small as evidenced by her huge belly drooping over the front of it. Crimson, Cleo, and Shelby all looked at each other knowingly.

"Hey J'ai! How have you been, girl? It's been a long time," acknowledged Cleo. They all made their way through the crowd to greet the longtime friend they hadn't seen in over five years.

They lost contact with her when her affluent parents shipped her off to some expensive drug rehabilitation joint down in sunny Florida. Her demise all started that fateful night she met Marvin Gallagher, a self-described drug lord from Detroit who moved his emerging drug business to Naptown during the mid-1980s.

His 'business venture' saturated the community with crack cocaine and soon devastated Indy's most down-trodden neighborhoods, and also reached affluent neighborhoods including Carmel and Fishers. Now, just like many drug lord girlfriends, Janice was showered with all the latest gear from Prada, Dolce & Gabbana, and Gucci.

Her wedding finger was outfitted with an exquisite five-carat gem that shone so brightly, you couldn't look at it for very long because it could blind you, though they never stepped one foot down nobody's aisle. Oh, yeah … he wined and dined her, took her out to the finest restaurants and on frequent trips across the States and overseas. She didn't want for anything. But, just like the Cinderella story—minus the happy ending—all good things had to come to an end. J'ai started innocently enough, with the occasional joint "just to take the edge off." Snorting cocaine came a short time later, and the next thing they knew, she was downin' ecstasy and anything else she could get her hands on.

Watching a childhood friend's life spiral out of control was unnerving. No one thought she'd ever show her face again after that ugly fall from grace. A few years after arriving in Nap, Maurice's mutilated, lifeless body was discovered by some fishermen in the White River. The local news alleged he was killed assassination-style. His killer was never found. But here J'ai stood unflinching, tall and proud.

"Well, I'll be damned, if it ain't Cleo and the gang all up in Club Isis. How y'all been? It's been a minute."

"We're all doin' pretty good. No sense in complaining no way 'cause don't nobody wanna listen to somebody else's problems in this day and age," Donnieka rattled off.

"I know that's right, girl! Boy, it sure is great seeing y'all. An unexpected surprise fo' sho'," J'ai lamented.

Cleo leaned forward and placed her forearms on the bar top. "Yeah, same here. When did you get back in town?"

"Oh, I've been back just over a month. I'm trippin' on how everything looks so different. Everywhere I go, I see all these new neighborhoods, like the ones off Michigan Road. Man, oh, man, they sho' crowded dem lil' cracker box houses together, huh?"

Before anyone could reply, Crimson chimed in.

"Hey, those people just left that table over there in the corner and it's close to the restrooms. Let's make our way over there before someone else swoops down on it." She was already en route to the black-topped, round table that was surrounded by just enough chairs for everyone.

"I know, girl. Ain't it a trip? I don't know what makes these builders think folk wanna live right on top of each other. What happened to something called privacy?" Donnieka asked as she waddled her wide hips over to the table. Her skirt engulfed her bottom half, making her appear even bigger than she was.

"Hey, what's up, ma? I figured you'd be here when I neva got a call back from ya." Javon took his sultry gaze off Cleo for a moment and turned his attention to Cleo's friends. "And how y'all ladies doin' tonight?"

Shelby's nostrils flared up. She really couldn't stand his black ass and only tolerated him because her BFF was still dealin' with him, much to her dismay.

The first thing Cleo saw was his dimples. "Well, if it ain't Mr. Javon McCoy, what's up? My bad. I thought I'd already told ya this was my night out with the girls."

"Oh yeah, I remember sugah." He possessively wrapped his massive arms around Cleo's waist. "You know I couldn't let your fine ass be all up in 'dis club without me bein' here to watch ova my piece."

True to his Afrocentric style, tonight he was sporting a navy-blue traditional ensemble, looking like the African Prince Akeem Joffer of Zamunda, Eddie Murphy's main character from *Coming to America*.

Before Cleo could respond, the D.J. switched out a fast tune in favor of something more romantic. All the ladies began swerving in their seats to the oh-so-sweet melody.

Still holding her tightly around the waist, Javon asked, "Oh, baby, this is my jam! May I have this dance?"

Once again, his bright puppy-dog brown eyes made her melt inside. "Oh, all right, Javon, but keep in mind that you cannot be stuck up my butt all night. I'm here to party with my girls, hence the words, 'girls' night out,' ya hear me?" Cleo exclaimed.

"Yeah, yeah, I hear ya," Javon replied while leading her onto the dance floor by hand. As they made their way through the thick, sweaty crowd, the eyes of the other persuasion swayed in tune with every move of her generous hips. While Cleo was enjoying the attention, she also watched as Javon took notice of the googly eyes of a few dudes holding up the wall just to the left of them. He gripped her hand tightly. She gleamed, watching Javon hold his head up high and puff out his formidable chest.

His face had the look of a dangerous mix of jealousy and pride as he graciously led his would-be-wife-someday onto the dance floor.

Cleo felt a deep prodding inside. Javon's penetrating eyes gazed down upon her. Her eyes shimmered under the sparkling colors of red, blue, and green bouncing off the dance globe above their heads. At that moment, discerning questions ascended upon her.

Is he the one? Could he be the one that I will share the rest of my life with?

Do I truly, earnestly love him?

Does he really care about me like he always claims he does?

Can I see giving myself to him, fully and completely ... 'til death do us part?

"Baby, whatchu thinkin' 'bout? You got that far-away look in your eyes." He gently used his index finger to lift her chin. "Wha'dup?"

The dance floor was packed with people grinding on each other as if they were about to take things to the next level.

A slim cat with a golden upper grill and yellow teeth to match yelled out to one shameless couple who were damn near taking their clothes off right on the dance floor—not that the skank had much on to begin with. Whoever told her red stripes make tubby girls look slimmer lied. And, to add insult to injury, every roll, lump, dimple, and fold on her jellied body was highlighted by the stretched stripes of her spandex mini dress.

"Damn! Y'all need to get a room!"

They ignored his comment and continued their carnal dance as if nothing had been said. Cleo and Javon chuckled and shook their heads at the hilarious escapade that unfolded before them.

Suddenly, he spoke the words that she'd been wishing he would have said years ago. "I love you, Cleo. I mean, I've fallen deeply in love with you and I don't want anyone else to have you. I know in the past I haven't always shown you the kind of love you deserve, but I now realize my true, undeniable feelings for you, and I really want us to stop playing around and get married."

Cleo was speechless, staring blankly into his suddenly serious eyes.

Javon cupped her face with his massive hands and whispered those aching words again.

"I love you, CeeCee, and I hope you feel the same. Please tell me the love you had for me at the beginning ain't completely gone," he pleaded.

The song had ended, and the D.J. threw on some rap song that was bragging about shootin' cops and having a female on her knees pleasing him.

Slowly, they walked off the floor, only this time she took the lead.

"Javon, I really don't know what to say right now. So much has happened over the last eight years and, you're right, I do not trust you."

She fought back tears and longingly stared into his eyes, searching for at least one ounce of truth in the words he'd just uttered. But then her attention was averted toward Shelby standing at the bar. A tall, lanky guy with buck teeth, rumpled clothes and a nappy Jim Kelly was tryin' to get his mack on.

Cleo giggled when she observed her BFF's continuous eye-rolling, a sure indication she had no interest in the would-be suitor. True to form, she read Shelby's lips saying, "Nigga, please. How about you go find your barber and have him tighten up that fucked up ass Jim Kelly on top of your head? Now be gone."

"Babe, what are you looking at?" Javon asked, impatience etched in the fine creases on his forehead.

Cleo pointed at Shelby, who was walking toward them. When she drew closer, Cleo could see anger and curiosity cloaked in Shelby's beat-up face.

"Humph," Javon grunted loudly as he crossed his arms.

You could cut the tension with a knife. It was no secret that Javon couldn't stand Shelby, and Shelby hated Javon's guts. Cleo took a step back from Javon and placed her attention on her BFF.

"CeeCee, is everything OK?"

Cleo watched as Shelby rolled her eyes at Javon. "Yes, everything's fine, Shelby."

Perturbed, Shelby cocked her head and put her hands on her hips, a sure sign she was not satisfied with Cleo's response.

"Are you sure? You seem upset and if everything is really okay, then why are you crying?" Shelby pulled out a Kleenex and wiped away the tears that had stained her friend's flushed cheeks and smeared eyeliner.

Irritated by Shelby's interruption, Javon chimed in. "Damn, Shelby, she done already told ya everything's fine, so why you hounding her? She a grown-ass woman that knows how to handle her own. Too bad we cain't say the same 'bout you." Javon laughed loudly.

Incensed, Shelby replied, "Why, you triflin' ass nigga!" Wagging her finger in his face, she continued. "You got some nerve with your low-life ass. I know about everything you've put Cleo through, from standin' her up on numerous occasions, your nasty ass hoes callin' her phone in the middle of the night—"

Not liking where their conversation was going, Cleo stood between them. "All right now, you two! Stop it! Just stop it, dammit!"

"Naw, naw! Fuck her, fuck her! She just wants you to be a lonely bitch like her!"

"You dumb-ass, triflin' ass punk!" Shelby yelled.

True to the black woman head-rolling mantra, Shelby twirled her neck as if she was the one who invented it. "You wanna get personal, that's cool, too," she exclaimed.

Oh, boy, here she goes, thought Cleo. She relented because she knew there was no turning back now.

Like any other club in the world, it wasn't out of the ordinary for little spats to go down at Club Isis. But this lil' run-in was gettin' worse and worse by the second. People began turning their heads, giving them the 'shut-the-fuck-up' look. It was half-past one in the morning, and both Shelby and Javon had clearly had too much to drink. The fact that they already couldn't stand each other only added fuel to the fire.

"I know all about that night you called CeeCee and begged her to join you at that hotel—"

The smug look that was spread across his face only seconds ago dissipated like morning dew on a lush green lawn. Shelby had hit a home run. And she knew it.

"Girl, you don't know what happened! Yo ass wasn't even there!" he shouted.

Shelby took a few steps toward him, and now they were face to face. "It don't matter if I was there or not," she said, pointing her finger in his face, "I know what happened. Like I said a moment ago before you rudely interrupted me, CeeCee gave in to your pleading and made her way to spend the night with you, and shortly after she arrived, she got prepared for bed while you were in the other room smokin' it up with ya homeboy.

Now, let's stop and think about this for a second … you get a hotel room supposedly so you can chill out with my girl since you was still livin' at home with ya momma at the time—only to call ya boy over to smoke some weed and got my girl waitin' in the bedroom. Now, this is the real fucked-up part … Cleo pulled the sheet and cover back only to discover cum stains on the bed, you nasty, triflin' fucker!"

That did it. Cleo yanked Shelby's left arm and said, "Okay, Shell, that's enough, let's go back to our table now!"

Still filled with rage, Shelby yanked her arm back and got right back up in Javon's face again. "You ain't shit," she roared. "Cleo is in a whole other league that you don't know nothin' about and will never know 'cause you from da hood and all you fit to do is eat her pussy, you jackass!"

"Cleo, you better get that wench away from me! I ain't into hittin' females, but she sho' askin' for it and if she don't get on somewhere, I'ma dot her eye!"

Cleo glared at him as a roller coaster of emotions shot through her, leaving her to wonder what she ever saw in him. She rolled her eyes directly at him and literally dragged Shelby back to their table.

"CeeCee, wait! Wait a minute!" begged Javon. He ran to her and yanked on her arm. "How you just gon' leave me like dat?"

Cleo twirled her head around like the actress in *Poltergeist*. With eyes slanted, she hissed, "Nigga, if you don't get your hands off me, I'ma fuck you up!" Her response caught him off guard. He stepped back and stared blankly at her.

Satisfied with the startled look on his face, she continued to drag her BFF to their table where all their friends were still planted like tree stumps. As they approached, all eyes were fixed on them and, true to form, Shelby was still letting all kinds of 'F' bombs drop.

"What the hell happened?" Crimson and Donnieka asked in unison.

After the fiasco between Javon and Shelby, Cleo was totally drained and not feeling the club scene any longer.

"I don't know why you still deal with that triflin' fucker!" Shelby slurred. By this time, she was so tipsy, drool ran down the side of her mouth and she could barely keep her composure in her chair.

"Shut the fuck up, girl. Yo ass is so damn gone, you can't even sit still in your chair. You know you never could hold your liquor and that still ain't changed," Cleo replied. She could feel her heart beating faster. She was not trying to get in a big-ass argument with her pissy, drunk-ass friend, 'cause it was doomed to get real ugly if their confrontation continued.

"All right, all right, that's enough," J'ai chimed in. She threw her arm around Cleo's shoulder. "I ain't seen y'all in forever and ain't tryin' to hear no arguing all damn night, shit. Besides, I know y'all came here to have a good time, not fuckin' argue."

Just then, their waitress walked up. She stood maybe four and a half feet, wearing all black, with long, platinum ringlets tumbling down her back. Except for her hook nose and pudgy stomach, she was kinda cute. Kinda.

"Is there anything else I can get you, ladies? This is the last call for drinks." Her voice was at odds with her appearance, sounding like Maude from the popular 1970s TV show.

"Yes ma'am," J'ai replied. "Could you please bring a round of Patrón shots for me and my long-lost friends? I think a celebration is in order for this reunion tonight!"

She was a bit tipsy herself from the slurred words that eased from her glossy lips.

"Oh no, Shelby sho' don't need nothing else to drink, please believe. Besides, I'm about to take her home before she starts up again with Javon," Cleo said, gathering her best friend and their purses.

Crimson watched without uttering a word, but a look of concern was firmly etched on her face.

"Ah, dang it! I ain't ready to go yet. Man, I thought we was gonna rock it out till closin' time," said a disappointed Donnieka.

"Stop pouting like a five-year-old, Donnieka. Nobody said you gotta leave and you sho' don't need our permission to stay," Cleo said.

Reluctantly, Crimson piped in, "Oh, what the hell, I'll stay with you, girl. Besides, I don't want you up in this club by yourself. These niggas is crazy and ain't no tellin' what they might do, especially if they ain't found a piece of ass to take home with 'dem."

"Ah, excuse me! Excuse me! Waitress, could you hurry up and get ova here so we can order drinks before cut-off time? Damn, you been at their table for a long-ass time. There are other people here, ya know."

Everyone turned in the direction of the screeching voice, only to see a feeble-looking woman probably in her late 60s with almond-colored skin, deep-set chocolate eyes and a wrapped-up coif. Her multi-colored ensemble was at least five sizes too big for her petite frame, and she had the audacity to wear six-inch stilettos.

Grinning, the waitress cried out, "Oh, stop it, Beulah. Why you always tryin' to start up some shit with me? I'll be over in a minute, so don't get your britches all up in a roar, ol' lady."

By now, Beulah couldn't control the penetrating roar rising from her gut as she laughed her way back to the dance floor and started getting her boogie-oogie on with a few other solo dancers who apparently thought Club Isis was holding an audition for S*o You Think You Can Dance.*

The D.J. had just thrown on some hip hop joint that was constantly ridin' the radio waves at WHHH, 96.3.

"Ladies, it's been great, but we gotta say good night. One of y'all call me tomorrow sometime and let me know how it ended," Cleo said as she dragged Shelby—who was now drifting in and out of the real world—toward the exit.

"And make sure Shelby stays put tonight. You know how she do. Hell, you may have to stay the night with that girl. I sho' ain't tryin' to bail nobody out of jail tonight," Crimson chimed in.

Looking over her shoulder toward their friends, Cleo replied, "Girl, I got this. It ain't nothin' new to me." Of all the things that had happened tonight, the one thing she knew for sure was that she was going to finally end things with Javon, kick Craig and Reese to the curb, and concentrate on what she and Kennedy had started.

Though she wasn't sure she was ready to put all her eggs in one basket, she'd begun to believe that eventually something true, something real could happen between them.

⚢ 8 ⚥

The weekend came and went so fast, it was all a blur. A bit lethargic, Cleo sat slumped down in her chair and began picking at a sore on her arm. *Where the hell did this sore come from?* She couldn't recall how or when she got it.

"Good mornin', good mornin', good mornin'! How's my girl this glorious Monday mornin'? Oh, it's so lovely outside and I really don't wanna be here. Shit, I shoulda called in sick today!" lamented Shelby

who had all but forgotten her behavior a few nights before at the club. She at times reminded Cleo of Jekyll and Hyde because of her mood swings and the liquor sure didn't help.

"How are you feelin' this morning, Shell? How's the headache?"

Shelby cleared her throat before she spoke, trying to mask her age-old pain. "Oh, girl. I'm fine, just fine. You know how I do, you been knowin' me all my life. Headache's gone, I'm refreshed and ready to take on the world!" she cheered.

But Cleo knew better. She was keenly aware of her BFF's long-time struggle with alcohol. But the drinking was just a cover-up for the real deal. The truth lied in the death of her only child, but she chose to save that conversation for another time.

"You know, we didn't get the chance to talk about you and James while at the club. So, what's up with him?" Cleo couldn't help but notice an uneasy look covering her face before one word found its way out of her usually loudmouth and her refusal to look Cleo directly in the eye.

"Well, um, you know James and I were really diggin' each other in the beginning. I thought he was so fine with 'dem deep-ass dimples, that thousand-watt smile. Girl, I know you remember that wide-ass smile that just engulfed me ever since that day at StarWing. Wow, what a fool I've been over his sorry-ass!" Shelby hung her head down low.

Cleo could sense the anger rising up and out of her friend like a dark cloud darkening a bright, sun-drenched sky. "Hey, slow it down there, lil' lady. Don't let that nigga get your pressure up. He ain't worth it," she said sincerely.

Cleo continued watching Shelby as she walked from the window to one of the old chairs in front of Cleo's desk. As she slumped her seemingly lifeless body down, the deep creases in her forehead provided evidence of the hardships she'd experienced over the years. They reminded Cleo of the deep-seated creases in the old leather chair she just sat in.

Cleo reached across her desk and grabbed her trembling hands. "Hey, Shell, we don't have to talk about this now. Besides, that damn Katrina is probably standing at my door with a glass trying to decipher our conversation with her nosey ass," she joked, trying to lighten the mood.

By now, a slow steady stream of tears began flowing down her perfectly blushed cheeks. Her once flawless mascara was now totally ruined, but Cleo realized this was good for her best friend, in a way. A release of penned-up rage and pain that she so desperately needed to shed.

"Dammit, Shelby, you should've done as I asked years ago and gone to see a counselor after losing the baby. Now here we are, all these years later, and you're still struggling. Matter of fact, you seem to be getting worse. Hey, tell you what, why don't you come over tonight so we can get into our girly-girl chat." Cleo looked directly at her tear-stained face and wiped them away.

Shelby sniffled and finally looked up. "Nice color," nodding her head towards Cleo's nails.

Cleo smiled at the dazzling aqua blue splashed on her nails. "Why yes, my dear, you know Monica got them skills unlike no other. You remember Craig turned me onto her, right?"

Cleo looked on as Shelby managed a half-smile. "Yes, I remember."

Cleo leaned back and commenced picking at her nails. "Anyway, enough about all that, back to you. I can see you need a listening ear and as your very best friend in the whole wide world, it is my duty, no, my honor to be there for you in your time of need."

Shelby breathed a sigh of relief. "Oh, CeeCee, you're the best friend, a true friend any girl could ever ask for. I appreciate you so much, you just don't know. "Sometimes," she said, her eyes falling shut "I feel so helpless, so ashamed because you always have to come to my rescue like I was your child or something instead of a grown-ass woman."

"Shelby, look into my eyes." Cleo echoed what she'd already said earlier. "You've known me all my life, shit, you know me better than anyone else in this world, including my mama, my daddy, and my siblings. We've been there for each other time and time again. That's the way we've always done it and that's the way it's always gonna be, agreed?"
A glint of relief appeared in Shelby's eyes.

"Agreed."

"Ah damn, it's that time," Cleo looked up at the wall clock and began gathering her things.

"Oh, shit, it sure is. I hope Samantha is on her best behavior today or else she's gonna catch these hands 'cause I'm tired of her foolishness," Shelby said as she wiped tears from her eyes with the Kleenex, she grabbed out of Cleo's tissue box.

Cleo wriggled her index finger. "Girl, now don't you start. We gonna let that chile be, shit, you know she got some issues she obviously ain't never dealt with. We can stop by your office to grab your stuff on our way down to the staffing room, okay?"

She looked on as Shelby blew her nose one last time and tossed the tissue in the wastebasket.

"Okay, cool," she replied and rose from the chair and took a deep breath.

Secretly, Cleo was anxious about seeing Kennedy and hoped they would be able to talk afterward.

⚢ 9 ⚥

"Samantha was on her best behavior today, huh, CeeCee?" Shelby implored as they departed the meeting.

A covert gaze was shared between Cleo and Kennedy as she passed them in the hallway. "Yep, thank the Lord or like my brother, Sasha says, 'Yahweh'. That was the most respectful and humble she's been in a long time."

"Indeed, and I'm glad 'cause I really thought I was gonna have to serve up a knuckle sandwich," Shelby laughed.

Cleo pinched Shelby's arm. "Girl, stop. Get yo butt to your home visit, with your crazy self."

"Ouch!" Shelby yelped. "Okay, okay, I'm going, but I'm just saying!" They arrived at Cleo's office door, Cleo shook her head and watched Shelby continue down the corridor.

With Kennedy heavy on her mind, Cleo rushed into her office to call her, but before she could pick up the receiver, there was a knock on her door. Her heart jumped from her chest to her throat when she looked up and saw Kennedy waltzing through her door. Once again, she was enamored by her alarming beauty.

"Oh, good afternoon, Kennedy. How are you?" asked Cleo as she nervously adjusted her trembling body in her chair.

"I'm fine. Can we talk?"

"Of course."

Settle yourself down, Cleo. Damn.

Kennedy closed the door behind her and sat in the chocolate brown chair placed directly in front of Cleo's desk.

Her make-up was flawless, as always. Her coif was done up in an exquisite French roll with a few strands of her honey-coated hair swept to the left side of her gorgeous, oval-shaped face. Today she was sporting a simple, but sophisticated alabaster-colored Gucci pantsuit, a cream-colored camisole and a sleek pair of cream-colored four-inch heels. She embodied radiance to the umpteenth power.

"About our, um, well you know …"

"Yes." Cleo interrupted. She felt that stirring inside her, gripping and tugging at her very soul—*or was it the prodding, lesbian-infused desire rising from her sex?*

Kennedy shifted nervously in her chair, seemingly struggling to find the right words. "Um, I don't know what came over me. I apologize." Her uncertain gaze met Cleo's stunned eyes.

Suddenly, a trickle of sweat sauntered down Cleo's brow, though the thermostat was set to a very cool sixty-five degrees.

It's getting hot in herrreeee.

"I … I don't know what to say, Kennedy. No other woman has ever kissed me, so I was taken aback … but to be honest with you, I rather enjoyed it," Cleo admitted.

Like a dissipating dark cloud threatening rain on a bright sunny day, the gloominess that was present on Kennedy's despondent face disappeared before Cleo's eyes.

"Oh, my God. I wasn't sure … I've been feelin' this way all my life Cleo but scared as hell to let that side of me show," Kennedy stated as she leaned forward on Cleo's desk. Before she could utter a response, the phone rang. Cleo glared down at the black telephone as if her glare was going to stop it from ringing.

"Hold that thought," she requested and reached for the receiver. "Thank you for calling E.R.C. This is Cleo Stinson. How may I help you?"

It was one of her client's advocates calling to cancel a meeting they had planned later that day. She couldn't help but be aware of Kennedy's penetrating gaze on her, or more specifically, her physique, as she nervously fumbled with the twisted phone cord.

"Okay, Belinda, I understand completely. You can plan, plan, plan, but sometimes things just come up unexpectedly that we have no control over." Cleo cleared her throat. "They call it *life happens* when you're making plans, right?"

"You know, I do believe you are correct, Cleo. I tell ya, it always seems to be something to mess up your plans. Thanks for understanding and I'll be sure to call you sometime tomorrow morning to reschedule," Belinda replied.

"That will be fine. I will await your call tomorrow to reschedule. Have a good night, Belinda and tell that beautiful daughter of yours I said hi. By the way, how old is Adeline now and didn't she have a birthday recently?"

Kennedy nodded in agreement, sliding back into her seat, not breaking her gaze.

"Oh my God, Cleo! Adeline just turned twelve last week! I still can't believe how my baby girl is growing up on me. You know, the older she gets, the more she reminds me of my grandmother. I'm so glad I made that fateful decision to name her after my Granny, but I digress. Well, I'm sure you've got plenty of work to do just like me. The heap of files on the right side of my desk is beginning to put a permanent dent in it. I'll talk to you tomorrow, bye, bye."

Relieved that the conversation finally came to an end ignited Cleo as she was all too eager to get back to the star of her lesbian fantasies. "Bye, Belinda."

"Sorry, that took so long. Lord knows I didn't mean for it to," she said as she hung up the receiver.

"Oh, that's okay. You know I know how it is," Kennedy replied as she eased her hourglass frame forward once again, her full, welcoming bosom at arm's length from Cleo's grasp. Afraid of what the closeness might lead to, Cleo rolled her chair back a few inches for she was not so sure she could keep her probing hands to herself much longer.

"Yeah, I know you get it," said Cleo, her twinkling sugary brown eyes took in Kennedy's sparkling radiance all over again.

Kennedy stifled a cough. "As I was saying a short time ago, I've been having these, these sexual urges for gorgeous women like yourself since childhood, but I never dared to act on them because I knew my family, especially my parents, would've thought I was mentally ill and had me locked up in some God-forsaken mental institution or something off the wall like it."

Did she just refer to me as gorgeous? Wow, who woulda thunk it?

The conversation was already deep and she wanted to continue, but knew it wasn't the time and damn sure wasn't the place for such revealing dialogue.

"Kennedy, I can relate to everything you've just said, and, though I don't really know you like that, I'm finding myself very eager to share some things with you as well. I want us to finish talking, but in a more private environment.

Like I've mentioned many times, these office walls are so damn paper-thin and I know you don't want that damn Katrina Williams gettin' wind of this."

Kennedy's dreamy oyster-gray eyes looked a bit sullen, giving them that far-away look.

"Yes, once again, you speak the truth, Cleo. Okay, well, I have some time after work today, how about you?" she asked, her earnest eyes penetrating Cleo's soul.

Cleo's eyes opened wide with anticipation of them being alone later, but it also shook her core. "Well, um, okay, um …"

Kennedy laughed. "Oh, caught you off guard, huh?"

Cleo's cheeks flushed red as she watched Kennedy wiggle her index finger at her. "Why yes, yes ma'am, you did, but—"

Why has this woman got me feeling like a schoolgirl all over again?

"You seem to be wise beyond your years and it seems that can be a blessing at times and also a curse. And, please don't take me the wrong way, I don't mean to sound pompous but I have to ask, am I correct in my thinking?"

She stood up and walked over to Cleo who also stood up and once again they were face-to-face.

Damn! Why did she have to get so close to me?

***Nowhere to run, no need to hide,
all the doors are locked,

baby and I have you inside

The lyrics from 'Don't Be Afraid' Aaron Hall's 1992 hit rang in Cleo's ear like a tidal wave crashing down on a dwarfed steamboat that didn't have a chance in the world. However, she was determined not to get consumed like the pitiful steamboat. No, instead she stood tall and firm in her posture and was determined not to give in to the soaring heat rising from her kitty-kat. *Damn, this chick acts like she really knows somebody, don't she? Gutsy and fine all rolled into one, a combination that was almost too good to resist. Almost.*

Cleo boldly looked dead into the eyes of the femme fatale that would be her lover someday, dare they act on the true, reverberating essence of their attraction for one another.

"Well, Miss Kennedy, I must say you are very observant, aren't you?" asked Cleo nervously shifting from her left heel to her right. They were so close, she couldn't help but take in a whiff of her tantalizing perfume that smelled of lilacs in full bloom.

Kennedy giggled. "Why, yes, I've been told on a few occasions that I'm quite observant. This trait has served me well, not only in my personal life but also in my career."

"Hmm, I see." Cleo swallowed hard. Her mouth felt like it was full of cotton and there was not a drop of water, soda or anything in sight to quench her thirst. "Not to toot my own horn, but yes, your statement rings true."

"Thanks for being honest with me, Cleo. I really appreciate it," she acknowledged as she drew even closer to Cleo.

"Please call me CeeCee. That's what all my close friends call me."

"Okay, CeeCee. May I ask just one more thing of you?"

It was too late now. The heat that was rising from between her legs morphed into something more liquid-like.

"Sure, go ahead," Cleo affirmed.

The next thing she felt was Miss Kennedy St. Martin's oh-so-soft glossy lips pressing against her plump lips. In an instant, their stolen moment was gone. Cleo's mind had already been blown by the sheer, utter beauty of Kennedy and the funny thing was she had yet to revel in the real tender, sweet nugget that awaited her between Miss St. Martin's opulent thighs. At least not yet.

"Mmmmmm, thank you. I've been wanting to kiss you ever since I walked in here," Kennedy admitted.

Kennedy ran her hands down her blouse, revealing the stiffness of her nipples. A blush spread across Cleo's face. "Oh, wow," she managed to say. Thunderous giggling could be heard through the thin walls, along with what sounded like a runaway train speeding down the hallway.

"Hey, Jermaine, Que, and the rest of y'all stop runnin' like heathens down the hallway. I done already told y'all once and I'm not gonna repeat it again," a lady yelled out.

"Okay-yuh!"

"Sorry, Mama."

The running came to a quick halt. "Yeah, okay," the mother's voice said.

Cleo and Kennedy looked at each other and burst into cackles. "Kids, what can you do?" Cleo said matter-of-factly and shrugged her shoulders. Cleo observed Kennedy slowly licking her lips which were painted in a soft pink shade that reminded her of Bubblicious Bubble Gum. *I wonder how her lips would feel on my skin.*

"Yeah, you're so right. I can picture my own kids doing the same thing. They're so rambunctious, especially the boys. Anyhow, I have a question," Kennedy asked, breaking her spell.

Oh, great. Another reminder that she's technically taken and has little ones. Cleo shook her head and moved back towards her chair.

"Oh, yeah, sure. We can meet at my place, say around seven-thirty?" She grabbed a purple sticky note and quickly scribbled her address and cell number down, then handed it to her.

Kennedy reached for the note. "Okay, that works. I'm so looking forward to sitting down with you, Cleo." She rose from the chair and headed toward the door.

Cleo began gnawing on the pen absentmindedly as she watched her walk out of the door, her mouth salivating with every single step she took. "Me, too. See you later."

⚢ 10 ⚦

Even though Cleo couldn't explain her sudden attraction towards women, she could not deny the magnetic pull that persisted between her and Kennedy. And the fact that *she* was pursuing her so boldly was simply incomprehensible.

Mere words could not express the inconceivable chain of events in the last several weeks of her life. Craig showing up again, Javon still circling around, Reese vying for space in her life, and now a woman. Cleo wasn't sure what to make of any of it.

Dressed in a relaxed pair of fitted jeans and a plain white tee, Cleo decided to go braless and not because she wanted to entice the sexy feline with her tender, erect nipples peeking through her tee, it was simply because she was at home on a breezy Monday evening, chilling out and waiting on her company to arrive. When home alone, which was most of the time since she lived alone anyway, she never wore a bra. It gave her a sense of freedom, especially because she always had to wear one outside her home as her more than generous bosom often garnered unwanted attention.

She heard a soft tapping on her front door precisely at seven-thirty.

Oh my God, that's her. She really came!" Cleo said to herself as she headed to the door.

"Well, hello there Kennedy. Please come in." Her eyes quickly swept up and down Kennedy's physique, stopping briefly to admire the way her voluptuous hips glided from side to side with every single step.

"You look lovely in that outfit, by the way."
Kennedy floated over the threshold. "Oh, this old thing?" said Kennedy, sheepishly gliding her hand down her shirt, smoothing out nonexistent wrinkles. A broad, beautiful smile lit up her face.

Cleo cocked her head to the side, admiring her and her gloryness-ness like she'd done countless times at work ... only this time she didn't have to do it on the down-low. Miss Kennedy was rockin' a dark pair of Levi's and a crisp, white linen button-down shirt. Adding to her usual sexiness, she also wore a beautiful, multi-colored beaded necklace that hung just right on her chest, highlighting her exquisite bust. Along with matching earrings and gold bangles. She looked good enough to eat ... in more ways than one.

Cleo let out a low, slow laugh. "Well, let me just say this, you look marvelous!"
Kennedy's rosy cheeks turned a deeper red color. "Oh, thank you, CeeCee."
They both headed down the hall to the living room. Cleo motioned toward her sofa. "Have a seat, make yourself comfortable."

While Kennedy got comfortable on the sofa (just where Cleo was hoping she'd sit so they could be *close, but not too close*), she continued walking into her newly renovated kitchen that featured clear, glass-faced walnut cabinets, environmental-friendly bamboo flooring, and quartz countertops. "Would you like something to eat or drink? I didn't think to ask if you were a vegetarian, so I decided to forego anything with red meat or pork. Instead, I whipped up a light spinach salad with some tasty mesquite turkey."

"Oh, I'll just take some red wine if you have any. I see that you've remodeled your bungalow. What year was it built?" Kennedy glanced leisurely around the room, taking in the original craftsman ornate woodwork, alcove ceilings, and the large built in cabinet that served as the centerpiece in the dimly lit dining room.

"No problem, one glass of red wine coming right up. This gem of a bungalow was built in 1941. And, yes, since moving in a few years ago, I've been taking on various projects since it was in serious need of some TLC. I'm an HGTV junkie, so whenever I see something I like on one of their shows, I try to incorporate at least some aspects into my home." Cleo quickly dished up a small portion of spinach salad and poured two generous glasses of red wine and placed everything on a tray, then headed back to her guest in her living room.

"Here you go, Kennedy." Cleo slightly bent down to allow her to retrieve her wine glass and then it happened. The women fell into a trance staring deep into each other's eyes. Suddenly, the memory of their encounter a few weeks earlier in Cleo's office flashed through her mind.

Oh, why is she looking at me like that—again? Doesn't she know what that look does to me? Um, is that wetness I'm feeling down there? Snap out of it, girl. Damn.

Before speaking, Cleo counted to five, and then took a long gulp of wine. "Okay, we're finally alone to talk about the things we briefly touched on at work a few weeks ago. I don't know about you, but, honestly, I counted down the hours for this conversation while we were at work. I know I'm not the only woman who has discovered her attraction towards the same gender later in life, but you are the first woman I've known to admit it to me. I must say, it's comforting to know beyond a shadow of a doubt that I am not alone in this."

Realizing she was rambling, Cleo grabbed her fork, stabbed at her salad, and then quickly shoved a bite into her mouth. She nervously brushed her hair back with her left hand. She could feel herself trembling and prayed Kennedy hadn't noticed. It would be so embarrassing if she did.

Kennedy looked at her reassuringly. "Oh, Cleo. Let me say this—and I hope this will settle your nerves a little bit 'cause I can see you're nervous and I don't want you to be. This is a chance for us to come clean about this … this lesbian thing and I think we'll get more out of it if we let go of our doubts and just be honest with one another."

Oh, damn, she did notice. Shit! Cleo held her head down in shame.

Kennedy edged closer and wrapped her slender, yet strong arms around her shoulder. In turn, Cleo did the same. For a long while, they just held one another. Muted cries and moaning flooded her home, so many years of pent-up frustration, hesitation, and uncertainty concerning not only their sexual orientation but also their self-worth. Convictions that ran deeper than the Pacific Ocean for both women threatened their very being.

"Thanks. I needed that," Kennedy said breathlessly. She withdrew from their embrace but remained close to Cleo.

"Yeah, me, too apparently," Cleo lamented.

After getting all that out, the ladies gathered themselves, reached for their wine glasses, and continued their discourse.

"So, as I was telling you at work, I think I've always known, but just didn't have the words to say what it was. I just knew what I was feeling was different somehow, but I'd been attracted to girls since early childhood," Kennedy revealed.

"Wow! Are you serious, that young?" Cleo was taken aback by her statement. "But, *how* did you know?" Cleo's ears perked up like a feline in the same way Shelby's ears did when she was listening to a juicy story.

"Well," said Kennedy as she kicked up her knees and placed them under her bottom on the sofa. Her stylish sandals were already resting on the floor. It was obvious she was comfortable in Cleo's home. "… I can remember when I was in first grade, and I kept getting busted for sniffing my teacher's chair. I believe her name was Mrs. Armstrong and she was so beautiful to me … kinda reminded me of Lynda Carter when she played *Wonder Woman* on T.V." Kennedy grabbed her belly. She was rolling on the inside. "I can't explain it. There was just something about her scent, it was so … so seductive, so enticing to me for some reason …"

Cleo's eyes bulged in disbelief. "Hold up, hold up. Did you just say you got caught *sniffing* your teacher's chair?! What were you thinking?"

Kennedy burst into a deafening cackle and all you could see was her full set of pearly whites gleaming. "Ah, CeeCee, I couldn't tell you what was going through my mind, but the one thing Mrs. Armstrong said gave what I was a name, *gay*."

Kennedy had that faraway look in her twinkling grey eyes. Once again, Cleo was completely smitten with her striking looks, but instead of letting lust take control, she remained calm, cool, and collected.

A few moments passed as Kennedy pondered that time in her life. Speechless, Cleo remained silent as Kennedy's words settled in her mind.

Kennedy reached for her glass but realized it was empty. "May I have more wine, please?"

Cleo jumped. She was so attuned to the movie playing over and over in her head, that Kennedy's sultry voice startled her.

She placed her hand on Cleo's right knee and at that same moment, the phone rang.

"Ugh! Why is it the phone always rings when you're around, Miss Lady, jeez."

Kennedy gave her an innocent look that said *it's not my fault the phone is ringing*. She fluffed the large cushiony sofa pillows behind her, while Cleo pranced over to the counter to retrieve her phone.

"Oh, it's my sister, Symone. This won't take long, Kennedy." Cleo answered the phone. "Hey sis, what's goin' on?"

Kennedy rose from the sofa and stretched her succulent body. Her opulent eyes fixed on the watercolor painting that was strategically placed above the original, wood-burning ornate fireplace.

"Okay, that's fine, Symone." Cleo fingered the phone cord while her eyes enjoyed her company's backside. Once again, she felt herself getting aroused, her panties wet. "Tell my nieces I love them and I'll see you all soon. Bye!"

"You did ask for more wine, didn't you Kennedy?" she asked as she headed to the glass coffee table to retrieve their empty glasses.

"Yes, I did, thanks. Hey, who is Austin Timberland? I've never heard of him, but this painting is exquisite. I love the blend of rainbow colors."

Cleo grabbed a bottle of Oliver Soft Red Wine from her fridge and held it up to show it to her. "Will this do?"

Still transfixed on Austin's art, Kennedy nodded in response.

"His approach to watercolor is something out of this world, isn't it? Austin is a frat brother of one of my ex-boyfriends, Craig. I became an instant fan since I first saw his work, so I'm not surprised that the painting has captured your attention."

The nervousness Cleo felt before Kennedy arrived had finally begun to subside. Surely all the wine they were indulging in had something to do with it.

Cleo once again filled her glass to the brim, then slinked over to the star of her wet dreams and topped off her glass. As the bubbly flowed throughout the rest of the evening, the heat between the two women grew to a fiery pitch. The hour hand struck nine o'clock on the huge antique wall clock as the women's tongues delighted in a carnal dance, just as they had a few weeks before in Cleo's office. Slowly, they began undressing one another as they headed to Cleo's bedroom.

Though she was enthralled with what was happening, Cleo couldn't help but think about how things had gotten out of control.

One button, two buttons, three buttons, four. She counted each one on Kennedy's shirt as she released them, only to reveal a seductive, black balconette lace bra, nipples so hard they threatened to burst through the garment.

She didn't want to stop the tongue lashing going on between them (they were oh-so-hungry for it), but once Kennedy's bosom was on front street, Cleo commenced to kneading her right breast as her tongue dug in and out of her inviting, wet mouth.

"Oh, God, you are so beautiful, Kennedy."

The women barely made it to Cleo's bedroom which was tastefully decorated in soft, muted earth colors of creamy caramel and burnt sienna gave testament to her taste in décor and HGTV flair.

"Take off your clothes and lay down on your back," Cleo demanded. "Alexa, play 'Do Me Baby' by Prince." Prince's falsetto voice immediately filled the air, bathing them in the tantalizing melodic verses. She looked on as Kennedy followed her command, letting what clothes remained on her body fall into a puddle around her ankles. She seductively stepped out of the puddle, eyes still glued on her soon-to-be lover, settling onto the cushiony mattress and held out her hand, inviting Cleo to join her.

The excitement brooding inside Cleo was almost too much to bear, but that didn't stop her from stripping naked and hopping into bed to join the beautiful Kennedy.

After months of dreaming and fantasizing about her co-worker being in her bed, her fantasy was becoming reality.

Indeed, for the first time in their lives, they were embarking on a new journey that both had dreamed of many times, but never really thought would come to fruition. Gone were their fears and inhibitions. They anxiously gave in to what they were feeling for each other and just let it *flow* like Niagara Falls.

Cleo slowly crawled on top of her, taking it all in, touching, rubbing, feeling, caressing, licking and kissing every single part of Kennedy's sultry body, from her wonderfully manicured toes, to her soft, but firm calves, thighs, and full hips. Before she arrived at her wet-and-sexy V, Cleo was already drunk on her tantalizing scent. Meanwhile, a very limber Kennedy obliged by opening her legs wide, revealing her delectable pretty-in-pink pussy.

"Damn girl! I didn't know you had it goin' on like *that,"* she exclaimed just before her wagging tongue slid inside. Kennedy's legs quivered and shook like spiraling waves, while her body writhed with pleasure.

Though this was her first time tasting a woman, Cleo dove into her new lover's soft peach like a pro, a testament to how often she'd fantasized about doing this very same thing, and now, she was experiencing it in living color.

"Oh, Cleo, it feels sooo good, so good! I can't believe how good this feels, oh my God. This is crazy, oh, yeah, that's it, keep strokin' her, oh, don't stop! Yes! Oh, Tink loves that!"

"Uhmmummm," Cleo managed to say in between slurps, her tongue continuing on its course, hands firmly gripped and kneaded Kennedy's plump ass, traveling up to her heaving breasts where they found Kennedy's hard-as-nails round nipples aching to be sucked on.

Almost two hours went by before Cleo came up for air. Kennedy's intoxicating nectar was just too good to pull away from. After the first time, she exploded into her mouth, Cleo thought she was going to lose it. The taste was just that breathtaking.

Damn, I'm in love.

Not to bc outdone, Kennedy was overly anxious to do some exploring of her own. Once again, their tongues found their way back to one another. Cleo's entire face was covered in Kennedy's wetness, sending them both into ecstasy once again. Now the commander-in-charge, Kennedy flipped the script by having Cleo stretch out on the bed on her stomach. Cleo nestled her nose into her pillow, gleefully giving up control to the beautiful gazelle.

"Now, close your eyes and don't move," sweet seduction dripping with every word. "There are some things I've been aching to do to you for a long time," stated Kennedy as her hot tongue trailed up and down the inviting crevices of Cleo's backside.

A glimmer of light shone through the amethyst-colored French-pleated curtains, casting a warm glow onto her milky-smooth skin. Her heart was thumping hard, and her body shuddered at the mere thought of what was to come.

Kennedy first touched and caressed Cleo's soft derrière and velvety smooth back, long tongue strokes soon followed and all that was heard were oh's and ah's coming from Cleo. Hearing her moans increased her horniness ten times over, leading her to do even more exploring … only instead of using her hands, her hot, thirsty tongue was in search mode.

Kennedy flexed her arms, lifted Cleo's back half and dug her wet tongue into her firm butthole, sending cascades of tremors up and down her body. Indeed, they were so entrenched with the lovemaking or fucking, whichever was the more appropriate term for their unexpected sexcapade, before she knew it, she yelled out Kennedy's name over and over and over again.

Pure. Unadulterated. Pleasure.

The ladies eagerly took turns, graciously letting one another take the lead as the sizzling sex continued throughout the evening.

In the back of Cleo's mind, however, reality kept rearing its ugly head. The very stark reminder that her newly appointed femme fatale was a married woman, with children.

"What's wrong? Kennedy asked as she turned to look Cleo dead in the eyes.

All the shuckin' and divin' the women were doing in Cleo's bed was beginning to mess with her head, but she was determined to not let it show.

"Oh, nothing, babe," Cleo lied, shaking it off. She brushed a few strands of Kennedy's hair back, then drew her in for a deep tongue kiss. She felt her body melt like butter in her grasp and in that moment, she pretended Kennedy was all hers … even if it was for a few fleeting moments.

Besides, Cleo's heart was still set on finding Prince Charming and starting a family of her own someday. She wasn't ready to give up on that long-held dream… at least she didn't think she was.

⚢ 11 ⚥

Cleo was just leaving her client's southside apartment, where the roaches, bullets, and bodily fluids roamed freely, when her cell went off. It was her basic ring, meaning that whoever it was, their number was not pre-saved. Typically, it was a bill collector or some company trying to sell her something or wanted her to donate to their worthy cause. She reached into her purse and retrieved her mobile phone. "This is Cleo Stinson. How can I help you?"

"Hey there, lady. It is sooo good to hear your voice."

She tossed her purse and work bag inside and settled into the driver's seat.

"Hey there yourself Javon. How are you?" The sun was just beginning to set, revealing an array of glowing late summer hues like citrine, crimson, and ochre. It reminded her of all the sunsets she and Javon used to relish in at their favorite parks, Eagle Creek and Riverside.

"Oh, yes. I'm here. Sorry, my cell isn't getting a good reception out here," she lied. "Now, what were you saying?" She cranked up the engine, secured her seatbelt, and backed out of the parking lot.

"Oh, I see. Well, where are you anyway?"

He got some damn nerve, she commented to herself. With certain irritation in her voice, she replied, "Javon, who's phone number is this? You better not be calling me from one of your hoe's phones, I know that much," she popped off, not allowing him to get a word in edgewise. "Now what have I told you about askin' me about my whereabouts? I am NOT your woman, so you ain't got no right to be asking me personal questions, you hear me?! And another thing—"

"But, wait a sec, I just wanna—"

"Look boy, don't be interrupting me when I'm talkin'!" she shouted into the phone. As I was saying, I haven't heard a peep out of you since that night at Club Isis when Shelby read you all up and down like a book!"

"Cleo, please. Just listen for one moment, damn!" Javon yelled on the other end. That did it for her. She hung up. "Good riddance," she hissed under her breath as she rolled into her garage and turned off the engine. All she wanted to do once she walked inside her home was peel off her clothes and check her handbag for roaches. She noticed several crawling up the dingy white wall in front of her during the discussion she was having with her client Shalonda Wilkins, a barely nineteen-year-old mom who'd just given birth to her fifth child. The poor girl was on the verge of losing her kids for the third time because of her long-time struggle with crack.

She drove all the way to the south side of town to drop off information about a few community resources available to her, but Miss Wilkins seemed more interested in the baby daddy drama that was unfolding on *Maury* than anything else. Now that Tomika Grimes had resigned, Cleo had to pick up all of Ms. Wilkin's cases until the position got filled, but who knew how long that was going to take. Cleo groaned inwardly as she made her way home.

⚢ 12 ⚥

"Hello?"

"Hey, baby, where you been? I been callin' and callin'. Why ain't chu answer yo phone?"

Cleo's ears felt a bit painful from hearing Javon's poor English. "I've been busy, Javon. What do you want? And besides, didn't I just tell you yesterday about yourself?" Cleo finished emptying the last grocery bag. "Look, I'm preparing for company. It's my turn to host the book club I started a few months ago."

"Hey, slow down there, baby. What, you tryin' to be like Oprah now? You tryin' to be white?"

A vexed Cleo leaned against the kitchen wall and took in several deep breaths before responding. "You know Javon, I expected something that ignorant to come out of your mouth. You need some culture. You need to venture outside of your small world, and you just never know, you might learn something."

"Girl, you trippin' me out with that stuff. Anyways, you always talkin' that smack about me not spending enough 'quality time' with you, but I've been tryin' to contact you and you ain't been returnin' my calls, so, you tell me what's up with that? Did you go and meet someone new or something? Betcha he can't lick you like I can.

Matter of fact, why don't you come pay me a visit so I can taste you. I miss that fat pussy of yours."

Automatically, Cleo felt wetness on her panties. *That fucker knows how to hit it home. Argh! He gets on my last nerve, knowing full well how I love getting my pussy licked by him.*

"You ain't nothing but a freak, you know that? And whose pussy besides mine have you been licking here lately?" asked a now horny Cleo as she cut up celery for the vegetable tray. The veiled, yet tantalizing memory of her time with Kennedy crept into her mind.

Uh oh, not again. A warm, instantaneous squirt seeped through her panties. Cleo grinned ear-to-ear.

In his old swaggering voice, Javon replied, "Girl, you know you 'da only one. I ain't been messin' with none of 'em hoes. You are my number one anyways, so don't even play me like dat. Now, come on, whatcha gonna do? You gonna come through tonight or what?"

Reluctantly, she replied, "Well, I'm hosting our book club this evening, so I guess I'll come through later tonight. Say around eleven, eleven-thirty. I'll see you then. Bye."

"Bye, baby. See ya tonight."

Well, once again, I ain't one to pass up some bomb-ass head, so if he wanna taste these juices, I'ma make sure my punani flows like a waterfall while I ride that nigga's face.

****

"Hey sis, what's up?" asked a rather cheery Symone. Standing at five-foot-eleven, smooth, cocoa-brown skin and a sleek 'grown and sexy' short hairdo, like her younger sister, she commanded her fair share of attention from the opposite sex as well. Today, she was dressed in a pale blue halter top sundress and matching sandals.

"Hey, what are you so happy about?" Cleo asked as she closed the door.

"Ah, nothing, girl. I'm just in a good mood is all," she replied with a sheepish grin on her face.

"Girl, it's me, okay? I can see the excitement dancing in your eyes. Now, come out with it." Giggling, Symone dangled her left hand.

"Oh, my God!" exclaimed Cleo. "Look at that humongous rock on your finger!"

She was sporting an exquisite, beautifully cut marquise diamond ring. It had such perfect clarity, it twinkled like the crystalline stars in the late-night sky.

"Yes!" screeched Symone. "David replaced my wedding ring since my original one was stolen from our jeweler's shop last year. You remember that don't you?"

"Of course, I remember. You had taken it in because one of the doo-hickeys had come loose, right? Did the police ever find out who did it?" she inquired as they walked back into the kitchen.

"Doo-hickey? For real, CeeCee? You mean a prong; it's called a prong." Symone shook her head.

Cleo threw her hands in the air. "Well, damn sis, I just couldn't think of what the dang thing is called, okay?"

"Girl, sometimes you make me wonder about you. No, they haven't, and it is so damn frustrating! But we can still count our blessings. I'm glad no one got hurt that day when those damn thieves waltzed up in there in the middle of the day like that. That was some bold-ass shit," said Symone as she sat down at the kitchen counter and began arranging soda crackers, saltines and wheat crackers on the serving tray.

"That's a scary thought, isn't it?" Cleo said as she glanced at the wall clock. "Oh, shit. It's already six-thirty. Let's get this food ready before they start knocking at my door. You know Donnieka will be looking for food as soon as she walks in, but what she really needs is a Slim-Fast," said a repulsed Cleo.

"How is Donnieka doing with her weight loss? I haven't seen her since our meeting last month."

"Well, to be straight up with you, she is not faring so well. She told me that her doctor wanted her to lose fifteen pounds before her next check-up with him, but instead of losing, she'd gained another ten!" exclaimed Cleo.

"No! You've got to be joking. The last time I saw her, she looked like she weighed at least three hundred pounds, damn!" Symone said, concerned.

Cleo added, dejectedly, "I wish I was. I've tried to get her on the track with Shelby and me, but she always comes up with an excuse. But I tell you, her weight scares me to death. She's inching closer and closer to three hundred pounds, and she has such a pretty face and cheerful personality. It's a shame. I can't remember if I told you, but recently, one of my coworkers passed away because of complications from obesity. It ain't nothin' to play with, ya know?"

"Wow, CeeCee. That's really sad," said Symone as she added the last cracker and garnishment to the serving tray. Well, I guess all we can do is just be there for her and encourage her."

"Yeah, you're right. I will keep after her because I don't wanna see her get so overweight like those humongous people I see on *My 600-lb. Life.* Man, some of'em be weighing as much as 700 and 800 pounds! Sis, I tell ya, that shit is so crazy!"

"I know, I know," Symone shook her head, then picked up the tray and headed to the living room.

Cleo was in tow, carrying a few bottles of their favorite Moscato. "Hey, by the way, I've been meaning to ask you how your MBA classes are going."

Symone set the tray on the small folding table Cleo had put up next to the sliding door. "Oh, girl, they're kicking my ass, but I must say, I'm glad I chose an online program."

"I know that's right. School ain't no joke, no matter the subject you're studying," Cleo lamented as she straightened the red plastic cups next to the wine. "Okay, looks like we're ready. Our guests should be here any moment now."

Exacerbated, Symone trudged over to Cleo's sofa and kicked up her heels. "Whew," she said, "I don't know why I'm so out of breath suddenly."

"You know, I've noticed you've been short of breath the last few times we were together," sipping her freshly poured Moscato.

Symone rubbed her aching temples. "I know, sis. I'm not sure what's going on, but I did schedule an appointment with Dr. Michelson for next week."

"Speaking of the doctor, I'm due for a check-up myself. I'll be sure to get on her schedule next week, too, if I can."

Just then, the doorbell rang. Cleo sucked down the last drop of Moscato, then rose from her comfy seat to answer the door.

⚢ 13 ⚤

Her company didn't leave until well past eleven. Cleo's bed was calling her name and she was all-to-ready to succumb to her sleepiness. The horniness she felt earlier during her conversation with Javon had waned. She didn't bother calling him to let him know she'd have to take a rain check on their midnight rendezvous.

Hell, he can get a little taste of the shit he's always dishing out to me for once, Cleo thought as she prepared for bed.

Her bedroom walls were flawlessly painted in a soft shade of primrose and her queen-sized bed was situated in the middle of the room against a wall with windows on both sides. When she first checked out the house, the room she fell most in love with was the master bedroom suite. The large windows brought in lots and lots of natural sunlight, making the room warm and cozy. The walk-in closet had plenty of storage space for all her clothes, handbags and shoes. And, lastly, the master bath offered double sinks, a jacuzzi tub and exquisite light fixtures that she'd added herself shortly after moving in.

In her birthday suit, she crawled into bed and pulled the lavender flat sheet and bedspread up to her neck. She reached for the TV remote control and turned the news on. More bad news.
The anchor was talking about some little girl that had been kidnapped by her play uncle and there was a story about a young boy walking home in his neighborhood minding his own business when suddenly he was shot in the crossfire of two battling gangs. Before she knew it, her mind drifted into dreamland.

"Come here, Cleo."

Cleo nervously sauntered over to this strange, sexy feline who was sprawled out over her bed, naked.

"You don't mind if I kiss you, do you, sweetheart? Your lips look so soft and I've been holding back my urge to lick them all night long," said the enticing woman.

"No, I don't mind at all. I've been wanting you to kiss me but wasn't sure of how to tell you. I've never done this before, so I'm kind of nervous. I'm not sure what to do, how to act …" Cleo admitted as she sat down on the bed. Her hands and knees began to shake uncontrollably, small beads of perspiration formed on her forehead. Knowingly, the anonymous lady reached out and put her hand on Cleo's thigh. "Ah, it's okay, baby. It's really no different from kissing a man. We're just a whole lot softer, is all."

Cleo's chocolate-brown eyes become transfixed on her gorgeous honey-dipped body laid out on the bed. Her small round nipples were already standing at attention and Cleo's mouth began to salivate.

Watching Cleo admiring her curvaceous, silky-smooth body, the nameless and faceless vixen placed her hand on Cleo's narrow chin. For a moment, they gazed into each other's eyes, and then it happened. The vixen's hungry mouth inched closer to Cleo's lips. Cleo, whose initial nervousness had her shaking earlier, was now calm. She wrapped her firm arms around the feline's soft, thick waist. She was enjoying everything about what was happening.

The sexy vixen slowly, methodically nudged her tongue into Cleo's wanting mouth. Following her lead, Cleo was so alarmed and amazed at how soft and sensual the vixen's lips felt as they touched hers. Instinctively, Cleo's hands went on a journey on the woman's heavenly body. Cleo said to herself, "Ya know, she was right. It really is no different from kissing a man ... but then again, it is." This woman was tonguing her down unlike no man had ever done before and it left her wanting, yearning for more.

⚢ 14 ⚥

The sultry sounds of Art of Noise's 'Love' echoed through her Ridgeline's interior as she drove down North Michigan Road, the song's beautiful melody echoing her mood, reminding her of the titillating waves of pleasure she experienced when she and Kennedy kissed for the first time and was looking forward to spending time with her. She so yearned to experience that kind of affection again; to discover and rediscover the sweet nectar between Kennedy's thighs, to touch the soft spot hidden behind her left ear and the tiny crevices in the back of her right arm and behind her kneecaps. It wasn't long before she felt something wet and warm down below, causing her to tighten her thighs, keeping her climax avalanche under control.

Cleo rolled into the parking lot with just a few minutes to spare. She noticed Kennedy's silver Volvo parked on the opposite side and breathed a sigh of relief that she showed up as she said she would. She stole one last look in the rearview mirror, before bouncing out of her ride and headed inside the coffee joint. As she entered through the door, she was greeted by a bubbly barista, with a high, squeaky voice, "Hi! Welcome to Starbucks, how can I help you?"

Cleo smiled. "Thank you, but I'm gonna check out the menu first." Her eyes were transfixed on the chalk written menu above the barista's head.

Like all other Starbucks locations, this location was decorated in warm, earthy colors, and boasts of light-colored wooden tables and chairs, a half dozen window-facing bar stools, and a few comfy brown leather chairs situated in one corner.

Several dozen people peppered the space, including a group of college students who were all hovering over the table looking at something on a laptop, a freckle-faced woman dousing her Danish into her coffee, scrolling through her iPhone, and chatting up a friend sitting across from her. A weird-looking older Arab man with beady eyes bore a hole into her as she walked by him on her way to the small table where Kennedy sat, just about to take a sip of her steaming latté. Cleo gave him a look and shook her head, a sure sign that his rudeness did not break her stride.

"Hello beautiful," she stated as she sat down across from Kennedy. "You look great as always."

Kennedy blushed. "Hello to you, too, Miss Stinson. She gestured towards the counter. "Are you going to get something to drink or eat?"

"Um, maybe later," she shrugged, she didn't really want anything right now. How's your latté? What flavor is that?" she asked as she leaned forward, peaking into her cup.

Kennedy's face lit up as if she'd just won a prize or something. "Oh, CeeCee, this is my favorite drink ever, it's their skinny latté and it tastes so damn good, you just wouldn't believe!"

Kennedy gazed longingly at Cleo, licking her natural-hued lips, "… almost tastes as good as your kisses did a few weeks back."

Cleo nervously rubbed her chin and giggled, not sure of how to respond to her obvious flirting.

"Wow, it must really be 'cause you just about leaped from your chair a moment ago," she laughed. "My favorite is their caramel macchiato—now that's some good stuff right there!" She exclaimed, trying to take her mind off Kennedy's statement, but finding it very difficult to do so.

"But, CeeCee, that drink has way too many calories, oh my God! It's just too fattening, girl!" A look of terror spread across her face.

Cleo smirked and shook her head. "Okay, okay, enough with this jibber-jabber. We came here to discuss *us,* not the fat content in my favorite Starbucks drink, wow."

Before she knew what she was doing, Cleo's hand found its way to Kennedy's exposed thigh. It felt taut and warm to the touch and the smoldering fire deep down in Cleo's belly got a searing jolt from the interaction.

She averted her eyes towards Kennedy's and watched her pouty, yet wonderfully clear lips spread into the most magnificent smile she'd ever seen. Though the temperature inside the coffeehouse was nice and cool.

Small beads of sweat rolled down the nape of her neck. She had to grab one of Kennedy's napkins to wipe her neck.

It's getting hottttttt in herrrreeee.

The weather was simply perfect that evening in Nap, having cooled down from close to ninety degrees to a much cooler seventy-two degrees. "Do you want to sit out on the patio?" Cleo asked.

"You know, it has cooled down a lot and I do love feeling the sweet summer breeze across my skin," Kennedy responded, rising from her seat.

"Okay, great, I'm gonna go ahead and order a drink right quick, so I'll meet you outside," she said as she headed toward the counter.

****

Iced coffee in hand, Cleo walked onto the patio only to discover Kennedy engaged with another woman.

"Hey Kennedy, I decided on an iced coffee this time." A concrete smile appeared on her face.

"Hello, I'm Cleo and you are?"

Kennedy interjected, "Cleo, this is my sister-in-law, Saquarah. Saquarah, this is one of my good friends from work, Cleo."

Cleo's heart dropped to her stomach. Saquarah had obviously made herself comfortable and appeared to have no intentions of leaving anytime soon. Damn, it would seem that their tête-à-tête would have to wait.

Cleo sat down across from Kennedy. An apology was written all over her face, but it was especially apparent in her beautiful eyes.

"It's nice to make your acquaintance, Cleo," stated Saquarah, a stout woman with cocoa-colored skin, big bubbly hazel eyes and the tiniest hands and feet Cleo had ever seen on a woman. The ladies spent the remainder of the evening talking about everything under the sun and though the conversation kept Cleo's attention, she couldn't help but think about the discussion she and Kennedy had already planned. Saquarah just so happened to live in the neighborhood, decided to test out the brand-new bike her husband had just bought her and found herself at her neighborhood Starbucks.

How great for her.

Saquarah's presence confirmed that there would be no discussing their budding relationship (dare she refer to it in that way since Kennedy was a married woman … all day, every day).

It wasn't long before Cleo was over the discussion that was not to be had that evening and especially Kennedy's intrusive sister-in-law. Cleo drank the last few drops of her beverage, then she excused herself as she scrolled through a few old text messages and began walking towards her truck.

Kennedy swiftly jumped to her feet, a glimmer of sadness still evident in her weak smile, "Okay, Cleo. I'll call you!"

"Sounds good, chat with you soon," she replied as she clicked the alarm button on her keychain. Shortly after leaving the parking lot, her cell buzzed.

"Hi, baby. Can we talk?" It was a message from Javon who she'd been avoiding for the past few weeks. Cleo had no interest in dealing with him, especially since Craig was now back in the picture; and then there was still fine-ass Reese and most recently, Miss St. Martin. Whew, with all these options, what was a girl to do? *I think it's time to tell Javon he can go kick rocks.*

She silenced her phone, turned on some old-school Loose Ends and continued on her merry way.

⚢ 15 ⚤

The alarm sounded promptly at six-thirty. Cleo immediately checked her phone to see if Kennedy had texted her. Much to her delight, she had,

Once again I apologize for the interruption with Saquarah. I was just sitting there sipping my latte when suddenly I heard my name being called—then I saw her and my heart sank. SMH. I promise I will make it up to you soon. Smooches □

Yes! That woman really is digging on me, sweet! She sprung out of bed and immediately felt wetness between her legs. She'd cum in her sleep while dreaming about Kennedy. *Oh, damn! It's happened again. Why am I dreaming about her like this? Why did I let her kiss me?* She asked herself, no longer able to shake it off anymore. Thinking about being intimate with another woman was something that had never entered her mind when she was younger. And, yet, she could not explain why she was having these thoughts out of the clear blue.

The dreams and fantasies had increased ever since the day Kennedy first laid those lips on hers, causing her much discomfort and confusion. And yet, she could not deny the very real tugging, fluttering in her belly. Her curiosity was aroused in ways she'd never imagined.

Still, she longed to meet and eventually marry her Mr. Right. Her biological clock was moving at warp speed, and she didn't want it to expire before she could feel a bundle of joy growing in her womb. She'd always imagined having a baby girl and had already chosen her name: *Anya Marie Clementine*. She was waiting on her man to come claim her as his wife. But, every day, it seemed like a far-fetched dream that was never going to come true.

⚢ 16 ⚥

Cleo peeped out of her bedroom window. It was a beautiful Saturday morning, the sun casting off a stunning, morning glow, reminding her of blooming daffodils—her mother's favorite flower. *Well, the Lord must be happy today for the Creator has lavished us with wonderful weather* she commented to herself as she peeked at her watch and saw that it was half-past seven. With Kennedy and what would have been their first discussion on her mind, she headed north on Lafayette Road to meet Shelby and a few other friends, Donnieka Williams and Crimson Thomas at Northwestway Park for their weekly walk together. It was always the same scenario. Shelby and Cleo would lead the pack. Donnieka seemed to always become afflicted with some type of ailment after the first mile. Today, it was a Charlie horse. Well, that was no surprise, hell the girl weighed close to 350 pounds and was only five-foot-five. Her family doctor told her that if she didn't make some type of effort to lose weight, she was never going to be able to have the gastric bypass surgery she wanted so desperately.

Over the last year, she was diagnosed with diabetes, her high blood pressure had skyrocketed since she put on another fifteen pounds, and it was not likely to come down anytime soon.

At the midway point, Crimson began complaining about her back hurting. Now, she was nowhere near the size of Donnieka, but would still be considered 'overweight' by American standards, weighing about 139 pounds, but she was also just short of being six feet tall like her model mother.

"Come with me over to the picnic table, Crimson. We can wait there until Shelby and Cleo finish the rest of their run," said Donnieka, panting as she began walking towards the table.

"Okay, here I come," said Crimson as she headed toward Donnieka at the table, all while rubbing her lower back with her right arm.

"Boy, I swear. Donnieka pulls this shit every time we come to the park. She always talkin' that smack about how she wants to lose weight. Hell, just the other day, she came over to my house crying because she's so fat and nobody likes her or wants to be around her," Cleo huffed.

"Ah, come on, CeeCee. Cut her some slack. You know her self-esteem is shot to shit," Shelby said as she began to pick up the pace around the track.

Cleo increased her stride to stay in line with Shelby. "I know girl, but I'm just frustrated with her. She constantly asks for our help and I've been going out of my way with trying to keep her on the right track. But, when it comes to puttin' in work, she is forever coming up with excuses. I've just about had it with her!"

"Well, CeeCee, all I can say is, don't give up on the girl 'cause it sounds as though she really needs people in her corner while she tries to tackle her weight problem. I mean, it ain't like you and I both don't know what it's like to struggle with our weight. But it's all good. Okay, enough with the chitchat, let's handle our business and go around the trail a few more times before calling it a day. Are you with me or what?" asked Shelby.

Steady with her breathing, Cleo responded, "Hey, girl. I'm with it!" Then she took off, leaving Shelby in the dust.

****

After getting into her truck, Cleo checked her cell for messages, hoping at least one would be from Kennedy. There were three missed calls, two of which were from her, much to Cleo's delight.

"Cleo, I'm so sorry about last night," she said breathlessly. "I truly was not expecting to run into my sister-in-law, but I definitely want to meet up sometime today, that is if you have some spare time.

Right now, I'm on my way to take my son to his karate lesson and I have to run a few errands but will be done no later than four. Give me a call as soon as you can. I really hope we can connect later this afternoon."

Cleo grinned cheek-to-cheek. *Wow, maybe she really is digging me, even more than I originally thought.* She was so tickled and anxious, she called Kennedy immediately.

"Oh, hey, it's me, Cleo. I got your message and yes, I'd love to see you today," she blurted.

"Hey CeeCee. Great to hear, so let's pick up our conversation at your house, is that okay?" Kennedy asked.

Well damn, she might as well hit me over the head with a sledgehammer... of course, we can't talk at her house or anything else for that matter.

Where. She. Lives.

With. Her. Husband.

And. Children.

A biting chill ran down Cleo's back. *I've got to keep my perspective with whatever this is with her. Get it together girl and put your game face back on.*

Cleo bit her lip. "Oh, okay, sounds good."

"Wonderful. What time should I arrive?"

"Let's say six o'clock, that cool?"

"Great. I look forward to it. Ciao for now."

"See you then, bye-bye."

⚢ 17 ⚦

Cleo had just finished sprucing up her home in anticipation for Kennedy's arrival. Gerald Levert's "Baby I'm Ready" rang out from the wall speakers she recently had professionally installed. Gerald's lyrics permeated her feelings for Kennedy, though she questioned them often. *Do I really love Kennedy or is it just the sex?* …was the one burning question she didn't have an honest answer for…at least not yet. She continued using the Swiffer dust mop on the living room wood floor and singing along with Gerald when her cell dinged, notifying her of a text from Kennedy,

Pls, pls, pls don't be mad at me, CeeCee. I'm not gonna be able to make it over due to unforeseen circumstances. I promise to make it up to u soon!

"Fuck, here we go. I hate this shit!" Cleo shouted. "It's bad enough she can't spend the night with me, and now this again?! Arghhh!!!!" Cleo threw the dust mop across the room in a fit of rage, then stomped down the hallway to her room, stripped naked, tears streaming down her cheeks, jumped into her bed, snatched her bedspread from the end, covering her whole body up with it, and continued crying into her pillow.

I know you ain't surprised.
Shut the fuck up! I don't wanna hear it.
I done told ya ass many times that woman is married with children and ain't gon' neva leave her family fo' ya ass, so you may as well finally come down from the blue sky, take them rose-colored glasses off with the quickness and get real dummy!
Fuck you!
Yeah, OK, keep it up. She's gonna break your heart, just you wait and see.
Whatever asshole.

⚢ 18 ⚥

"Hey baby, what's up?"

"Oh, God. Here we go," Cleo said, grabbing her lighter and a box of chocolate-flavored cigarillos lying on her living room table. *I can tell already I'm gonna need this.* "You're just not gonna leave well enough alone, are you, Javon?" She pulled out a cigarillo, stuck it in her mouth and lit it. *I'd much prefer to be talking to Kennedy instead of your ass. I can't believe she hasn't text or called me yet, damn.*

"Now, see. There you go, talkin' all that mess when all I wanna do is make you happy, make you mines forever. I done already told you, I ain't tryin' to be wit' nobody else but you. But you be actin' all funky and shit whenever the mood hits you. Sometimes I think you don't want to be bothered with me, but I still love you, though."

Cleo cringed at the words that just left his lips. "As always, you are full of shit, Javon. You ain't foolin' nobody but yourself."

"Why is it that just about every time we talk, we gotta argue? Can't we have a pleasant conversation sometimes, damn! Look, the main reason why I'm callin' you is because I want to take you out for dinner and a movie. I was thinkin' we can check out Kevin Hart's new flick."

"So, am I supposed to just forget about that mess at the club with you and Shelby?" Cleo shot back.

"Baby, I done apologized for that a million times now. I was drunk 'n' didn't know what I was saying, okay? Now can't we just get past that now, please? Now, whatcha thank 'bout checking out Kevin's new movie? I know you dig his brand of comedy."

Cleo savored the taste of chocolate after taking another pull. "Yeah, I do like his crazy-ass movies 'cause he's hilarious." She paused for a minute, then responded, "Well, I guess that will be cool. What time are you talkin'?"

"Oh, yeah! That's my baby girl, you know I love yo' ass so stop playin' with me. Hold on while I go check the website. I looked at it earlier, but now I don't remember the time."

Cleo could hear the faint clicking sound of his huge fingers on the keyboard of his laptop as she waited impatiently on the other end.

Fumbling with the receiver, in his raspy voice, he said, "Okay, it starts at 7:35 p.m. It's only about a quarter past three now. Can you be ready by 6:15 p.m?"

Only half interested, Cleo said, "Um, yeah. That's enough time for me. Wait a minute, do I have to drive again?"

"No, silly! I will swoop you up at 6:15 sharp. Just make sure you're ready."

"Okay. You know I got to check with you since you don't have a car. By the way, whose car will you be driving this time anyway?" Cleo asked as she headed down the hallway to her bedroom.

"Oh, that's real funny, CeeCee. Anyways, a buddy of mine let me hold his whip while he's out of town for a couple of days. But it won't be long before I get my own ride. I've been savin' for almost six months now. So, whatcha think about that, woman? See, I'm making all these changes just for you—for us. You're going to be my wife one day soon, ya know."

She ignored the 'wife' comment. "Well, it's about time, my man! That is great news and I'm so happy for you! Hey, I'ma get off this phone so I can be ready when you get here. See you shortly, bye." *Shit, it will be nice to have that nigga come pick me up for once.*

"Alright, see you soon, sweets."

After getting off the phone with Javon, Cleo checked and double-checked her cell to see if there had been any word from Kennedy.

Crickets.

****

At 6:50 p.m., they pulled into what used to be a Cubs grocery store parking lot. They stepped out of the souped-up 1970 Chevrolet Chevelle, which had been painted money-green.

"Hey, Cleo, let's hurry up and get inside. There are more people pullin' in and I wanna get a good seat," said Javon as he walked around to the passenger side. Cleo took a long look at him, remembering what had attracted her to him so long ago. He wasn't all that tall, only five-foot-eight, slightly on the chubby side with a chestnut brown complexion. His light brown eyes reminded her of a puppy dog because they drooped slightly in the corners. Tonight, he was neatly dressed in a honey-brown Dashiki and a pair of dark brown slacks. She'd decided to wear her favorite ebony-colored blouse and a long, heather-gray flared skirt.

"Okay, Javon. I'm ready," Cleo said, reaching for his hand. "By the way, Donnieka and Crimson saw it last night and said we will not be disappointed."

"Oh yeah? My partner Darrell said the same thing." He smiled, then bent over slightly and kissed her on her hand. "Did I tell ya that ya look good, gal? Damn, ya sho' do, baby."

Cleo blushed. "Yes, you did, but a lady never tires of hearing how good she looks, so do go on." They both started cracking up.

"Girl, get yo tail on in here," Javon said, holding the cinema door open for her.

****

"So, what did you think of the movie?" asked Javon as they strolled back to the Malibu, holding hands.

"Actually, I thought it was pretty good. Lots of crazy-ass humor like only Kevin can deliver. But I don't know if I would go as far to say that it was his funniest stand-up act ever, like Donnieka and Crimson said," replied Cleo as she slid into the passenger seat for the second time that night. She wasn't used to this kind of treatment from Javon as *she* was usually the one driving *him* around. *Hmmm, I could get used to this.*

"Yeah, I agree. I think he was much more hilarious in his first stand-up special, but, eh, everybody got they own opinion, right babe?" he said as he closed the passenger door. "One thing I do know fo' sho' is that ol' Kev got good taste in 'dem skirts, though."

Cleo rolled her eyes at his juvenile statement.

"Well, my lady, what would you like to eat for dinner? And I hope you gon' be my dessert, eh?"

He stuck his long, thick tongue out of his full brown lips just so she could be reminded of what his lil' trooper—as he called it—could do to her milky-pink clit. As much as she hated to admit it, he was THE ONE man that knew exactly how to stroke her plump, juicy clit the right way. Every. Single. Time. What made the situation worse was that he was well aware of this very fact, too.

Ignoring his reference to her being his dessert, she replied, "Well, I'm pretty open to whatever. As long as it's not Golden Corral or a Chinese restaurant," Cleo said as he opened the passenger side door for her.

"Um, aren't you quite the gentleman, opening doors for me now? You haven't done that since the days when we first began dating," noted an impressed Cleo as she settled into the black leather passenger seat and crossed her legs.

Javon laughed. "I know, I know. I'm tryin' to switch up some things, ya know. Make things like they used to be between us. We had such a good relationship and I'm just tryin' to show ya that I can be that man again for ya, baby. Like I said before, I want you to be my wife one day."

Cleo could feel the tiny hairs on her neck spring up after hearing Javon's words. She had dreaded him bringing up *marriage* again. "Javon, we've already been through this. I don't see it, us being married any time in the future, so why can't you just accept that and move on?"

Cleo noticed that as he gripped the steering wheel tighter, his jaw tightened as well. "Baby, I don't want to get in no argument. Things are going good so far tonight and I want it to continue. Consider the subject dropped. Now, back to dinner, how about Rick's Boatyard? I got a taste for some nice, lean steak and theirs are the best!"

Glad he dropped the subject, Cleo's mood suddenly felt a little brighter. Bobbing her head to some hip hop song that was blaring out the sound system that had a slammin' beat, but unintelligible lyrics, she said, "Cool with me."

"So, whatcha got up fo' the rest of the night, baby?" Eagerness was written all over his face.

"Why do you ask? What's on your mind, Javon?"

"Well, ya know ... you did stand me up the other night, remember? And, just to think, my tongue was all set and ready to taste all your juices, gal. I was so ready to sop ya up with a biscuit. So, what do ya say? After dinner, ya thank we can mosey on over to my crib so I can make love to you?"

The mere thought of him tonguing her down made Cleo's clit somersault. She squirmed in her seat and tightly clenched her thick thighs; a meager attempt to calm her now throbbing clit. After regaining *some* of her composure, she mumbled, "That sounds like a plan to me."

****

They arrived at Javon's apartment around eleven. As he slid his door key into the old, rusted lock, he slid his hot tongue into Cleo's hungry mouth. Her body was already on fire from the ride to his apartment, thanks to the little sightseeing his fingers did inside her crotch. He'd always been pretty good at fingering her ... and it didn't help that he knew her voluptuous curves like the back of his hand, having caressed, sucked and licked every inch of her so many times in the past. There was no time for chit-chatting tonight. One thing was on both their minds as they walked into his small, cramped apartment. While leading her down the short, narrow hallway, he instinctively began taking off her clothes.

. There was no time for chit-chatting tonight. One thing was on both their minds as they walked into his small, cramped apartment. While leading her down the short, narrow hallway, he instinctively began taking off her clothes First to disappear from her thick frame was her favorite ebony-colored blouse, followed by the ebony-colored lace bra she'd gotten on sale at Ashley Stewart, along with the matching sexy thong. He tugged at her skirt zipper; it was not coming loose as quickly as he would've liked.

Using her best enactment of a southern drawl, Cleo said, "Hey there partner, ya got a lil' trouble on your hands? Well, jus' let me see if I can help ya out there, son." Javon gently moved his large, chestnut-brown hand from her zipper, then took her left-hand thumb and index finger and pulled down on the zipper, allowing her skirt to fall to the floor. Javon's puppy dog amber eyes bulged out of his head, his mouth opened wide, revealing saliva sauntering down the left corner of his thick, greedy lips as he gazed at her heaven-sent figure.

"Oh, baby. You are beautiful. There is nothing else to say," declared Javon as he edged closer to her, encasing her dulcet waist with his heavy arms.

"Big Daddy, you know I'm hot and ready for you," she squealed, wrapping her arms around his neck.

Ever so slowly, Javon leaned into her aching body, with her ample breasts swollen and cherry-brown nipples standing at attention, he effortlessly gripped her right breast with his large palm, bent down and suckled her ripe nipple. Enraptured, Cleo threw her head back and shrilled in pure, unadulterated ecstasy.

Unable to contain the passion any longer, they both stripped off Javon's clothes, revealing Mr. Marvelous standing at attention like a real soldier, ready to take care of business. It was Cleo's turn to take control. Extending her arms, she pushed him onto the carpeted bedroom floor, then enclosed her sexy, thick thighs around his head, allowing his long, ardent tongue to dip into her pulsating, dripping wet pussy.

"Oh, yes, Big Daddy! That's it… don't stop, ohhhhh yesssss! Suck on my clit, make me feel it, baby. Let me know how much you want this sweet, fat pussy!" she yelled, swaying her hips back and forth, up and down, side to side, in his eager mouth.

In response, Javon reached his arms up to her round, buxom ass and rubbed, squeezed and kneaded her apple bottom with his knowing hands.

"Mmmmmm, oh, baby, you taste so good," he grumbled in between licks. "Ah, yes. I love eatin' yo pussy, suga."

Keeping with the beat, she grooved along with his rhythm as his fiery tongue found its way to the crack of her ass. The next thing she knew, his tongue was doing a delightful dance up and down her crack and inside her asshole. This made them both screech with fervor.

Not wanting to waste another minute, Javon swiftly slid Mr. Marvelous inside her moist snatch. And, just as she'd done on numerous occasions in the past, she bounced, gyrated and stroked Mr. Marvelous like nobody's business. Like clockwork, she felt him squirming underneath her, then, suddenly, his body became as stiff as a two-by-four and as his eyes rolled back in his head, Mr. Marvelous exploded inside of her. With every fiber of her being, she could feel him pulsating between her thighs, then she, too, followed suit. Arching her back and clenching her thighs as tight as she could around him, allowed her riveting climax to reach a new height, where no man had ever gone before; her love jones flowed down like a tidal wave of pure passion.

"Ahhhhhh!" They breathlessly said in unison. Cleo's thick frame was now glistening with droplets of sweat as she rolled off of him onto the floor.

Panting, she muttered, "Mmmmm, that was so good, so damn good, Javon. You had it goin' on real strong. And, once again, Mr. Marvelous delivered an Oscar-worthy performance."

Completely drained and out of breath, "Umm mmm," Javon mumbled, drifting off to sleep, bathed in Cleo's ambrosial scent.

Cleo stretched out her limbs then turned over in the opposite direction of Javon. It wasn't long before images of her encounter with Kennedy entered her mind. *If I breathe in deep enough, I can still catch wafts of Kennedy's scent in my nose, how her nipple hardens when I'm suckling it in my mouth and how she giggles when my finger teases her clit ... but, seriously, what's going on with me? I just fucked Javon and as always, I enjoyed myself and yet here I am fantasizing about being with a woman, but not just any woman, Kennedy St. Martin is the only one I desire.*

Flustered, she ran her hand through her hair and felt a strong urge to check her cell to see if Kennedy had called or at least texted her. She reached for her handbag on Javon's bedside table and was not disappointed,

CeeCee, I can't seem to get you off my mind. Our time together was everything I'd imagined it would be and then some and I hope you feel the same way. And even though my circumstances are not ideal, I want you to know that I'm really into you and I ask for your patience as I figure things out. Don't give up on me, please. Yours, Kennedy

Overcome with emotion, a single tear made its way down her cheek. She quietly returned her phone to her handbag, deciding to respond after she left in the morning. She flipped over to spoon Javon, wrapping her arms tightly around him and concentrated on trying to get some sleep.

⚢ 19 ⚥

Cleo's night at Javon's was a restless one. So much in fact that she showered, brushed her teeth, quickly styled her coiffe and retrieved one of her several outfits that remained in Javon's tiny second bedroom closet and exited his place early while he was still calling the hogs. As soon as she stepped into her Uber, she retrieved her cell from her bag, took a deep breath and slowly typed out a reply to Kennedy,

GM, got ur message last night ... it was a pleasure hearing from you, my dear. I most certainly enjoyed being with you too and can't wait to do it all over again. Indeed circumstances are not ideal and I know we both still have many questions that can't possibly be answered all at once. But believe me when I say that I have all the patience in the world for you, love ... no worries. I walked into this with eyes wide open and I'm down for the long haul. All my love, CeeCee

Cleo read and re-read her text before clicking the send button. The driver revved up the engine and headed west on 38th towards her home. She had to ready herself for her breakfast date with her BFF.

****

"Girl, where were you last night? I tried calling and texting you several times," asked Shelby as they were being seated for brunch at the Original Pancake House off West 86th Street.

Pulling out her chair, Cleo replied, "Oh, girlfriend. You gon' trip if I tell you what I got into last night, but hold up a minute, I gotta chit-chat with Pam for a minute.

"Who's Pam?"

"Oh, that's right. You haven't met her before because you've only been here, what once or twice, right?"

"Yeah, and? Just because you've made it your mainstay, doesn't mean everyone else has followed suit, young lady."

"Okay, I hear you, ma. Pam is a waitress here. In fact, I'd go as far to say she's the best one they got in this joint," she revealed.

Throwing her worn brown leather backpack over her left shoulder, Shelby said, "Oh, yeah. Well, it's too bad we didn't get seated in her area. Do you think they'd move us to her section if we ask? Since you've already bragged on her, I'd like for her to serve us today."

"Well, I don't see why not. Let me flag our waiter right quick." Waving her neatly manicured right index finger in the air, she got the attention of the tall, lanky white boy who had so many red pimples on his face that he reminded Cleo of an old high school classmate. His acne was so awful, that he'd earned the nickname *pizza face.*

Glancing at his nametag, Cleo stated, "Adam, we'd like to change to Pam's section. Do you think you can make that happen for us?"

Adam dug his hands down into his pockets. "Well, uh, I guess so. Let me go check and make sure she has a table available for y'all," turning on his heels in the opposite direction.

After a few minutes, he returned and escorted them to Pam's section. The restaurant was painted in a muted green color, with gold-tinted light fixtures secured on the ceilings throughout. Additionally, there was fake greenery placed among the booths and tables.

As they rounded the corner, their eyes met Pam's who had a Kool-Aid grin across her flawless face. She stood at five-foot-seven with a slim physique, short, hair and a complexion as smooth as a Hershey's dark chocolate bar.

"Hey, lady! How are you doing?" Pam asked as she embraced Cleo.

Welcoming her embrace, Cleo stretched out her arms and hugged her back. "I'm doing good, can't complain, you know. Things could always be worse," lamented Cleo. "I'd like you to meet my best friend in the whole wide world, Ms. Shelby James," as she gestured towards her.

"It's a pleasure meeting you Shelby," stated Pam.

"Likewise, Pam. I tell you, my girl has been bragging about you, so I'm hoping you won't disappoint us," Shelby said jokingly.

"Well, I always aim to please my customers and I hope to impress you enough to come see us again. Ladies, take your seats, and here are your menus. Can I start you with some coffee, tea or water?"

Cleo and Shelby took their respective seats across from each other. "I'll have a cup of coffee, please," they said in unison.

"Hey, girl, don't be jinxing me up in this establishment." Cleo laughed as she looked over the top of her menu at Shelby.

"I feel the same way, girl," giggled Shelby.

"Okay, ladies, that's two coffees coming right up. Cleo, I know you like a lil' coffee with your cream and sugar." She turned to Shelby. "Would you like cream and sugar as well?

"No, thank you. I prefer to drink my coffee black. But could you please bring me a glass of water with lemon?

"Not a problem. I'll be right back. Take your time scanning the menus." Pam left the table and walked towards the kitchen.

"CeeCee, I think you're right on the money with Pam. She really does seem like a real, genuinely nice person. Don't come across too many of them these days, ya know."

Scanning the breakfast menu, Cleo answered, "I know, that's right. There just ain't enough 'real' folks in the world today. Pam is definitely an exception. Which menu are you going to order from? The dinner, breakfast or lunch?"

"Well, everything on the menu looks so good, but I think I'ma go with one of their delicious-looking baked omelets. Girl, get a load of the picture. They look mouth-watering, don't they?" Shelby said as she thrust her menu in Cleo's face.

Laughing, Cleo said, "Girl, I know. I've seen it a million times, already. I'm telling you, they are the bomb. The Belgian waffles have captured my attention, but so have Nelly's banana pancakes. Oh, what is a girl to do? Should I be a greedy pig and order both? Or play it nice and choose one of them?"

"Now, girl, you know you don't need to be a glutton like that. Eating all that would be just defeating the purpose of us exercising like we do, ya feel me?"

"You're right. I need to stop. I will go with one of their healthy choices like turkey egg white omelet and call it a day." Cleo looked up from her menu. "Oh, Pam is coming with our drinks."

Balancing her serving tray like a real pro, Pam expertly set a coffee cup in front of both of them, along with a coffee pitcher and extra sugar and cream for Cleo.

"So, have you ladies decided what you want to eat today?" Pam reached into her apron for a pen and order pad.

"Why, yes, Pam. We've made up our minds. Shelby, go ahead and order first."

"How gracious of you, CeeCee. Pam, I'm gonna go with the oven-baked mushroom omelet."

"And would you like the sherry sauce or salsa?" Pam asked as she scribbled on her notepad.

"I'll have the sherry sauce, please."

"Well, because I've never tried them before, I'm gonna go with Nelly's banana pancakes and a side of bacon," Cleo said, slyly licking her lips, forgetting all about the lighter choice.

"Oh, Cleo, you're going to love them," Pam said. "Many of my regular customers swear by that entrée. Okay, ladies, I'll get these orders turned in right away. It shouldn't be too long."

"Okay, Pam. Thank you," said Cleo.

"Yeah, thanks a million." Shelby took another sip of coffee. "Hey, by the way, this coffee is really good!"

"Well, I'm glad you're enjoying it. Y'all just let me know if I need to refill your pitcher." Pam turned and left.

"Okay. Now, it's time for you to tell me what kept you from answering your phone last night."

Grinning from ear-to-ear, Cleo said, "Well, Javon called—"

"Oh, boy. I should've known," Shelby groaned.

"Hold on just a minute. Do ya want me to tell ya what happened or what?" She threw her hands up in the air. "I know he's not one of your favorite people but take a chill pill and hear me out."

Shelby leaned back into her chair and rolled her eyes.

Cleo took her spoon and stirred two packets of Splenda and one packet of sugar into her coffee, then proceeded to dump six half and a half creamers into her cup that now threatened to teeter over the side with all the cream she'd put in it. "Anyways, as I was saying. Javon called and asked me out for dinner and a movie. So, we went to see Kevin Hart's new flick at Georgetown Cinema. After the movie, he suggested we eat dinner at Rick's Boatyard because he loves their lean steaks and I have to admit, I think they have the best tasting steaks as well."

Cleo noticed Shelby chewing on her bottom lip while she was talking. This could only mean one thing: she was holding back what was really on her mind. It was burning her up to keep her pouty mouth closed.

Ignoring this, she continued, "Dinner was delicious, and we actually ran into some distant relatives of his. They were celebrating the matriarch's seventy-fifth birthday."

"Oh, yeah, that's nice," Shelby commented.

Just then, Pam had returned with their food.

"Ladies, I got some good stuff for y'all." Pam approached them with a large tray filled with their food. "Here you go, Cleo," handing her entrée.

"Thank you, Pam."

"Shelby, here's your food, ladies. Please enjoy and I'll be back to check on y'all in a short while." Pam placed her hands on her slim hips and smiled.

"Thanks, Pam. It sure looks delicious!"

"Now back to our conversation." Cleo took a bit of the crispy bacon on her plate and once again, Shelby rolled her eyes in disgust.

"Ya know, Javon and I discussed that and we both agreed it will be a while before we go back there again, if at all."

"Shit, I know that's right, girl!"

"You've probably already figured it out. We ended the evening gettin' busy at his apartment. Now, I know I said I was going to leave his triflin' ass alone. But, oh girl, when he got to talkin' about eatin' my pussy, I'm sorry, but I could not resist. Shit, I mean, I already told you how good that nigga can eat pussy ... the only problem being is that mine ain't the only one he likes sticking his tongue in. But, oh well. I got my nut and at this point, that's the only thing that matters," Cleo said as she took the last bite of her pancakes.

Nibbling on her jellied toast, Shelby said, "Yeah, I knew you fucked him. I remember you talkin' about how fierce that boy's tongue is. Well, not that I'm all for it because that negro just put you through too much and I don't want to see my girl get hurt again, ya know? Sometimes we get so caught up in the sex and then, there we go—smack dab back into Alice in Wonderland and don't know what done hit cha. So, just be careful ... keep your perspective and remember it's just sex. Nothin' more, nothin' less. Your Prince Charming is coming. You just wait and see."

Raising a curious brow, Cleo responded, "I appreciate your concern and I feel everything you said. I have to admit, that boy's tongue is hard for me to resist. When someone's lickin' it right, it's just too fuckin' hard to give that shit up."

They both laughed, raised their fists, and did their little fist bump. Shelby took a sip from her glass of water which was filled to the brim with ice cubes and several wedges of lemon. "Hey, speaking of all your men friends, what's up with ya boy Craig, you haven't said anything about him in a minute."

CeeCee shook her head, "Girl, that nigga done pulled one of his infamous disappearing acts on me again, even after all that bullshit talk about wanting another chance, how he knows he fucked up, blah, blah, blah."

Shelby pulled her signature move and sat up straight, ears perked up like a cat ready to take in some juicy gossip. "Damn, girl, no he didn't. I'm so sick and tired of these fuck boys out here always on game. After we ran into him and that exquisite dinner he made for you … damn …" her voice trailed off.

"Yeah, I know, Shell. But, eh, I really don't have time to be sweatin' his ass when I'm already got my hands full with Javon and Reese, ya know?" *I ain't saying nothing about Kennedy, 'cause I ain't ready to delve into all that with Shelby ... not yet.*

Instead, she changed the subject. "So, speaking of having someone around to lick it right, what's up with that Cole Crawford dude? Ever since he started working at Exodus, I've noticed he tends to keep to himself, but damn that nigga is sexy as hell and I'm sure he can lick it just right," she joked.

"Oh, he likes to lick, all right, but just not what you're thinking," Shelby replied.

"What did you say?" she asked, her curiosity aroused.

Shelby's bright eyes lit up even more as she was always up for sharing hearsay.

"Oh, CeeCee, you won't believe this, but dude is a gay blade!"

Cleo blinked a few times, unsure of what she'd just been told. "Say what?"

A few nosey white people swiftly turned their heads in their direction.

Shelby noticed what happened, so she slid her lithe body from the opposite side of the booth and planted her bottom right next to Cleo to avoid feeding the outsiders what they did not need to hear. Disbelief blanketed Cleo's face as she stared into Shelby's, searching for any sign that this was all just a joke.

There was none to be found. She was serious.

Cleo shifted uneasily in her seat. The very real possibility of *her* being gay panged her, but she refused to let it show. If she did, she knew her BFF would become suspicious and start asking probing questions; questions she did not have answers to—at least not yet.

“So, you're telling me that that fine ass glass of water likes men?” Cleo's mind would not accept this alarming news. “Are you sure? Who told you this?” she demanded.

“I know it's true this time, CeeCee. Do you remember my gay cousin Bryonn?”

Cleo solemnly nodded her head.

Shelby gulped down the last of her orange juice and then continued. "Well, girl, you know he knows everybody in Naptown who lives that nasty lifestyle, especially anyone who is black."

Cleo noticed how she turned her nose up when she said, “that nasty lifestyle.” Her stomach flip-flopped after hearing her friend-for-life say something that was so mean-spirited—senseless in fact. Even though they'd known each other all their lives, the subject of homosexuality rarely ever came up. They both were aware of gay folks in their neighborhood and families, but most were on the down-low … not to mention the ones that sternly kept that closet door shut tight.

Well, except for that one crazy chick named Felicia in high school who everybody knew was lesbian because she was always goin' around cracking on any and everybody, no matter if they were a fellow student or even a teacher. Felicia was an equal opportunist, so gender was no matter to her, either. But she was cool with them, and they even hung out with her sometimes. On the flip side, she and Shelby were well-known for being 'boy crazy' back in the day, leaving many broken-hearted boys in the dust.

Shelby continued. "Bryonn knows the guy he was kickin' it with last year! He used to see them at all the lil' gay parties, and at that one annual event at their club back in the day." Putting her thinking cap on, she held her manicured right index finger to her temple, then continued. "Damn, for the life of me, I can't remember what it's called …"

Cleo immediately took note of the vibrant cherry-red nail color on Shelby's nails. It was an exact match to the ensemble she wore, a cherry-red halter top and blue jean cut-off shorts. "Nice coordination you got goin' on there, by the way."

"Oh, thanks CeeCee. I think red is my new favorite color…" Shelby wiggled her fingers. "…makes me feel all fiery inside and out."

"Yeah, I can tell." Cleo relaxed her rigid body by leaning back in the booth and quietly sipped her lukewarm coffee. "You're really enjoying telling yourself, aren't you, Miss Gossip?"

Shelby gave her an innocent look. "What do you mean? It's all true, you know I ain't lying!"

Cleo shook her head. "Hmmmm, OK."

A light bulb suddenly went off in Shelby's head.

"Old School Matinee, that's what's it's called! I knew I'd think of it," she exclaimed, damn near jumping out of her seat.

"Okay, okay, I believe you, Shell. It's just like *wow*, ya know?"

"Oh, I know, girl. Who would've thought someone who looks like him would prefer dick over pussy? I mean, what the hell."

Cleo did not respond as she was done with the conversation. Their tête-à-tête had the wheels in her head spinning out of control. She had a lot of thinking to do once she was alone again. Standing up, she asked, "You ready to get out a dodge?"

"Yeah, let's get outta dodge," laughed Shelby as they headed out of the restaurant.

⚢ 20 ⚥

"Good morning, Pepper. How was your weekend?" Cleo asked as she approached the center's receptionist area. "I got here early so we would have time to chitchat as it's been a while and I picked up breakfast sandwiches from Hardee's." She handed Pepper her bag and sat their drinks down on the desk by the switchboard. "I got your favorite."

Pepper accepted the bag and quickly yanked it open. "Oh wee! You got me the Monster? Oh, thank you, thank you, thank you!" She took a bite of the hot sandwich. "Ummmm, tastes delicious! I haven't had it in a while, so thanks. My weekend was a relaxing one, just did some reading, housecleaning, and took a short solo hike at Eagle Creek. How was yours? Anything new with Javon or Craig?"

Cleo joined Pepper behind the receptionist desk area, sat down, opened her Hardee's bag, retrieved her sandwich, and took a big bite.

"Well, I haven't heard from Craig in a while. He's back to doing his disappearing acts again and as for Javon, I kicked it with him at the movie theater."

"Oh, so he's still hanging around, huh? Let me guess, he still wants to get married, right?" Pepper asked, then tossed a hash brown in her mouth.

Cleo shook her head. “Girl, you already know. He’s always bringing marriage up in our conversations, but I ain’t studdin’ him. The love I once had is long gone, especially after that ugly episode at Club Isis with Shelby. But I can’t lie, the boy sure knows how to eat some pussy, straight up! I think that’s why, if I’m being honest, I keep dealing with him after all these years.”

“I hear you, Cleo. It can be hard to give up sex from someone you’ve been dealing with for a long time, and they know all the right buttons to push every single time.”

Cleo took a sip of her beverage. “Yes indeed, yes indeed. How was the hike? I keep saying I need to get myself over to Eagle Creek to check out their kayaking. Do you kayak?”

Pepper shook her head. “It’s been some years. The last time didn’t go so well. My kayak flipped over and I almost drowned.” She dropped her head. “I never learned how to swim.”

“Oh, my goodness! Sorry to hear that, so how did you get out of the water?” Cleo asked.

“Cedric, my boyfriend at the time was with me, so that’s the one thing he did right during our turbulent years together.”

Cleo ate the last bite of her sandwich. “Oh yes. I remember you telling me about him a while back. Did you ever learn how to swim?”

"Honestly, I thought about it because that was the second time I almost drowned, but I haven't been able to bring myself to do it. I'm terrified but have so much love for the water. Is that crazy?"

Cleo tossed her bag into the trash can behind her. "No, not at all, Pepper. However, I encourage you to tackle that fear and just do it. I think you'll be very pleased with yourself." Cleo stood up to leave.

"I'm glad we got to chat this morning dear, and I hope your Monday goes well."

Pepper ate the last bite of her Monster sandwich. "Thanks again for the breakfast, and yes, I will seriously consider those swimming lessons again."

Cleo stuck her pinky finger out. "Pinky swear?"

Pepper giggled and did the same. "Yes. Pinky swear."

****

Cleo was making her way to her office when her cell dinged. It was Kennedy,

Hey u, my apologies again for having 2 cancel at the last min. I'll be out doing home visits all day today, but wanna spend some time with u this evening…think u can get away from the ofc early so we can rendezvous at our fav park? I really wanna c u □ □

Cleo smiled ear-to-ear. Yes! She wants me just as much as I want her. Cleo immediately text her back,

Most def beautiful. I wanna see u 2. Let's do 3:30 at Holliday Park, k?

OK, c u then.

****

“Oh hi, Jim. You decided to get here early like me, I see.” Cleo sat in one of the chairs across from Jim, then retrieved her laptop from her computer bag.”

Jim looked up from his laptop. “Hey you. Yes ma’am. I figured I’d get settled in before Samantha arrives.” He leaned back into the chair, ran his freckled fingers through his thinning red hair, and crossed his legs. “I want to make sure I have the right answers for any questions she conjures up, no matter how irrelevant it’s likely to be.”

Cleo shook her head in agreement. “Yep, sounds about right.”

⚢ 21 ⚥

Butterflies took flight in the bottom of Cleo's stomach. The anticipation of her impending rendezvous with Kennedy later at Holliday Park was almost too much to bear. Puddles of discarded clothing surrounded her as she stood in front of her full-length mirror one last time, carefully inspecting her chosen ensemble: her favorite pair of jeans that deliciously coated every curve of her voluptuous five-foot-nine frame and a new purple-hued, paisley print halter top.

Ah yes. This is perfect. She glanced at the wall clock which had just struck one o'clock.

Damn, two more hours to go. What am I gonna do with all this time? A moment later, her phone rang. Crimson's name flashed across the screen.

Cleo plopped down on her unmade bed, grabbed her cell off the bedside table and clicked on the green button. "Hey lady, how's it going?"

"Oh, all is well. I was just checking in. Everything good?"

Cleo's heart sped up a few beats. *Damn. How much longer am I going to go without telling her and the rest of them?* She shook her head and bit down on a hangnail on her left thumb.

"Yeah, everything is alright with me. Why do you ask?" Her curiosity was aroused.

Fuck! Did she learn about me and Kennedy? Did she somehow find out about the change in my sexual preference? Ah, calm down. You're just acting paranoid.

"Oh, it's just that we haven't seen you in a while ... thought maybe something was going on."

Cleo breathed a sigh of relief. *Okay, good. My secret is still a secret. At least for now.*

"Ah, I see. Naw girl. I've just been busy with my niece since Symone decided to return to school and I've also been working late these last few weeks," she said. Well, it was partly true.

"Oh, well, okay," she replied.

Cleo detected something was off with Crimson. It was the way she emphasized the word 'okay'. Hell, she probably just don't believe me.

"How's your mom doing?" Cleo asked, changing the subject.

"Oh, she's good. As a matter of fact, she's preparing to go out on her first date since my dad passed, can you believe it?"

Cleo stretched out across her bed, reached for the remote to turn down a song by Loose Ends she wasn't already familiar with.

"Wow, no, I really can't, that's pretty sweet. I know you've been trying to get her to date for a while. How long has it been since your dad passed away, five, six years now?" she implored.

"Yeah, it's coming up on six next month. I can hardly believe it."

"Wow, Crimson, I can't believe that much time has gone by, but I am happy to learn the news about your mom." Cleo rummaged through her handbag for her Bluetooth earbuds as the conversation was taking longer than she anticipated.

"Hold on Crimson, I'm gonna put my ear pods in."

"Okay," Cleo heard her say before placing her mobile down next to her on the bed. Cleo put her plugs in and grabbed her cell to make sure the Bluetooth was activated.

"Okay, I'm back. Now back to your mom. Who is the lucky man that has the privilege of taking out a supermodel turned clothing boutique business owner?" Cleo resumed her position on her bed.

"Oh, it's a local entrepreneur named Rowen Bradley. He opened up that high-end footwear store for men in Broad Ripple a couple of years ago."

Hearing the word 'entrepreneur' excited Cleo. "I think I know the place, isn't it called *Bradley's Viatu*?"

"As a matter of fact, yes, it is. How did you know?" Crimson asked.

"Girl, that is both Devin's and Sasha's favorite shoe store, you hear me? They both were there at the grand opening and as a matter of fact, Rowen happens to be a good friend of my dad's. They grew up together!"

"Say what? Are you serious right now CeeCee? Wow!"

"Yes, Crimson, dead serious. He's a cool dude and I hope they hit it off. Your mom deserves to be happy after losing your dad in that car crash." Cleo reached for her glass of Moscato and took a sip.

"Agreed," Crimson replied. "My dad was a terrific husband to my mom, and he was a fantastic dad. I know he'd want mom to be happy with the right man. I'm excited for her."

"Yes, your dad was so much fun, too, but your mother deserves some happiness," Cleo lamented.

"Yes, indeed, CeeCee, yes, indeed. Well, I'm gonna get off here, but I'm glad we got the chance to catch up and I look forward to our next outing."

Cleo sipped the last few drops from her glass and rolled over to her side, "Okay, girl, talk to you later."

After hanging up, Cleo went back in the history of her YouTube channel to find the unknown song by one of her all-time favorite groups, Loose Ends. She found out that it was called 'So Where Are You?'

How in the hell did this one get past me? I'll never know, but I absolutely love it!

She spent the remaining time rewinding it over and over until it was time for her date with Kennedy at the park.

⚢ 22 ⚥

Cleo arrived an hour early at Holliday Park for her afternoon excursion with Kennedy. Ambiguity enveloped her as she pictured what was going to take place once her lover arrived. She prayed nothing or no one would disturb their time together this time around. The park was secluded, albeit for a scattering of a few souls jogging along the weaving paved street that circled the vast grounds, and a large Asian family taking photos around The Ruins, a favorite photogenic spot centrally located at the park.

After coming to the T-intersection, Cleo turned left, steering her Ridgeline towards the parking lot across from the nature center. She backed her truck into a secluded parking space and did her best to relax. The bright sun rays flashed through the tall sprawling trees populating the luscious green grass while Cheryl Lynn's 'Encore' filled the truck's interior. She spent the time listening to one of her favorite CDs filled with old school jams, and before long she had drifted off to sleep, not stirring until she heard Kennedy's familiar tap on her driver's side window.

Sleepily, she opened both eyes and saw Kennedy's smiling face. Butterflies took flight deep inside her belly, causing her clitoris to twitch.

Damn, she is fine. Why does she have to be so dang-gone good-looking?

Cleo clicked the automatic window button. "Hello there, beautiful."

"Hey yourself, you ol' sexy thang, you."

Kennedy stuck her head in and kissed her deeply for several long minutes.

Finally, Cleo pulled away. "Come on around to the passenger side. We have much to discuss," she hesitated, then said, "and *do* before the evening gets away from us."

Always the fashionista, she sported a rose-colored, button-down silk blouse, charcoal black wide-legged linen dress pants and a sophisticated pair of sling-back heels. Her long soft curls tumbled down her back; she was as exquisite as exquisite could be.

Kennedy hurried around to the other side and happily jumped in.

"So, what do you want to talk about first?" Kennedy asked.

Her YouTube playlist was now playing 'Girl, I Got My Eyes on You', an oldie but goodie by the 90s group, *Today.* Cleo looked on as the groove took hold of Kennedy immediately. Her curvy body began gyrating to the rhythm of the old school jam, making Cleo salivate. She wanted to take her right then and there.

How in the hell can this woman turn me on like this?

Cleo mentally undressed her, exposing her supple breasts and ample derriere. Mere words were no longer needed at that moment. Kennedy swiftly unbuttoned her blouse, peeled off her pants, crawled into the back seat, opened her legs and waited for her lover to join her. Just then, Kennedy's cell started buzzing. Cleo looked on as she retrieved her cell from her handbag. It was probably her husband wondering where she was, but that had no bearing on what was taking place at that very moment.

Kennedy sat up and smiled meekly at Cleo, "Sorry baby, it's him, but it won't take long."

Feeling dejected, Cleo simply nodded, watching her lover answer the call. "Yes, Bernard, what's going on? No, I didn't forget. I already told you what I had to go do. Yes, I know, you don't need to remind me, okay." She rolled her eyes. "Okay, I'll see you later." She hung up, then said to Cleo, "Come here you."

"What did he want?" Cleo found herself asking Kennedy shook her head again, "Oh, he just called to make sure I didn't forget to stop by the store before returning home. The kids asked for some deli lunch meat is all." Cleo looked on as Kennedy laid back down and opened her legs and rubbed her herself.

Cleo quickly forgot all about the abrupt interruption, clumsily turned the music down—it was important to be able to listen to the slow, methodical whimpers and moans that would soon fill her truck's interior—then hurriedly jumped in the back seat with the sexy, purring kitten who was waiting impatiently for her to dive in.

Cleo did just that. Her thirsty, wet tongue dove deep inside of her lover, causing her to twist and turn. Throaty moans rose from Kennedy like she'd never heard before, which made her even hotter; made her want to explore every single inch of her unbelievably sexy and alluring pudenda until she just couldn't take it anymore. Their periodic sexcades allowed for a deep and lasting understanding of her lover's body and what turned her on the most. Like following an ancient treasure map in search of precious gems, Cleo began her search by pinching and biting Kennedy's large, sugary brown nipples, ample derriere, and deliciously thick legs and calves.

Cleo gripped Kennedy's hardened right nipple with her left hand and began kneading and squeezing the butterscotch morsel, much to the delight of Kennedy, who was squirming, shuddering, and whimpering with every single stroke.

Cleo's wet tongue expertly moved in, out, and around, drinking every single drop her tongue could savor as Kennedy's avalanche of juices flowed. Her beatifically shaped honey pot was already rock-hard; the sweet aroma wafting from her sex left Cleo feeling high as if she'd just smoked a blunt. It was, in a word, euphoric.

"Oh my God, babe!" Kennedy blurted out, wiping sweat from her forehead. "That tongue of yours does amazing things to my kittykat that are just beyond belief!" she exclaimed.

Cleo had just finished flicking her tongue across her lover's plump pussy lips and deliciously salty inner thighs, then rolled over onto her back and locked her hands together under her head. A smug smile appeared in the corners of her slick lips. "Baby, you know I love tasting you, always." She propped herself up on her forearms and peered over at her. "It is my mission to please you."

Birds were flying from tree to tree chirping away, causing a stir among the expansive trees and their inhabitants. A family of green-winged geese waddled close by making that annoying clucking noise that drove Cleo nuts.

Kennedy's toothy grin said it all. She rose from a prone position, then straddled Cleo, her hand tugging at Cleo's pant buckle, nail polish dazzling in the sunset.

The unmistakable look on her face confirmed the message: she was hungry too. So, Cleo obliged, and let Kennedy take what she needed. Undoubtedly, she was soaking wet and could use a good tongue-lashing as well, so she laid back and propped her thick, chocolate thighs open, her heart's rhythm speeding up with each caress from her lover.

Shit, she needed this. So much pent-up uncertainty and frustration were too much to handle. A release was just what the doctor prescribed; Kennedy was the medicine she needed to relax and enjoy multiple orgasms that had laid dormant far too long deep down in her groin.

Kennedy's long tendrils dangled around her face as she buried it into Cleo's sweet spot, her long, recently pierced tongue gently licked and sucked on her thighs, down the slight crevices where the thigh and buttocks meet. It had become her favorite spot to nibble on.

"Ohhhh, ahhhh, ohhhhhh. Oh, baby, that feels soooooooo good." Cleo stroked her soft curls, wrapping strands around her fingers.

"Mmmmmm, damn, baby, you know I love it down here," Kennedy whispered but didn't break her stride.

Cleo arched her back and began rubbing, thrusting her hips into Kennedy's wide-open mouth, her pierced tongue gently, earnestly licking and slurping, thoroughly enjoying Cleo's ambrosia, giving her a high unlike anything else in the world.

"Oh, yes, yes, yes, yes! Right there, Kennedy, baby. Right there. Oh, God, I feel it, I feel that ring stroking my clit ... oh, ohhhhh, ohhhhh, it's, it's so hard, it's throbbing, yearning, please give me more ... don't stop, don't you dare stop, please," Cleo pleaded.

Using both hands, she gripped Kennedy's head and smashed it into her wet, up-in-smoke pussy. "Ahhhhhh, it's coming baby, it's coming, oh God, right, right there, that's right, go deep, go deep, baby, don't stop!"

Kennedy was panting, holding Cleo's legs up and back as far as she could. There was no way she was letting not even one drop escape her hungry mouth. She had to have every single drop as if her life depended on it. Cleo relished the euphoric feeling she was having while being pleased by Kennedy in a way that no one had ever pleased her orally before...including Javon.

⚢ 23 ⚤

"Where's your twin, Ava?" Mother Stinson asked. Cleo overheard her question as she walked through the threshold of her parents' door, balancing her handbag and a bowl of her tasty potato salad.

"Once again, he's at work, puttin' in some overtime," Ava replied.

"Hey everybody, I'm here," Cleo yelled out on her way through the dining room to the kitchen. Mother Stinson was standing at the sink, rinsing off the last wine glass and setting it on the counter.

"Oh, hey baby. It's about time you got here. Your father was just asking about you."

Cleo opened her parents' shiny new black stainless-steel French-style refrigerator and placed the potato salad bowl inside. "Oh, sorry. My neighbor, Mr. van Deveer held me up again," she replied while rubbing the back of her neck, "as he often does whenever he sees me." She eyed Ava as she walked back into the kitchen and plopped her narrow behind into one of the bar stools.

"Hey there, lil' sis."

"What's up, CeeCee? I heard you mention ol' Mr. van Deveer. How is he and didn't you tell us a while back that his wife passed?"

Cleo observed Ava flinging her box braids back behind her slender shoulders and leaned forward, placing her head into her propped-up hands.

"Oh, he seems to be doing okay, considering the circumstances," Cleo responded, taking a seat across from her little sister. "They were married for more than sixty years before she died," Cleo responded, setting her handbag on the marble counter.

"Oh, what a blessing that was for them 'cause not everyone gets that lucky," Her mother chimed in. "Or, they were blessed, at least" she added.

Cleo had that faraway look in her eyes, imagining what it would be like to share a life with someone you loved who *also* loved you back just the same. If only.

"Shoot, I know that's right, Ma!"
Cleo heard Ava's high-shrilled response, snapping her out of her daydream. "Yeah, I know that's right," she added to the conversation. She turned her attention toward her mother. "So, what are we having tonight, Mom?" Cleo turned on her heels and began walking towards the stove on the opposite side of the kitchen, her nose guiding her along the way.

"Now don't you go sticking your nose in any of my pots, CeeCee, or else I'm gonna have to get my switch out and chase you around this here kitchen, young lady!"
Cleo stopped dead in her tracks, just before she reached for one of the pots simmering on the stove.

"Yes ma'am, yes ma'am." Begrudgingly, she walked back to the stool she rose from moments ago. "Where's daddy?" she asked.

Ava replied, "Where is he whenever he's not sleeping?"

"Down in his man-cave," they both said in unison and began giggling.

Her mother chimed in, "Ugh, ever since we renovated the basement, that father of yours practically lives down there. He is mesmerized by that humongous, curved TV he and Sasha picked up from Best Buy a few weeks ago. I think he loves it more than he loves any of us," she said while stirring something up in one of the pots on the stove.

The Stinson girls looked at each other knowingly and smiled. "Daddy's always been a TV junkie, ain't that right Ava?" Cleo asked, rising from the stool and began heading toward the basement door.

"Yes, Lord," Ava replied, taking a drink from the half-empty water bottle in her hand.

"I'ma go holler at the ol' man. Be back shortly," Cleo said.

"Okay," Cleo heard her mother say. "Tell your father dinner will be ready in about twenty minutes."

"Yes, Mom, I will." Cleo walked down the steps and turned the right corner in the direction of her dad's man cave.

She passed the fancy new Olhausen pool table that replaced the family's other table they had for more than two decades and walked a few more feet to the closed door of Father Stinson's man cave. Out of respect (because her parents taught her that), Cleo knocked a few times before opening it.

"Hey Daddy. I'm here," Cleo announced. She walked over and planted a kiss on her father's bald head.

"Oh, there's my baby girl, so you finally came to spend some time with your family, huh?" he quipped, turning down the volume on the Pacers game he was watching. "I'm glad you've made us a priority today, my child."

"Ha-ha, funny dad, real funny." Cleo playfully rolled her eyes at her father, then walked around to the L-shaped grey sofa. She lovingly admired the gazillion framed photos of her family, some from their annual King's Island vacations, birthday celebrations at Holliday Park, and the professional holiday photos that her mother insisted on every year.

"So how are you liking the renovations, Daddy?" Cleo set back and curled her legs onto the sofa. She looked on as her father reached onto the coffee table and retrieved a half-smoked cigar, placed it in his left hand and used his right hand to retrieve the royal blue hammer-shaped lighter she'd bought him a while back. His slate grey eyes twinkled in the light coming from the fire-spewing lighter.

"CeeCee, I absolutely love it!" he exclaimed. Cleo watched as her dad stood up and gingerly walked over to the wall, a sure sign of the toll his right bow leg was taking on him.

"Check out this color, CeeCee," he said, pointing at the wall as if it were some kind of trophy or something. "They call it Valspar Almost Charcoal," he said proudly. "Picked it out myself."

Cleo took in the newly painted wall. "Yeah, Daddy, I love it, complements the sofa perfectly," she said, rubbing her left hand across the surface on the sofa next to her.

"Daddy, you seem to be having more trouble than usual with that bowed leg of yours," Cleo stated, watching him tread back to his worn-out Lay-Z-Boy that he refused to let go of. Since the renovations had been completed, it was the only thing left that was old.

"Are you experiencing more pain?"

Her father waved his hand and shrugged. "Ah, CeeCee, I'm fine, it's the same as it's always been," he responded, dismissing her concerns and settling back into his chair.

Cleo knew that wasn't true but decided to drop the subject for now. "Well, alright, Daddy, just making sure, is all."

"I know baby, I know. Hey, I've been meaning to ask you about the lil' black Bible I gave you when you were around ten years old. Do you still have it?"

Cleo sat up and batted her eyes, perplexed, picturing her beloved pocket-sized Bible she had cherished ever since her father gave it to her. It had a permanent resting place on her bedside table.

"Yes, Dad, why do you ask?"

"Oh, just wanted to make sure you still had it, is all. You know it's the greatest book of all time, right, CeeCee?"

Cleo nodded her head. She watched her dad settle back into his Lay-Z-Boy and kicked up his feet onto the footrest.

"Whenever you're feeling lost, unsure, upset, unhappy, you know you can turn to open up the Good Book. All the answers you seek to any questions you have are in that book, never forget that, okay?"

Cleo was unsure of what to say or how to act. Though he was a God-fearing man, her father rarely talked about anything concerning religion, let alone attend anybody's place of worship. "Okay, Daddy," she responded, shifting uneasily in her seat.

"Oh, I forgot to tell you Mom said dinner will be done in about twenty minutes."

Her father rubbed the back of his bald head and inhaled his cigar that was resting in the ashtray. "Oh, yes, my stomach was just beginning to touch back, as you young folk say," he laughed, obviously tickled with himself.

A few moments passed when they heard her mother's voice calling down from the kitchen. "Dinner's ready!"

Cleo and her father looked at each other and grinned. “Let’s eat!” Cleo yelled excitedly. She watched as her dad slowly rose from his Lay-Z-Boy. “Yes, Lord, I’m ready.”

⚢ 24 ⚥

The weekend flew by as quickly as it came, which was like warp speed to someone Cleo's age. It was Monday morning and Cleo found herself sitting at her desk, wondering how she got there. Her mind was muddled with images from the last bombastic lovemaking session with Miss St. Martin. So many unsettling thoughts ran through her mind, and she just couldn't shake the deep feelings she was already having for Kennedy.

Out of the blue, Shelby burst through the door, interrupting her thoughts, as she did practically every day. Dressed on the conservative side today, Shelby donned a simple, but sophisticated grey pantsuit with an eggshell blouse and matching pumps.

"Hey, girl, what happened to you on Saturday?" She promptly plopped her ample bottom onto Cleo's desk, causing papers and files to scatter onto the floor.

"Me and the girls waited for you almost thirty minutes at Northwestway for our walk and I tried calling your cell and house phone when I couldn't get you, I figured you were laid up with Javon or Craig or, perhaps, a new piece of ass?"

Cleo shook her head, all too aware of just how nosey Shelby could be most of the time. It sure made it hard sometimes to share or trust her with her most intimate thoughts and feelings, hence the very reason she chose not to disclose her feelings for women, let alone their co-worker, Kennedy. At least not just yet.

"Sorry, to disappoint, Shell, but the answer is no, I did not layup with Javon or Craig or anybody else over the weekend. I just needed some *me* time, is all."

Shelby raised her eyebrows in suspicion as if to say *heifer, I know you lyin' to me,* but she didn't say anything and let her continue.

Surprised by Shelby's silence, Cleo crossed her legs and continued. "Girl, as a matter of fact, I haven't heard from Javon since that night at the movie theater and Craig pulled one of his disappearing acts as you know he often does and when I say, I am not missing them either—"

There came a knock on her door, interrupting their conversation.

"Come in," Cleo said as she sat up in her chair. It was one person neither of them cared to see, Samantha Merriweather.

"Excuse me, but I overheard some of your conversation and, well, frankly, I don't think this is the right place for it and you are both on the clock, so let's get back to work, ladies."

Before either could respond, she exited just as swiftly as she had pranced into Cleo's office. After the initial shock dissipated, an incensed Shelby jumped up and headed for the door.

Cleo knew what her BFF had on her mind, and she was not going to allow her to get fired today, so she sprang into action. Cleo grabbed Shelby by the arm before she could step one foot out the door.

"Hold up, girl! I am not gonna let you get yourself caught up in that bitch's spider web. Hell, you already know she's already fishin', tryna to find something on us to get us fired, especially me because I can tell she's still threatened by me."

Shelby jerked her arm back. "But, damn, did you hear her? Who the fuck does that wench think she is talking to us like we somebody's child up in here?" Shelby balled up her right fist and pounded it into her left hand. "I just wanna pounce on her just ONE good time, that's all. Is that asking too much? Argh!"

Shelby stomped back to the chair she rose from and planted her ass back in it.

"Girl, if I didn't know any better, I could've sworn I saw steam pumping from your ears. You're that pissed off, huh?" Cleo said.

Shelby folded her arms. "Hell yeah, I am! The nerve of that heifer!"

"Hey, boo, don't sweat the small stuff." She glanced at her wristwatch. "You know you are better than that and, shit, it's midday, let's go out for lunch. We need to get away from this office for a while."

They gathered their belongings and headed out for a much-needed break from Samantha Merriweather. Like always, the office was so quiet you could hear a pin drop. The ladies made their way to the elevator, laughing and talking about the crazy things they went through at North Central back in the day.

⚢ 25 - This chapter features Shelby's POV⚥

Cleo awoke the next morning to birds chirping loudly outside her bedroom window, a sure-fire reminder of Naptown's balmy mid-summer mornings. She was glad it was Saturday because she was bursting with energy that would serve her well at Juan Solomon Park, affectionately known as the tennis courts, for a match with her friends. She reached for her home phone as she rolled out of bed and dialed her BFF's number.

Excitement overwhelmed her about the performers scheduled for this year's Indiana Black Expo's free outdoor concert she'd just heard on WTLC that she almost tripped over the bedpost on her way to the bathroom.

"Girl, guess who's gonna be at the free concert?!" She blurted out as toothpaste spilled from her mouth.

Shelby was just waking up from a deep slumber, eyes puffy and swollen after a long night out with James. But she dared not speak of him in Cleo's presence, even if she was several blocks away. She could almost smell the smoke booming from her truck's engine racing over to her home to beat some sense into her from continuing to deal with the nigga when she'd promised to stay away from him during their last girl-talk session a while ago.

"Who?" Shelby managed to say as a sharp, throbbing pain traveled through her head making its way to her engorged left eye. "What the fuck …"

"What did you just say?" Cleo asked as she put her toothbrush away and reached for her Biotène mouthwash.

The sudden realization that she had a black eye pained and infuriated her to no end, but she knew the beat down that would surely come from her BFF would be much worse, so she played it off.

"Um, girl, Oshun just jumped up on the bed, scared the mess outta me. I love my baby, but, damn, she sure can be sneaky as hell sometimes." Silently, she prayed Cleo would buy her story. For extra measure, she crossed her fingers just for the false sense of extra security.

"Oh, yeah, cats are famous for being sneaky, as you well know. Anyhow, it's gonna be the shit this year 'cause the S.O.S. Band, the Zapp Band, and Keith Sweat are gonna be in the house, woot, woot! And, you know how much I LOVE ME SOME KEITH almost as much as I love me some Gerald Levert, may he rest in peace."

"Whoa, yes I do know how much you love him," Shelby laughed, picturing Cleo doing her happy dance in her bathroom mirror and that made her giggle to no end, all the while hiding her age-old pain. "Girl, I'm not gonna make it this morning, sorry."

Cleo was getting her boogie oogie on to A Taste of Honey's 'Boogie Oogie Oogie', that WTLC just started playing, but upon hearing this statement from Shelby, her hips immediately stopped gyrating to the rhythm. "What the hell you mean you're not coming?!" she demanded.

"Girl, I just ain't feelin' good this morning. Got a stomachache," Shelby lied as she made her way to her bathroom.

Cleo heard the shuffling of Shelby's house shoes through the phone. She was never good about picking up her feet even as a teenager. "But it's our ritual, you can't just go and mess it up!" she pleaded while lotioning up her legs. Before Shelby could respond, she continued, "What am I supposed to tell Donnieka and Crimson, huh? You know those two are going to bc extremely disappointed."

In reality, they both knew who was the most disappointed, but neither said a word about it.

Shelby gathered herself before looking into the mirror that she and her BFF installed a while ago. It was now littered around the edges with brightly colored sticky notes. Some were inspirational in manner:

"We are what we repeatedly do; excellence, then, is not an act, but a habit" –Aristotle

While the neon green sticky notes attested to the importance of self-worth:

"It's all about falling in love with yourself and sharing that love with someone who appreciates you rather than looking for love to compensate for a self-love deficit"
-Eartha Kitt

And the hot pink notes were all reminders of how one can improve their lives, what NOT to do and WHO not to invite into your space:

"You can't keep a clean reputation hanging out with messy people"-Loreen Hall

"When the wrong people leave your life, the right things start happening"
"Manifest your dreams." -Oprah Winfrey

Her left eye was damn near all the colors of the rainbow. She expected some swelling, but nothing like this. There was no way she could leave her home for work, the grocery store, let alone a walk with her girls. Way too embarrassing, and the shame, oh, the shame she felt at that moment was completely and utterly devastating.

"I'm really sorry, CeeCee, but seriously, I just can't do it this morning, but I promise to make it up to all of you soon," she replied while continuing to assess the damage done to her face. *Oh, shit! Now I know that nigga didn't leave the imprint of his oversized fingers on my neck,* she exclaimed to herself.

"Hey hon, I promise I'll call you later on today to see how the walk went. Right now, I'm gonna dig through my medicine cabinet for some Pepto Bismol and lay it back down for a while. Love you, ciao!"

And, just like that, she was gone, leaving Cleo with her mouth hung open and no more time to plead her case. She shook her head, finished dressing, and headed to the tennis court.

****

"Hey ladies," Cleo said as she grabbed her tennis racket, shut her truck door and headed towards Crimson and Donnieka who were warming up on the court. In the distance, she could see the city's lawn service guys mowing the grass in the soccer area. The smell of fresh-cut grass invigorated her almost as much as the last climax she experienced with Kennedy.

"Where's Shell?" They said in unison.

Cleo shook her head and said, "She got a stomachache, so she won't be joining us this morning. How long have y'all been warming up?" she asked, stretching her lithe body into a forward bend.

Uh oh. Cleo's instincts kicked in. Something was up with her BFF, but she could not put her finger on it. As with all things kept secret, the truth would reveal itself eventually.

And as the true friend she was, Cleo would be there to support her lifelong friend, no matter what it was, because they were each other's ride or die chick-for-life.

"Oh, just for a few minutes," Crimson replied. "Well, I'm a little sad she's not gonna make it. I haven't seen her in a while and wanted to return her flat iron I've had since January."

Cleo began her warm-up routine and said, "Girl, I think Shelby forgot you even had it because she went out and bought one a few weeks ago, thinking she'd just misplaced it or something."

Standing a few feet from Crimson, Donnieka was trying to do forward leg kicks, but because she had so much girth centered in the front of her, she was having a hard time balancing herself.

Cleo glanced over at her to see if she could see any sign of weight loss. *Hmmm, seems she may have lost a pound or two …*

"Hey, Donnieka, how's that new diet workin' out for ya? Looks like you've lost a few pounds," Cleo stated as all three headed to the track.

A big Cheshire cat grin spread across her face as she replied "Actually, yeah, CeeCee. The diet's working out very well for me. Thanks for asking." Then she stopped in her tracks, sucked her stomach in and did a side pose for them.

"Girl, if you stick to that new diet of yours, you're gonna be skinnier than me one day soon!" exclaimed Crimson. "I'm so proud of you!"

"Me, too," Cleo chimed in. "All right, let's get into why we came today. Shit, if we all stay committed to our workouts, we're gonna be much lighter come this time next year."

"I know that's right, girl. Let's do this!" Donnieka agreed.

⚢ 26 ⚥

"Do you think you could ever live this kind of lifestyle, Kennedy?" It was a question Cleo had wanted to ask her many times but was afraid of what her answer might be. She'd bridged questions like this before, but Kennedy always managed to steer the conversation in another direction, much to Cleo's frustration. They'd just finished a late afternoon rendezvous at their favorite hotel.

A nervous frown blanketed Kennedy's delicate face.

"Well, remember a while back when I explained to you about feeling wary of being gone too much from home and how I don't want to chance getting caught, right?"

Cleo fought back the tears that threatened to stream down her worried face. "Yeah, I remember."

Kennedy bit her bottom lip and sat up on the bed. "Well, um, I'm trying to frame my response in a way that doesn't upset you or make you feel some kind of way, but I don't think I'm succeeding, am I?" She averted her eyes from Cleo's. "Well, um, CeeCee, I really, um …"

It was obvious she didn't know how to respond to Cleo's probing question. In turn, Cleo pulled herself up, along with the thick cotton white sheet. She tucked it around her chest as if she'd suddenly become shy and fought to keep the hot tears that were pooling in her eyes from tidal waving down her heated cheeks. "You know I've fallen in love with you, Kennedy—"

"I'm in love with you, too, CeeCee, but I—"

It was too late. The tears she had been fighting so hard to hold back began to flow steadily down her burning red cheeks.

Why did Kennedy have to be married?

Why did she have to have kids?

Why did she kiss me that day in my office?

Why did I succumb to her allure?

Why, oh why ...

"There are no buts," Cleo whispered. She started chewing on her fingernails, something she only did when she was upset about something or, in this case, extremely sad about something. "... truth is, you're a married woman and I have no right to even think I could ever take the place of your family."

Kennedy's eyes filled with regret. "CeeCee, I can't tell you how many times I thought about leaving Bernard so we can be together.

Our marriage is so unfulfilling and has been for a long time, but then I think about the kids and ..." She reached out for Cleo's hand, but Cleo withdrew from her and folded her arms, shutting her out.

"Please don't be like that, Cleo. You know I love you, don't you?"

Cleo stared at her, searching for some kind of recognition of their love—if it could be called that.

"Really? You really love me, *but*? There's always a *but* when it comes to this relationship," she retorted.

Kennedy reached for her arms once again, but Cleo stubbornly held tight, not wanting to give in to her lover. "Oh, so it's like that now, after everything we've shared and done together? You just gonna shut me out like that, really CeeCee?" Agitation flooded her words. She huffed, stood up and began putting her underwear on.

This was not going the way Cleo envisioned. She so desperately wanted Kennedy to say she loved her enough to run away together; to start a life together somewhere far away like in Fiji or even return to their ancestral land in Africa. Cleo didn't care where they ended up, as long as they were together. That was all that mattered.

"Wait, wait, Kennedy," she pleaded. "I'm sorry. I got upset because I just want to be with you, is all. I want you to be mine and only mine, is that so wrong?" Cleo released the sheet and went to her.

Kennedy began crying as she reached out to accept Cleo's trembling hand. "I know, CeeCee. I know how you feel about me because I feel the same way." She gently kissed away the tears streaming down Cleo's cheeks. In turn, Cleo wrapped her arms around Kennedy's waist and for several long minutes, they held one another, seemingly for dear life. "Baby, I really do love you." Kennedy cupped her face in her hands and looked deeply into her eyes that were now a faint shade of red from all the tears. "I love you so much it scares me sometimes because I never knew I could feel this way about a woman ..." Kennedy wrapped her arms around Cleo's shoulders and began rocking slowly. "... but I can't pretend I don't have a husband," she stammered, "... and a family I love too."

Hearing the word 'husband' made Cleo cringe. Even though she was all too aware of Kennedy's marriage, she found herself constantly trying to forget that very fact. The realization of sharing her first female lover with a man sickened her because she also realized she was putting herself at risk, too. Who's to say he wasn't having an affair with another woman or, hell, even a man for that matter? Cleo had E. Lynn Harris to thank for schooling her on the down-low brothas back in the day. She'll never forget that scene in one of his books where that freaky-ass football player Basil Henderson got caught red-handed by his woman screwing another dude.

Unequivocally, it was Harris that opened her eyes to just how real and how common the DL syndrome was among men—women too, if she was being honest. Cleo abruptly broke away. "So, what are you saying, Kennedy?"

Kennedy threw her hands up in the air, quickly finished dressing and left, once again leaving Cleo to wallow in her feelings all alone. For a while, she laid there thinking, pondering. Though she wasn't prepared to say it out loud, it was becoming quite apparent that their relationship was slowly coming to an end.

****

After her rendezvous with Kennedy, Cleo felt extremely restless and unsure of her next move as far as Kennedy went. The one thing she was certain of was that she was happy with the direction she was heading as far as her sexuality was concerned. Though the thought of coming out to her family and friends still frightened her, she finally felt comfortable in her own skin and more importantly, she was keenly aware that her faith had not wavered. She was not big on attending church, but always felt a strong and undeniable connection to her Creator. She was a child of God and nothing or no one was going to change that. After rolling into her garage, she walked straight to her bedroom, changed into her favorite zebra print loungewear, then made her way back to the kitchen to retrieve a strawberry-flavored Smirnoff cooler from the fridge.

Suddenly, she heard the faint sound of a cell phone tone coming from her bedroom and dashed to the room to answer the call. "Ouch!" she screamed out when her big toe hit the half-closed bedroom door. She retrieved her mobile off her bedside table on the last ring and saw that it was someone she had no interest in talking to: Javon.

What the hell does he want? Cleo wondered. She'd already cursed him out a few times over the phone and one day he even had the nerve to just show up at her home unannounced. Cleo was furious. Having no desire to speak with him, she let it go to voicemail, cozied up in her bed and opened her laptop. Time to check out the new posts…

Let's f*ck

AA FEMALE looking for another female to SQUIRT in my mouth while I suck in your juicy pussy...never had a squirter & now I would like to try one. I want your wet-ass pussy in my face...so pls don't keep me waiting b/c i'm so horny n so ready to please u. send pic to get one in return NO MEN AND HELL NO YOUR HUSBAND, BOYFRIEND OR WHO EVER U ARE FUCKIN CAN'T WATCH NOR JOIN IN...I don't do dick so don't even ask or waste my time! MUST BE DDD FREE, 420-FRIENDLY

My new agenda

The reason I am posting this is because I made a few stops when I got off work and found myself in crowded rooms but felt extremely alone and not wanting to be. I listened to ppl around me laugh and enjoy their conversations and I felt invisible. I began wondering if there is someone out here that is like me that prefers to have someone to spend time with. After a long week at work and as the weekend begins it would be nice to have someone to spend some time with. To do ordinary things with like go to dinner & a movie or stay in and watch Netflix, or just go to sleep with because the batteries need recharging from a busy week of work. I miss the human touch, no, I miss a woman's hand caressing my back, a whisper in my ear. I will soon celebrate my 40th & would like a mature, like-minded educated & professional lady to enjoy it with me. Pls be clean, HPW, disease & drama free. I also have a thing for women with cocoa-colored skin. Will you melt in my mouth? The sooner the better.

Friends w/ benefits?

Hiya! I am a married aa, discreetly bi laid back type of queen bee. I'm interested in meeting a real friend and experience the benefits of such a friendship. My husband is not aware nor will he be involved as I'm not trying to change my life, nor my life w/ my husband. I'm happy in my marriage, but just need to be in the company of a woman sometimes. I'm not interested in jumping into bed, I need someone who wants to first build a friendship, so if you are in a similar situation, contact me... hmu and let's see what happens. I'll be waiting…

With things getting so rocky with Kennedy, she found herself perusing the personals more and more often. She always found the ads to be very entertaining and never ceased to tantalize and amaze her. She was still getting used to the lifestyle and figuring out her feelings for men as the attraction was still there as well.

Could it be that I'm bisexual?

What does being bisexual really mean?

Are there many other women who identify as such?

These and other related questions flooded her consciousness more and more on a daily basis, leading her to conduct more research. She clicked on the Dictionary.com icon on her laptop and typed 'bisexuality.' According to the website, it's *a person sexually responsive to both sexes or ambisexual.*

"Hmmm, a person responsive to both sexes or ambisexual," she repeated to herself. Cleo tapped her finger on the keyboard, pondering the definition. "But, what in the world does ambisexual mean and how does it fit in with being bisexual?" This definition raised more questions rather than providing her with a definitive answer, so she shook her head, then clicked back to the personal ads.

Something different

1st of all I know this is the w4w selection. And that's cool; not tryna to change your orientation. I am a guy who simply just loves to eat, lick, suck on a woman n that it...no sex AT ALL!!! I am in the lake co area but cannot host. It can be at your spot, my ride, or even a storage unit...it don't matter. You can be single, married, bi, stud don't care let me eat and go about my day. Please be DDD free as I am ...I want to please and be safe as well. If ur serious please put location, pictures and email, kik, or number and let the eating begin.

What the hell is this dude talking about and why is he trying to get with a female who is gay? It's not like there isn't a casual encounters section on this site, so what gives?

Again, she shook her head in amazement and continued reading.

POLYAMOROUS LESBIAN!!- w4w - 30

What's up ladies? If the title caught u then let me tell u a little about myself. I'm a 30 y/o BBW sz 18 48DDs and a phat ass to match. Yesssss, thick in all the right places. I'm a sexy college-educated fun loving femme. Now let's get back to the title. I practice polyamory, so I am committed to a very sexy stud. Now let's talk about what I'm searching for. I'm looking for a stud but not just any old stud. I'm looking for a stud that likes femmes and studs cause u won't just b dating just me—u will b dating both of us.

I know ur thinking we're crazy but believe me these types of relationships can work with the right people. U must b DDD Free between the ages of 22-55. That's right, I don't discriminate cause age ain't nothing but a number, ya feel me? If ur interested hmu with a pic and tell me about yourself. I promise, u won't b disappointed. NO GAMES AND BS!!! NO FUCKIN MEN & I MEAN IT!!! Not down with drama, either. If you are, keep it movin!!! Don't do confused/bisexual females. So, if all this sounds good to u, hit me up & let's see what we can do.

Submissive needed for daytime online submission -w4w - 31
31 attractive WF looking for a submissive little slut who is available during the day to keep me entertained via email/messaging while I'm working from home. It may present the opportunity to lead to real-life contact, but no promises. Age/race not important to me, just your obedience. Type "Yes Madam" in the subj line…also, u will need to self-identify/voice identify & I promise, there will be no disappointments.

ULTRA SEXY FEMME SEEKS SAME - W-4-W—36

What it do ladies? Where are the sexy SGL professional women who from time to time enjoy the company of another female but due to their profession, must maintain a low profile? I'm looking for a sexy, HWP, ultra femme whose interested in some no-strings attached playtime as our schedule allows—like today would be great! I'm reaching out to the women who work hard, but can appreciate intimacy especially when it has been stimulated by intelligent conversation and a great personality. We can meet for a light lunch and converse & if there is chemistry, let nature take its course.

I can host today, but would like to take turns. My place, your place, a hotel, wherever we decide on works for me. I need you to exude sexiness, be single (I don't want to follow your man), and ready to voice verify. No studs-just my preference, no threesomes & pls don't ask). Your pic gets mine. ABSOLUTELY No MEN! You will NOT be disappointed 'cause I know I got what u want. Respond with "Let's do this!" in the subj line. Serious inquiries ONLY!

Sometimes it was inconceivable to think there really are so many women who desire other women, herself included. Cleo was still baffled by this fact but decided to continue reading more of ads up until she shut down her laptop and forced herself to go to sleep, dreaming about what it would be like to taste someone other than Kennedy.

⚢ 27 ⚥

The next three weeks flew by. In an effort to lessen the pain and hopelessness she was feeling since her encounter with Kennedy, Cleo submerged herself in all kinds of activities such as volunteering to take Thema to her soccer, ballet, taekwondo practices and play dates with her friends. When Symone asked her why she was suddenly so available to help out with her youngest niece, she explained that it had been her intention for a while to become more involved with Thema as she missed out on such affairs with Nahla who was now down in Bloomington pursuing a doctoral degree in Juridical Science at I.U.

Also, it would give her big sis some relief from all the running around she had to do in the absence of her husband, David, who was recently promoted to a sales executive position at Eli Lilly, but that often kept him away from home. The most positive thing about his promotion was the extra cash flow that allowed Symone to resign from her customer service position at a local call center. Shortly after she gave birth to Nahla, Symone began working at a call center to support their family. Over the years, she managed to work her way up to head supervisor, but knew she was stuck in a dead-end job. Like so many people, she yearned for something more satisfying.

On the other hand, David was blessed with not only depth-defying basketball skills that would rival those of MJ, but his skills also paved the way to a full scholarship to Butler University where he majored in biomedical engineering. Although they became parents at an early age, they defied glaring statistics by becoming *The Huxtables* of the Golden Ghetto. Resigning her supervisor position also freed up time for her to enroll in graduate school. She also had begun writing again but hadn't shared it with anyone except Cleo.

The sound of little footsteps could be heard as Thema made her way downstairs, rounding the corner into the kitchen where Cleo and Symone were sipping on sun tea that she'd made the evening before. The clatter of picture frames on the wall in the hallway shook when she sprinted to her favorite auntie.

"Hey, slow down, Thema, before you hurt yourself or break one of my picture frames!" Symone exclaimed.

"Auntie! Auntie!" she shouted as she leaped into Cleo's arms and gave her a big hug and a kiss. She was already suited up for her taekwondo class, hair pulled into a single ponytail, complete with pink and purple balls on the end.

"What'cha doin' here?" She squealed.

Cleo responded, "Hey, baby! I'm gonna give your mommy a break and take you to your class this evening, how does that sound?"

Thema's tiger eyes looked like saucers as delight spread over her face. "Yes! Yes! Yes!" she shouted as she stepped out of their embrace and started her happy dance.

"Ah, look at my oops baby." Symone put her hands on her generous hips and shook her head. " Cleo giggled. "Yeah, I remember that story."

"I'll never forget when my gynecologist gave me that surprise when I went in to get my I.U.D. checked out only to inform me that I was pregnant." Cleo embraced Thema and said, "Yep, now look at this beautiful lil' creature Allah gave you and David." She pinched Thema's rosy cheek who squealed in delight.

Thema engaged in her dance routine, leading Cleo to join her. All Symone could do was shake her head at the madness. "Alright, you two," she said as she glanced at the wall clock that showed the time to be half-past six. "Y'all better get going." She leaned down to Thema and gave her a big hug. "Now, you make sure to do everything the instructor tells you, okay?" she said as she smoothed her daughter's hair back. "Mommy loves you."

Thema pushed her mother's hand away and said "Okay, Mommy. I promise I will." Then she sprinted towards the front door, shouting "Let's go, Auntie!"

****

Cleo knew something bad was going on with her BFF because she hadn't heard back from her since their conversation Saturday morning, though she'd promised to call her that evening. She tried calling and texting her, but to no avail, leaving Cleo full of questions and concern. Moreover, Cleo was all too aware of Shelby's disappearing acts, too. Almost anything could trigger this kind of behavior. It had started after the death of her unborn baby.

Cleo struggled with deciding to just go over to her apartment and use the key Shelby had given her. In the end, she decided to let it ride, despite her instincts telling her otherwise.

⚢ 28 ⚥

Monday marked the week of the Black Expo and Cleo was getting more and more excited as each day drew nearer to her. She was itching to get down and dirty in more ways than one at the concert and the after-party that would follow. The countdown was on and poppin'! Monday almost down, four more days to go.

She was so revved up about the impending festivities, that her work ensemble reflected her mood: an ivory-hued button-down blouse and basic black linen slacks she'd been lucky enough to scoop up from one of her favorite vintage stores. To finish off the look, she paired her two-carat diamond earrings Craig had gifted her when she got promoted a few years back, along with a matching tennis bracelet.

Cleo was on her way to Jim's office when her phone rang, so she did a U-turn back to hers.

"Hello, thank you for calling the Exodus Resource Center—"

Before she could finish, a sexy and very familiar voice on the other end interrupted,

"Cleo, it's Kennedy. We need to talk."

She almost melted in the spot she stood in upon hearing Kennedy's sultry voice on the other end.

"Oh, hey, Kennedy," she stuttered, shifting from one leg to the other. "Um, yeah, um, okay."

Cleo was speechless. Her head was immediately filled with the sweet memories of their lovemaking more than a month ago. Just about every night, the various freaky things they did played out in her head like a movie reel … not to mention the incessant daydreaming.

"Hello, Cleo? Are you there?" The mere sound of her seductive voice shook Cleo to her core.

"Yes, yes, I'm here. It's just that, well …" she continued to have difficulty conversing with the woman who'd turn her world inside out … and yet, Kennedy had no idea of the impact that everything they shared that fateful night, from the deep, mind-blowing conversation, the authenticity and sincerity, and of course, the slamming combination of the sweetest taboo loving to the bombastic, toenail-curlin' fucking.

All right girl, snap the fuck out of it, damn!

By now, her skin shimmered with sweat beads under the dim light and her hand trembled as she ran her fingers over her pinned-up mane. Cleo managed to slither her limp body onto the sofa and continued, "I haven't heard from you since the last time and—"

"I know, I know," Kennedy interrupted. Cleo could sense her apprehensiveness through the receiver.

"Let me finish," she said with a little more authority in her voice this time around.

A little astounded by Cleo's stern reply, Kennedy responded, "Oh! Um, okay, I'm listening."

Her response made Cleo's confidence shoot up a few notches, her spine a pinch tauter. "Okay, see, this is the thing. I know a lot went on that night that was unexpected, but, well, honestly, I can't lie and say I didn't enjoy all of it 'cause I did, but we have to be real about this whole thing. I mean, you *are* married with children and that is a fact that I just can't shake."

Cleo's eyes were closed as she was spilling her guts to Kennedy. This woman had a hold on her unlike any man ever thought they did. Her allure left Cleo utterly defenseless … and she was having a real hard time making sense of it all. Never in her life did any of her boyfriends or male lovers make her feel like Kennedy did. The fact that they'd only shared fleeting moments made her question everything relating to her sexual orientation and personal life, which was in serious turmoil at the moment.

"Cleo? I can't hear you, are you still there?" Kennedy stated.

Once again, she was lost in her thoughts, but shook it off and continued, "Yeah, I'm here, sorry, lost my train of thought." Undeniable defeat echoed in her voice.

"Look, Cleo. I never meant to make you feel uncomfortable, upset, frustrated or anything like that. And please believe, above all else through this journey we have started together, I really care about you and want to see, learn, touch, feel, caress, suck, and lick everything on your sexy-ass body. I want to learn about what it means to be a lesbian in every way imaginable and immerse myself in the prolific writings of our foremothers like Audre Lorde, Barbara Smith, and Cheryl Clarke. Oh my God, CeeCee, if you only knew. If you only knew."

Cleo had no idea who those women were, so she made a mental note to look them up later. Before Cleo could respond, her office door flung open, interrupting their tête-à-tête.

"Hey girl, you ready to head out for lunch?" Shelby asked.

Cleo about jumped out of her skin. It didn't seem like that much time had gone by.

"Oh, Shell, you scared the bejeezus outta me! Jesus H. Christ!" she exclaimed.

Cleo's response caught Shelby off-guard. She just stood there glaring at her BFF, not sure of how to respond.

Immediately, Cleo could see she was being a little too harsh, so she regrouped and apologized for being so crass. "Hold on a sec," she said to Kennedy on the other end of the line.

"Let me finish up here and I'll be right out, Shelby. I'll meet you at your car in a few minutes." She sent her a reassuring look that let Shelby know she was being sincere. Cleo's rigid body relaxed when she saw Shelby smile back at her before turning on her heels and heading out the door.

"Thanks for holding, Kennedy. I was so caught up in our conversation, that I'd lost track of time," she said as she rose from the couch to gather her purse and keys.

"Not a problem, I understand," Kennedy replied.

"Okay, so about us getting together to chat. Would you have time later on in the week, say maybe Wednesday or Thursday evening?" Cleo imagined her beautiful gazelle waiting with bated breath on the other end of the line.

"Thursday will work for me. Let's say seven o'clock at the Starbucks on Lafayette Road?" she responded, closing and locking her office door.

"That's fine, Cleo. See you then," Kennedy replied. "Goodbye."

"Bye."

****

Just like the first-time Kennedy St. Martin waltzed into her office months earlier and planted that deep, penetrating kiss on her, turning her world upside-down, inside and out …

Cleo knew the journey with her was bound to shake her world even more as they continued to explore the uncharted territory of loving they'd only touched on during their first real encounter at Cleo's home. Cleo's feelings were all over the place as she was coming to realize her orientation was far from obvious.

At this moment, one thing was for certain: the enigmatic connection she shared with Kennedy was something that was not going away … despite her being a married woman with children. Cleo was quite aware she felt the same way … at least that's what Kennedy kept telling her.

They would continue to play this dangerous game and simply let nature unfold.

⚢ 29 ⚥

Cleo rubbed her aching, throbbing temples as soon as she walked through the door and tossed her handbag and keys onto the kitchen counter. She was completely and utterly drained from working with one of her most difficult clients, who also was her last home visit of the day. She flicked on the kitchen light and walked over to the fridge and opened it wide, only to be greeted with sparse pickings. *Damn, I'm out of milk, butter, and Kraft cheese slices,* she noted.

Looks like a turkey and Swiss cheese sandwich tonight. She retrieved the plastic bag of the few deli mesquite turkey slices that remained from her last grocery shopping day a few weeks ago, along with Swiss cheese from the middle drawer, and sat them on the counter. Then she grabbed the bread from the breadbasket. *Wait a minute, something's missing … ah, yes, I forgot the mayo, dammit.* She turned on her heel back to the fridge and grabbed the Hellman's from the door, along with a bottle of water. She nibbled on her sandwich and sifted through the mail that had been piling up over the past week or so.

After finishing her snack, she turned her attention to her laptop, staring into the monitor like it was a window into her soul. Hearing Audre's, Cheryl's, and Barbara's names had aroused her thirst to learn about them and others like them. She typed in Audre's name first into the browser. Millions of hits blanketed her screen. She decided to open *Biography.com* and devoured the paragraphs before her. As she read, Audre's life story began to unfold right before her very eyes. Cleo was fascinated by Audre's style of writing and the things she had to say that she didn't get to the others tonight. She decided to save them for another day and just let what she'd learn about the triple jeopardy of being a woman, lesbian, and black settle in the back of her mind.

Audre Lorde was a poet, essayist, educator, writer and activist. She was also a lesbian. She'd been married to a man and bore him two children. She raised her kids with her white female partner during the 1960s …

In the '60s, really? Wow, talk about defying the patriarchy, Cleo thought. She marveled at Audre's unbelievable self-awareness and determination to live her life as she, and only she, saw fit at a time in history when women's voices were often silenced by a male-dominated society.

Indeed, she was beyond a shadow of a doubt a warrior in every sense of the word. Cleo was in awe of the discoveries she was making and couldn't wait to get Audre's semi-biographical book *Zami: A New Spelling of My Name* from the library ASAP. *I cannot believe I never heard of Audre until now! Just another exam[le of certain voices being silenced. Damn, my mind is blown.*

****

"Caught Up in the Rapture of Love" sang out of Cleo's cell phone lying on her nightstand. She'd assigned Anita Baker's song to Kennedy because that was the way she felt about her: caught up in the rapture of love where nothing else could compare,

Hey, wanted to give you a heads up as soon as I realized I won't be able to meet with you on Fri at the hotel as planned. One of the boys has football practice and I'm gonna have to take and bring him home...sorry...promise to make it up to you...kisses all over (KAO)

Cleo's heart sank as she stared at her cell in disbelief. *Damn, not again. What the fuck? How much longer am I gonna deal with this shit?*

⚢ 30 ⚥

Monday, Tuesday, and Wednesday flew by without any warning. Cleo ended up receiving a second text from Kennedy,

> Hey lovey. We're on again for tomorrow…was able to get the parent of one Junior's team members to do the transport for their practice, yah! So I'll see you at our spot at seven. KAO

Cleo's scattered brain was chock full of thoughts, questions, and concerns she had for Kennedy. Indeed, there was going to be some serious exploring about what was going on between them and where their *relationship* was going, if anywhere. Adding to the scatter-brain syndrome, the Indiana Black Expo free concert was also on her mind. What was a girl to do? So much excitement was almost too much to bear, but she knew she had to take it all in stride. All the plans were made for the concert:

- ✓ Ava and Sasha, along with a few of their friends would arrive at the American Legion Mall at 7 a.m. to secure a spot for their clan. They were also responsible for setting up the tables and chairs and preparing the aluminum pans and burners for the smorgasbord.

- ✓ Devin and a few of his friends were responsible for buying the meat: baby back beef ribs, hot dogs, ground sirloin for burgers, and chicken wings.
- ✓ Shelby was on board with her famous potato salad, baked beans, and sliced bread.

Even though she was preoccupied with orchestrating the arrangements for the Expo, she was even more preoccupied with her impending discussion with Kennedy in less than an hour. She hurriedly dressed for her meeting with Kennedy, gathered her handbag and keys, and took one more glance at herself in the hall mirror before heading out the door.

"Well, howdy there, neighbor!" bellowed Mr. van Deveer, her next-door neighbor.

"Hey there Mr. van Deveer, how's it going?" she asked as she opened her truck door.

"Oh, you know, same shit, different day," he replied, shifting his weight from left to right. Hey, have you seen R.K. lately? I noticed he hasn't been eating the food I've been leaving out for him in the last few days."

Cleo could see the concern etched in his face for R.K., causing her heart to ache just a little. "You know, I sure haven't seen our lil' bundle of joy in a while, but if I see him, I'll be sure to let you know, Mr. van Deveer. Enjoy your evening," she stated shifting the gear into reverse.

She could tell he wanted to chat a while, but she had a more enticing tête-à-tête to get to with her female lover at one of their favorite spots, Charade Inn & Suites.

****

She pulled into the parking lot and took the main road all the way to the back to their usual suite tucked in the back for privacy.

Good, she's already here, she said to herself. She reached in the backseat for her overnight bag, then jumped out of her truck and pushed the button on her keychain to lock the doors and set the alarm.

"Hey honey, get yourself on in here. I have a surprise for you, love." Cleo looked towards the suite's door only to see Kennedy peeping out, obviously hiding whatever it was she draped her body in.

Cleo hoisted her overnight bag over her shoulder, grinning brightly, and picked up the pace to see what awaited her on the other side of the door. "Oh, yeah? Well, I just can't wait, lemme see what you've been up to before I arrived."

Cleo rushed in and shut the door quickly behind her, her eyes dancing. She could not believe the magnificent sight before her very eyes. "Wow," she managed to say.

Kennedy had laid out their love nest in style: purple and red rose petals and lavender and cream candles welcomed her into their abode, laid out in a pattern that ran through the quaint living room area all the way towards the short hallway that led to the bedroom.

"You like, my dear?" Kennedy asked, hands on her hips, smiling cheek-to-cheek.

Cleo grabbed her and smothered her in kisses everywhere. "Yes, my love, I love it. And look at you!" Cleo twirled her in a circle, admiring the silk and lace bra and panty set she was sporting, along with a matching pair of five-inch silver-encrusted stiletto heels. Her beautiful mane swept up in an elegant soft bun bundled atop her head, dazzling long silver earrings, and metallic silvery lipstick as a befitting finishing touch. A sight to behold in Cleo's eyes.

Suddenly they heard a loud knock at the door. They both froze in their tracks, unsure of what to do next.

"Open this damn door Kennedy Gertrude St. Martin right now! I know you're in there with her, so just open up the door before I kick it down," said a booming male voice.

Neither woman made a move. Cleo's heart dropped to the floor, feeling utterly defeated and incensed at the same time.

More swift, loud knocks could be heard from the door. "Open the door before I knock it off its hinges and you know I mean it, Kennedy!"

Welp, the jig is up now. Might as well sit back and see how this shit is gonna unfold ...

"I knew something like this was gonna happen at some point, but damn, why today," Cleo murmured under her breath, sighed, and made her way to the alabaster-colored sofa on the opposite side of the room.

She looked on as Kennedy quickly ran to the bedroom and returned dressed in her summer dress. All Cleo could see was the look of panic and dread painted on her lover's face.

"Okay, okay, I'm coming Bernard, damn!" Kennedy hollered at him through the door.

Cleo noticed Kennedy wouldn't bring herself to look in her direction as she took steps toward the door and opened it.

"What in the hell are you doing here, Bernard?" Kennedy demanded. "What, you following me now?"

Cleo crossed her arms and legs, instantly feeling uneasy after watching Kennedy's husband walk into their suite.

Bernard pushed her to the side, walked in, and made his presence known. A big scowl covered his hairy face while his hands flew to his hips.

"Move out my way woman. I think it's half past time I met the woman I've been sharing my wife with over the past several months, wouldn't you say?"

Cleo looked on as he took a few more steps inside the living area, closer to her. "So, you the one that got my wife out here licking pussy, huh?" He glared at Kennedy, then back at Cleo. "I didn't want to believe it, but here we are. Damn. Well, whatcha got to say for yourself, Cleo? I know you know she's married, and we got kids, so what the hell?"

"Bernard, leave her out of this, I'm your wife, not her! And, besides, you got some nerve after all the times you cheated on me, asshole!" Kennedy shot back.

Cleo's ears perked up. *Did she just say what I think she said?*

"Woman, you said you forgave me for my past transgressions, so I ain't even tryna hear all that, besides this shit right here," he pointed to Kennedy and then Cleo, "is all on you and *her.*"

"Okay, okay, I've heard enough." Cleo rose from the sofa, swooped up her bag and headed for the door. "I'm not getting in y'all's mess. Kennedy, I'm going to excuse myself and let you handle this with your husband." She almost choked on the word 'husband.'

Neither Bernard and Kennedy made a move; both stared at Cleo as she opened the door and walked out.

Cleo drove home in a complete fog, not able to make heads or tails of what had just transpired at Charade Inn & Suites, but she knew something like what just happened was bound to happen one day, she just didn't know when. Worst of all, she had nobody to confide in.

****

Once she arrived home and settled into her nightly routine, feverishly checked her cell to see if Kennedy had called or left any text messages, but there were none. *Damn, I can't believe that shit really popped off with Kennedy and her crazy-ass husband come charging up in their suite, interrupting our precious time together. I was sure ready to get into that ass, too, dammit, but oh well. Tomorrow's the free Expo concert so that is bound to help get my mind off things.*

At least that's what she told herself. She popped a few Melantonins to help her sleep 'cause her mind was racing forty-going-left.

⚢ 31 ⚤

Finally, the day had come. The Indiana Black Expo exhibit at the Convention Center was in full swing, but Cleo was over it because since its inception some thirty-odd years ago, she and her friends attended every year and after so long, it just got *old*. Too many negroes for her taste, and as her grandfather used to quip:

"Niggas and flies, niggas and flies, the more I see niggas, the more I like flies." Cleo knew just how deep that old quote meant back then and how it was still as relevant today.

She checked her cell over and over for any messages from Kennedy, but much to her dismay, there were none. *Girl, shake it off. You knew that woman was married with children, to begin with, so you should have already been prepared when the time came. You were going to get dropped like a bad habit any damn way!*

Cleo had done her duty by ensuring everyone was on point with their tasks and that everything that needed to be done was taken care of. She could hardly contain her excitement. She gathered her things to head downtown, locked her garage door, and set the alarm. Suddenly, her cell rang. It was her BFF's ringtone.

Cleo gulped deeply before answering. The two had only talked briefly over the phone or in passing at work as things had gotten crazy busy with so many new cases and the loss of Tomika, plus state had taken up residence over the last few weeks, combing through personnel and client files, the center's policies and procedure manuals, all in the effort to ensure state guidelines were firmly in place and were being followed. Even Samantha Merriweather could be seen walking around on eggshells as nervousness and uncertainty blanketed her face. But it was understandable. She had a lot riding on the impending report as the new lead supervisor. Hell, one could say her newly cemented position was potentially being held hostage by the state and if they found the center to be out of compliance, heads would roll, with hers leading the pack.

"Hey sugar, I tried to reach you when I first got up to see if you were still planning to join us at the concert," Cleo stated as she jumped into her Ridgeline and pushed the automatic garage door opener.

"Hi boo," Shelby replied, "Yes, of course, I will be there. Remember I'm bringing a few of the side dishes, duh!"

Cleo wasn't fooled. Something was up and it was high time she got to the bottom of it, but today was not the day.

The fiery sun rays blasted from the yellow-gold sun high up in the sky which was becoming encircled with smoldering grey clouds that threatened the day. Neighbors were everywhere, some with their young children in strollers, while others jogged alongside their beloved golden retrievers, brown Labradors, and German shepherds. She flashed a Colgate smile as they all waved as she drove by.

"Oh, okay, good. So, why didn't you answer earlier?" she questioned. She could hear Shelby's car door open through the receiver, confirming that she really was going to hang out.

"I was in the bathroom, jeez! What's with all the twenty questions this morning? I've nothing to hide, CeeCee; give me a break, damn!"

Hearing the exasperation in Shelby's voice jolted every fiber of her being. Cleo's chest heaved and fell as she seriously considered her words before speaking. "Hey now, I'm sorry, boo, I was not trying to make you upset or anything. I guess I'm just missing my best friend, is all. You've been distant lately and I can tell when you just need some space, so that's why I've stayed away."

Despite what began as a very promising and exciting day, melancholy enveloped Cleo just as the somber clouds had threatened to overtake the sun.

An eerie, quiet delay crept through the phone as the two best friends were at a loss for words—something that hardly ever happened. Just like most women, both liked to have the last word, no matter what.

No longer able to stand the stifling silence, Cleo finally spoke.

"I love you; you know that, right?"

"I love you, too, CeeCee. I'll see you soon." And, with that, she was gone.

Even though their conversation had ended on a civil note, Cleo knew her BFF all too well and because of that, she knew something was up with her. Knowing how Shelby could be when it came to the opposite sex, she was keenly aware that she probably fell back into the arms of that woman-beater James or some other low-life, trifling asshole.

****

Cleo reignited her excitement by switching the radio on to WTLC. Zapp's 'I Can Make You Dance' rang through the truck's speakers. Cranking up the volume, Cleo bobbed her head in rhythm to one of her all-time Zapp favorites. As with every free concert, locating parking was somewhat of a contact sport; you had to get in where you could fit in, no matter what. Cleo rounded the corner at St. Clair and North Meridian.

"Oh my God, I can't believe it!" she exclaimed. A hunter-green Mustang was peeling out of the one coveted parking space in the vicinity. *Wait a minute, could it be her?*

Cleo waited impatiently for the driver to turn her head so she could see if she was the same woman she'd seen leaving Culver's months earlier. Ever since that day, Cleo looked for her at the restaurant but never ran into her again, much to her dismay. Words could not describe the connection she felt towards the unknown woman. Her intuition told her this woman was surely lesbian.

Butterscotch complexion, check.

Long, sweeping locks, check.

Mesmerizing eyes, check.

Indeed, it was her. Their eyes locked on each other just like the last time, but their words were stifled by the unexpected encounter. Unlike the first time she saw her, the woman was not alone in her Mustang. The lady who occupied the passenger seat was older, probably in her late sixties. Her close-cropped salt and pepper hair framed her elongated face that was the same shade of chestnut as the unknown woman that had captured Cleo's attention.

While she and the nameless contessa fixated on one another, the older lady said something that broke the spell. A tantalizing grin spread across her face as she sped out of the parking space, leaving Cleo wondering what the lady had said to her.

Damn! I cannot believe our paths have crossed again.

What does it mean?
Does it mean anything?
Perhaps there is nothing to read into it at all. Who knows?

Disconcerting thoughts flooded her mind, but she knew she had to let them go. If the universe wanted them to meet, great. If not, well, it just wasn't meant to be—at least that's what she told herself as she gathered her things and headed to the prime spot Sasha, Ava, and their friends were holding for everyone.

It was only going on ten o'clock and the park was already filled with countless people from every corner of Indianapolis and beyond. Music blared outside, a mix of a local band on the stage and R&B sounds streaming from boom boxes. The air was filled with body odor, cheap perfume, and cigarette and marijuana smoke. Folks were congregating all around the park and the surrounding streets. White foam food containers, numerous plastic cups, straws, half-eaten rib tips, and cigarette butts were strewn in all directions, causing Cleo to wonder how much more trash would be accumulated as the night went on.

“Excuse me, please,” Cleo yelled as she squeezed through a thick crowd along the path she'd chosen to get to the spot. Finally, a clearing came to light, allowing her to see her people.

Waving wildly, she announced, "Here comes the party girl, so y’all better get ready!"

"Um, yeah, baby, you can be my party girl any day."

Cleo jerked her head in the direction of the throaty voiced creature. It was dressed in a worn leather biker jacket with 'Hoosier Homies' embroidered on the front right pocket and a pair of Levi's that looked like they could walk on their own.

Cleo glared at him, but that didn't stop the creature's murky, bloodshot eyes from staring her up and down as if she were a chunk of meat for him to devour.

"Nigga pah-lease! If you don't step off, I'ma—"

"Hey there CeeCee. Let me help you with all this stuff," said Sasha as he tossed her overflowing handbag over his broad shoulder with his right hand and then proceeded to escort her to their spot. Despite the chatter and music blaring out of several mobile stereos, Cleo's penetrating voice could be heard halfway across the park, causing folk to turn their heads in her direction to see what all the commotion was about. Thankfully, the fumes coming from her ears subsided upon being rescued by her baby brother.

"Hey Sasha, thanks for saving me from that ol' ugly, broke down creature," she said, her voice filled with disgust.

"Not a prob, sis," he replied as he glanced behind them to make sure the creature did not decide to follow. Turns out, he'd already moved on to the next female in sight.

Typical dog in heat.

Cleo looked up at her 'little' brother and marveled at his 6'11 frame. Like all the Stinson men, he was very handsome with Hershey chocolate-kissed skin, high, chiseled cheekbones and beautiful full lips, reminiscent of supermodel Tyson Beckford. His newly locked hair he began growing and nurturing two years prior was beginning to show signs of grandeur, much to his delight, and the ladies too, for that matter. True to his laid-back personality, he was dressed in a crisp white tee and a relaxed pair of dark blue jeans with a hole in the right butt cheek pocket where he kept his wallet and the beginnings of another hole in the right knee.

"My goodness, Sasha. Sometimes, I forget how tall you really are, but don't go thinking you all that just 'cause you got a lil' height on ya," she joked, then continued, "I'm still your big sister and I can still take you down." She playfully yanked on one of his locks.

In response, he immediately started twisting it again, then replied, "Whatever *big sister.* Need I remind you I am not that little boy you, Devin and Symone used to punk back in the day?

I'm a grown-ass man, now, I'm twice your height and outweigh you by just as much. And, I still haven't forgotten how y'all dogged me that summer I had to be in that damn wheelchair after my foot surgery!" He swiftly pinched her arm and took off running. "I ain't gonna ever be done gettin' you and the rest of them back for that!"

"Ouch!" Cleo yelped and took off after him. By the time they reached camp, they both were out of breath and laughing hysterically.

Ava, the smallest of the Stinson girls, jumped to her feet. "Boy, I can't take you two nowhere," wagging her finger and scolding them. Directing her attention towards her twin, she continued. "Now, look here Sasha, we are almost twenty-three-years-old and you still have not gotten over that wheelchair thing, jeez! What does that really say about you?" she demanded. Like their father's slate-grey eyes, Ava's darkened with irritation at her brother and sister. As tiny as she was, her personality commanded attention and obedience. Out of all of Cleo's siblings, she was the goodie-two-shoes who seemed to not have a funny bone in her body.

Cleo shrugged her shoulders as she and Sasha exchanged knowing glances as she unpacked her enormous handbag.

Annoyed with Ava's banter, Sasha retorted, "Look, Ava, it wasn't you in that wheelchair gettin' picked on."

He leaned against a nearby tree and began angrily twisting his developing locks. "Just be glad the bunion curse skipped you, shit."
Ava had walked over to check on the food, ignoring her brother's last comment. A short time later, the slight tension diminished, and the celebrating commenced. Shelby had arrived with all the goodies she promised to bring. Soon everyone was devouring potato salad, BBQ ribs and burgers, chips, baked beans, bread and a variety of spirits were flowing freely. It wouldn't be long before those who couldn't hold their liquor would either be sprawled out on the lawn, spewing their guts up or suddenly thinking they were super-human.

Cleo glanced at her watch and saw it was close to six-thirty when the opening act began their first set. For as far as the eye could see, folks began swooning to the groove of the band's infectious music. With so many clammed together, they made a huge, multi-colored ocean of people, each one ready to outshine the other. The police presence could be seen and felt as they constantly cleared the sidewalks that kept filling up with people squatting, marking their territory, chatting up long-lost friends, or those who were selling bottled water, beer and popcorn. But all of it was pointless because, just as every year before, folks would continue to fill in every single empty spot, anyway.

Even though Shelby acted as though nothing had happened, there was no fooling Cleo. She saw the days-old healing around her still puffy, blue-black left eye. Naturally, Shelby made the feeble attempt to hide the bruise under her wide-lens sunglasses. Now it all made sense. She had been avoiding letting her BFF see her because she'd obviously been with James again, even after she promised to leave that nigga alone. Cleo was searing on the inside, but she did not let it show. Nothing in the world was going to come between her dreamland husband Keith Sweat and the others in tonight's line-up.

"Girl, you're gonna break something if you don't stop it!" yelled Ava.

The moment Shelby arrived, she caught the dance bug, gyrating her full hips to the music pumping out of the surrounding speakers. Shelby laughed,

"Look sugar, I gotta shake what my mama gave me. Shit, it's in my genes and I can't deny it!" Undeterred, she continued shaking her booty in rhythm. Before long, Phredley, Sasha's best friend joined her. The way she was all up on the boy, one would think they were closer in age instead of the almost fifteen years that separated them. Amused, Cleo sat back, Crown mixed with a little bit of Coke in hand, chuckling loudly. She knew Shelby could easily get loose with Phredley if they kept carrying on like they were, but, hell, it wouldn't be the first time she let the cougar come out to play with a youngin.

Amused, Cleo sat back, Crown mixed with a little bit of Coke in hand, chuckling loudly. She knew Shelby could easily get loose with Phredley if they kept carrying on like they were, but, hell, it wouldn't be the first time she let the cougar come out to play with a youngin. There'd been two or three of them that got a taste of Shelby's brand of cougarism that had them coming back for more. Cleo thought her girl was a little touched in the head for carrying on with young men who didn't have anything to offer her, well, outside of a wet ass that is. It made her cringe just thinking about a youngin touching her, yuck!

As the night went on, laughter, jokes, jonein' and games of Spades, Uno, and Tonk proceeded until the crowd heard:

****More bounce to the ounce,*
much more

Cleo jumped out of her chair, spilling some of her drink on herself, and joined everyone on their makeshift dance floor.

"Look out there now, Shelby, you know I got them moves that will put y'all to shame!" she shouted, her booty moving to the rhythm.

Shelby was in her own little world, riding the melodic waves along with Phredley, not paying her any attention. Cleo wondered how much she drank or smoked before showing up at the park. Admittedly, she was worried about her BFF and was trying very hard to not say anything to her, but as the night wore on, she knew it was going to be difficult to keep her mouth shut.

"Ah, yeah, y'all know Zapp's my favorite band, right?" Cleo said while swaying her thick hips to the beat.

Sasha approached her, waving his finger at her.

"Sis, who you kiddin'? Everybody knows how much you love you some Zapp, but, let's not get it twisted 'cause we all know how much you love several old-school bands, it ain't just Zapp!"

Cleo teasingly glared at him. "What do you know about the old-school bands I enjoy, Sasha?"

Sasha rose from the lawn chair he was sitting in and once again began twirling one of his locks.

"Well, I've heard you say a gazillion times that the Isley Brothers were your favorite band, and also the S.O.S. Band was your favorite, and, um, what's the name of that other one?" He began snapping his fingers while Cleo just kept eyeing him, not ever wavering from her dance moves. "Oh, yeah, now I remember, the "Dazz Band" is another one, too!"

Cleo playfully yanked on the same strand of hair he kept twisting and re-twisting. "Ah, shut-up, lil' boy, you don't know nothing 'bout me and my music."

They both broke out in laughter and began dancing to the next number, 'Doo Wa Ditty (Blow that Thang)'.

"Ah, shoot! That's my jam!" Shouted Cleo as she began breaking down low. "Every time I hear a Zapp song I think of Roger Troutman. God, I miss him so much!" she exclaimed.

Suddenly, large, soft hands covered her eyes, shielding her from immediately seeing who had the nerve to touch her in such an intimate way. But, at the same time, the touch was somewhat familiar, sending a sizzling sensation down her spine.

"Guess who?" the unknown suitor said.

She instantly recognized Craig's sultry voice. "Hey there stranger." She turned to face him. Despite herself, she was glad to see him.

He wrapped her up in a welcome embrace, cheesing all the way. "Babe, it's always good to see you," he replied. "You lookin' good enough to eat," he quipped as his gaze remained transfixed on her curves.

Cleo blushed, nudging him in his rock-hard abs.

"Oh, boy, you need to quit it."

Taking his gaze off her just long enough to acknowledge everyone else, he returned his full attention to Cleo. "It's been a long time, CeeCee. I've missed you. How have you been?" he inquired.

Still grooving to the R&B sounds of the Zapp Band, she replied, "Oh, I've been all right, Craig, thanks for asking. How about you? How's life been treatin' you?"

He stood behind her, his hips in full swing with her own.

"Well, baby girl, you know how it is, what's that old saying, oh, yeah, 'Life's a bitch, then you die'." Cleo giggled out loud, then looked back at him, shaking her head. *Damn, his hands felt so good, so right around her waist,* she thought. Out of the corner of her eye, she could see Sasha boring a hole into Craig. For some reason, they never did hit it off, but she could never quite make sense of it.

After the Zapp Band finished their amazing performance, Craig invited her to go on a short walk with him while the S.O.S. Band members readied the stage for the concert's next set. He had said he wanted to fill her in with all the happenings in his life since he relocated to Detroit, two years ago. She wasn't so sure she wanted to hear about it but agreed to go along with him anyway despite her reservations.

"I'll be back in a little while," she told everybody. Shelby was too engrossed in whatever the young stallion Phredley was whispering into her ear to even notice, while everyone else was chatting up one another or stuffing their face with food.

As they strode down the overly crowded sidewalk, several male eyes became unhinged as soon as they noticed her deliciously round derrière. This invasion did not go unnoticed by the green-eyed monster, Craig.

Just as Javon had done months ago at Club Isis, he possessively gripped her hand to fend off the gawkers.

Inside, Cleo relished this cute act. She always loved the way her beaus displayed their affection and jealousy towards her; it made her feel special, wanted, and desired.

"So, what's going on Craig?" her voice filled with trepidation.

After they lost touch with one another, she'd heard he ran off with some woman who had his head all up in the sky. Word on the street said she whipped it on him so good, got knocked up real quick, and somehow convinced him to marry her and move to her hometown of Detroit. A short time after the baby was born, he learned it was not his, sending his world into a tailspin.

The problem with this scenario was that it was *just* a rumor and as the old-school group Timex Social Club says in their 1986 hit:

***How do rumors get started?
They're started by the jealous people and
They get mad about somethin' they had, and somebody else is holdin'

Much to their surprise, they found a somewhat private picnic table situated on the far back end of the park under a huge elm tree.

Craig hung his head low, then proceeded to confirm what she'd already heard. Though she had never experienced anything like what he'd been put through—it was on a whole other level—she felt his pain; an insufferable pain most adults encountered at some point in their lives at the hands of someone they loved.

There were no words for that kind of betrayal, but it reminded her of an old quote by Bob Marley, "Truth is, everybody is going to hurt you; you just gotta find the ones worth suffering for."

'Just Be Good to Me' rang from the speakers, causing all the women across the park to sing in unison:

***Friends tell me I am crazy / And I'm wasting time with you
You'll never be mine

"You know that's my shit, right?" Cleo rose from her seat and began swaying her hips to the groove.

Craig got up from the picnic table and stood behind her, his body quickly fell in step with her swaying hips. "Of course, I know how much you love the S.O.S. Band." They continued dancing to the band until they finished their set.

"Hello ladies, hello! Who wants to share this stage with me tonight, huh?" Keith Sweat's deep baritone voice rang through the speakers, causing a tidal wave of women of all ages to claw their way to the stage, trying to get the chance to be up close and personal with Mr. Beggar Man, himself. They weren't going to get far past the security guarding the stage.

Before Craig could utter another word, Cleo took off towards the stage, to the loving and inviting arms of her dreamland husband. She had every intention of being the chosen one tonight. Relying on her bearably primed athletic ability, she ducked, dived and pummeled her way to the stage. Under no circumstances was she not going to be denied her right, uh uh, no way José! Nothing short of a miracle, she made it onto the stage and into the melting embrace of Mr. Keith Sweat.

"Well, well, well, look what we have here," Keith cooed. A wide, open grin was plastered on his face as he showed her off to the crowd, who exploded into roars, whistling, and catcalls. She was glad she'd chosen to wear her favorite ivory halter sundress and four-inch, slingback ivory sandals.

"Ain't she a sight for sore eyes, y'all?" he stated as he held up her hand so she could do a quick twirl. Just then, a slight breeze swooped through, causing the bottom of her sundress to flare up, exposing her shapely chocolate legs. The crowd went into a frenzy.

Dashing as always, he was clad in white linen attire with matching wing-tipped Stacey Adams; his ivory belt adorned with a sprinkling of diamond studs. The exclamation point: his signature, meticulously groomed waves, and goatee. He was a vision to behold. They looked like the perfect couple up on the stage in their dazzling ensembles.

Even though Cleo had been sexually experimenting with Kennedy (really, what else could it be but an experiment because the lady was MARRIED with CHILDREN), she'd always felt an internal yearning for Keith Sweat. All he had to do was say the word and she would be his eternally. They danced and gyrated to a few of her favorites: 'Don't Stop Your Love', 'I Want Her', and 'I'll Give All My Love to You'. Always the gentleman (and who could also be-her-knight-in-shining-armor), bowed before her and kissed her sweetly on her trembling hand and flushed cheek.

Cleo's knees buckled and Keith moved to catch her before she fell to the stage floor. When it was time for her to vacate the stage, she floated down the steel stairway into heaven. She was in a dream state and her eyes had become slits and everything she tried to say was inaudible.

Standing to the right of the staircase was Craig with his arms folded and a scowl plastered on his face. He was trying to be mad, but he knew how big a fan she was of Keith's, thus there was no real reason to be upset … or was there?

"Hey honey," Cleo managed as she made herself come out of the trance Keith had her in. She swooped in close to his chest, making sure her full bosom rested against him.

He glared at her, not wanting to cave in, but once he felt her erect nipples through his thin shirt, that was all it took. He was putty in her hands.

"You know I'm mad at you for runnin' off like that," he lamented, wrapping his arms around her once more.

She returned his embrace and said, "I know, I know, but please don't be." She looked earnestly into his killer tiger eyes and continued, "You know how much of a fan I am, so surely you're not that surprised about what I did to capture my moment. Besides, it may be the only time I will ever get that close to him ever again."

Craig shook his head and embraced her even more tightly, then whispered, "You know I want to taste you tonight, right?" He encircled her hard nipple with his left index finger, kneading her full breasts with just the right amount of roughness, leaving her breathless. She gasped for air, caught off guard with the unexpected intimate moment they were sharing. "Um, yes, yes, I would love that."

She and Craig bounced and grooved to the tunes of the night's showstopper. True to his roots as a magnificent live performer, he put on a show that would forever be etched in the minds of all who were in attendance.

Just as he'd done earlier, Craig held her hand as they made their way back to the spot.

"Damn, sis, we thought you were gonna lose your mind up there on that stage with Keith!" Ava exclaimed.

Cleo laughed loudly, unable to contain the exhilarating thrill flowing through her aroused body. She noticed her unexpected date of the evening stood close to her side, a big Cheshire grin on his face.

Cleo looked around for Shelby, who was nowhere to be seen. "Where is Shelby?" She asked anyone who was listening.

"She snuck off with Phredley," replied Sasha, still throwing shade at Craig, who was looking somewhat uncomfortable.

Cleo shook her head, then began collecting her things. Craig quickly followed suit to get out of the line of fire. Now that the concert had ended, the crowd began to disperse. As Cleo predicted earlier, trash was strewn everywhere, and people both young and old waited impatiently in the mile-long line of port-o-potties, and the traffic was deadlocked.

Just another night at IBE's free concert.

"Y'all got this, right?" Cleo asked her siblings as she prepared to leave.

“Yes, Cleo. We got it,” Ava replied as she cleaned off the table of food. “I’ll call you tomorrow. Love you!”

Cleo blew kisses. “Love you too, lil’ sis.”

“Goodnight all,” Craig chimed in.

Walking hand in hand, she and Craig made their way to her vehicle.

“Running into you here has reaffirmed my faith in God. I’ve missed you so much, Cleo. You just don't know."

Why do they always have to bring G-O-D into the equation?

She leaned against the side of her Ridgeline, stared directly into his tiger eyes. "Craig, I know you went through some shit with that chick and I'm really sorry you had to go through all that. I can't imagine learning the child I thought was mine turned out not to be after all.” She opened her arms, inviting him into an embrace. From his sad eyes, Cleo could see the toll the whole ordeal had taken on his psyche. She ached for him.

Craig wistfully sank into her embrace, allowing her to console him. Forever the manliest of men, he tried but failed in holding back a tear. It wasn't long before a tidal wave came tumbling down his hardened face, fine creases etched around his beautiful eyes and emboldened on his forehead.

Cleo knew in that instant they would end up in bed together that night, each with their own reasons, good or bad.

⚢ 32 - This chapter feature's Shelby's POV⚥

"What the hell, Shelby? Why didn't you tell me you saw that nigga again?!" Cleo demanded as she stepped through her door. "And, why the hell did you just leave with Phredley like that without saying nothing?"

The ugly green and judgmental monster that threatened to rear his head at last night's concert was definitely present now.

"Well, hello, Cleo. Nice to see you, too," Shelby responded sheepishly. *Oh, boy, here she goes.*

Cleo continued storming down the hall towards Shelby's living room. The large, round-framed mirror hanging at the end of her corridor rattled as she rounded the corner. She planted herself in her favorite seat, a black leather chaise she and Shelby picked out together some time ago. She could hear Shelby's slow, methodical steps as she took her time returning to her living room. The sound of dread could be heard with every footstep.

Dressed in mauve-colored lounging attire, her soft curly hair stacked up on her head, and sleep still in her eyes, she appeared to be despondent. The swelling in her black eye didn't look as bad as it had the night before, but the damage was still visible.

"Would you like some coffee?" she whispered, sounding more like a wounded hound than the usually bubbly Shelby she knew.

Still fuming and unable to look directly at her BFF, Cleo responded with a frustrated *yes*. Shelby shuffled her way into her one-butt kitchen. Dirty dishes were strewn around on the counter and overflowed in the large, stainless-steel sink. Though Shelby was not obsessive-compulsive, Cleo could not recall a time when her kitchen was so unkempt. She believed in keeping her kitchen and bathrooms spotless. It seemed her friend was deeply hurting.

She retrieved the Folgers canister and coffee filters from the upper left cupboard next to the refrigerator. "Well, where should I begin?" she asked herself more so than her bestie as she scooped the dark coffee grounds into the filter and placed it into the brew basket of her Black & Decker coffee pot.

Cleo watched as she inhaled the wafting coffee aroma floating through the air. It seemed as though it had reawakened something in her the way it always did.

"I know I fucked up," her head hanging low, her voice barely a whisper. "I know I promised I would leave that bastard alone, Cleo, but—" Shelby struggled to find the right words as she returned to the living room. The sofa enveloped her as she sunk into it, then wrapped her arms around her knees, cradling herself in the same way she did whenever she was frightened or upset.

Cleo softened as she observed Shelby next to her. They'd been in similar situations countless times over the years; healing each other's wounds after being wronged by a host of men in their past. She moved in closer, then stretched her arms around her in a full embrace.

"I'm sorry for being such an ass when I walked through the door," Cleo said, wiping the tears away from Shelby's eyes.

"It's okay," Shelby whispered through her crying and sobbing. "I understand why you're so upset with me, CeeCee. I know I promised to leave James the hell alone, and then, without discussing it with you again, I stupidly decided he deserved another chance." Shelby pulled away from Cleo, shame written all over her face. Shelby caught Cleo rolling her eyes at her but decided she wouldn't respond to the negativity.

Cleo kicked her legs up onto the chaise and let her rigid body melt into it. The mere mention of that nigga's name was enough to make the smoldering anger inside start to rise again. But instead of interrupting her BFF, she cracked her knuckles and kept her comments to herself.

Shelby hung her head in shame. "Do you still want some coffee?" she asked, rubbing more sleep out of her weary eyes as she made her way back to the kitchen.

"Yes, please. Do you also have some flavored coffee creamer? You know I love me some Italian Sweet Cream, especially the International Delight brand." Cleo grabbed the remote control and flicked on the TV.

"I think I may have some vanilla caramel, but it's the Coffemate brand."

"Oh, that will do." Cleo began clicking through the channels on the remote.

A few moments later, Shelby returned with two steaming cups of coffee. "Here you go." She handed a cup to Cleo.

"Thanks, Shell. I left my house so early that I didn't get a chance to make a pot." Cleo's eyes closed as she took in a whiff of the aroma that was floating out of her cup. She continued clicking through the channels until she came across *AM Joy*.

"No, problemo, sugah." Shelby sat her cup down on the refurbished wooden living room table.

"I want to tell you what happened," Shelby said, picking up their conversation again. "James had been ringing my phone off the hook and sending bouquets of my favorite flowers." She chuckled. "Girl, he even went as far as to send me some of the edible flowers from Edible Arrangements!" she exclaimed, delight dancing in her eyes.

Cleo rolled her eyes again. "Girl, I know you didn't fall for that one."

Shelby took a long sip of her coffee. "Um. This is good. It's my first time using that flavor."

Cleo recognized her BFF trying to change the subject, but she wasn't going to let her off the hook. Not this time.

"Okay, back to how you let that snake back in your graces, please," Cleo retorted.

Shelby took an even longer gulp the second time around before getting back to her story. "Okay, okay, Jesus! You're just not gonna let up, are you?" Cleo glared at her.

Shelby relented, realizing she wasn't going to get out of it. "Basically, he coaxed his way back into my *good graces*. Had me really thinking we could give our relationship another go." She reached for her cup again and held it in her trembling hands for a few moments before taking a drink. "So, what led to our confrontation was his flirting … his excessive flirting, I should say. We were dining at one of our favorite spots, Rick's Boatyard when he started eyeballing that local singer, what's her face." She snapped her fingers, trying to recall her name. "Ah, hell, I can't think of it, but she was the entertainment that night."

"Oh, alrighty then." Cleo took a swallow from her steaming cup of coffee.

"He was like 'Oh, she is fine as wine' and 'I really dig them light-skinned broads'. Then, at the end of her last set, the bastard got up from our table-without saying a word to me, mind you, and waltzed his black ass over to her."

Soaring heat rose from Cleo's body. She was so pissed off at James, Shelby, Kennedy, Javon—at everybody at that moment—she didn't know what to do. As Shelby continued telling her the story, she began plotting the demise of James Connor. Indeed, it was time to call up some old friends to help her complete the task.

"Well, all I can say is that I trust you are over that damn nigga for real this time, especially after this latest episode." She took a few sips from the coffee mug that was outfitted with pictures of kittens, looking on as Shelby did the same. "Enough about that bastard. He certainly ain't that important for us to keep talkin' about. I wanna know what in the Sam hell is going on with you and my lil' brother's best friend."

Cleo watched as a big Cheshire grin spread across her face. "Well, um, see what had happened was ..."

"Come on, spit it out, Shelby."

Shelby ran her fingers through her hair, then rubbed her neck. "Okay, okay. Let me first preface what I'm about to share with you with this, alright?"

Cleo rolled her eyes impatiently.

"Okay, so you know I had been drinking and smoking on a fat joint that he had, and, well, you saw me, I was just enjoying myself, and well ..." Cleo looked on as Shelby nervously tugged on a loose string on the top she was wearing. Cleo also noticed that she was avoiding eye contact with her.

"What is it, Shelby? I know that look. You're holding back something, what is it?" Cleo demanded.

"Well, damn, okay … there is something I never told you about me and Phredley." She took another deep gulp from her coffee cup. "Back in the day when we used to babysit him and the twins, he was always trying to push up on me, but I would shut him down with the quickness. Well, until that one time …"

Cleo felt nauseous. "What the hell happened that one time, Shelby?" She watched her BFF squirm in her seat, an indication that she did something really fucked up.

"It was that one time I drove him home from y'all's house. He kept bugging the shit out of me about eating my pussy, claimed he was already a master at cunnilingus, and, well, shit, girl. I was already horny, hell you know how it goes when you're a teenager with all those raging hormones, so I let the lil nigga eat my pussy." She paused. "There. Now you know." She drank the last few drops of coffee, rose from the sofa and headed to the kitchen for a refill.

Cleo was stunned, speechless. *Well, I'll be damned. Did this wench just tell me she raped Phredley?*

"Hold the fuck up. How you just gon' walk away after telling me some shit like that Shelby, damn!"

Shelby shrugged her shoulders. "Fuck, what do you want me to say, Cleo? No, I'm not Miss Perfect, Never Do-Nothing Wrong Stinson, okay? You can be so fucking judgmental. That shit pisses me the fuck off!" She began stirring creamer into her coffee cup. "Besides, that was years ago and to be honest, he really was a master at it; told me some older female neighbor of theirs who used to babysit him taught him how to lick the kittykat right and he loves the taste."

Cleo folded her arms, eyeing her with suspicion. "I never would have thought in a million years you'd do something like that with a kid. Damn, Shell, what the fuck?" She looked on as Shelby made her way back to the living area, then set her steaming hot cup of coffee on the table and plopped down on the sofa.

"Look, I knew you weren't gonna be too pleased with this news, but, shit, it did happen and that is what kind of led up to us hanging out at the concert last night. Shit, he a grown-ass man now, and yeah, we did get our fuck on last night, but that's between him and me." Shelby reached for her cup and took a few sips.

Cleo stared at her. She was at a loss for words, which was so out of character for her. *Just when you think you know somebody and then find out something so crazy and off-the-wall about them.*

They both turned their attention to Joy Reid and a few of her regular guests, Tiffany Cross and Elie Mystal discussing the current state of political affairs going on in the country.

Cleo's mind was blown, no doubt about it. She found herself sneaking looks at her BFF as if meeting her for the first time. After all the secrets they shared among each other through the years, she never once mentioned anything about this thing with Phredley. It made her wonder what else was she keeping from her. Their sisterhood was now tainted, and Cleo wasn't sure how this situation was going to play out. *Damn, am I being too harsh on her, though? Am I so self-righteous and controlling that I can't look past my best friend's transgressions from years ago?*

"Well, are you just gonna sit there in judgment?"

Shelby's words snapped Cleo back into reality. Still somewhat speechless, she rubbed her temples and sighed. "Shelby, you know you really caught me off guard with all this and I'm not one to be at a loss for words. You really got me stumped."

"Well, I don't know what else to tell you, Cleo. Yes, I made a mistake, and no, I never told you about Phredley because I knew you would just judge me." Shelby was cradling her coffee cup, sipping it every few seconds or so.

"I kinda like him, though, much to my surprise. He's warm, very affectionate, and eager to please. He even talked about seeing where our *relationship* could go next." Cleo looked on as Shelby grinned into her coffee cup.

"So, you are seriously entertaining this with him?" She watched as Shelby's grin dissipated from her face, making her feel a little regretful for asking the question.

"You know what Cleo, I'm done talking and I think you should go—I need you to go before one of us says something that we might regret later."

"Oh, it's like that now, Shell?" Cleo responded, rising from her seat. Inwardly she knew her BFF was right, though she stopped short of saying it out loud. "Okay, okay, I know when I'm not wanted."

Cleo walked toward the front door. She noticed Shelby didn't even look her way as she vacated her homely abode when at any other time, she was the one begging her to come back so they could talk it out. But not this time. This time Cleo truly stepped into the wrong lane and Shelby wasn't having it.

⚢ 33 ⚥

Cleo's left eye perked open upon hearing her alarm go off. "Oh Lord, it can't be Monday morning already," she said to herself. She rubbed the sleep out of her right eye and pried both eyes open. Her bedside clock read six-thirty. After pushing STOP on her alarm clock, she rolled out of bed and began her morning ritual.

****

Anxiety was etched in the lines that framed Samantha's face, her skin covered with some kind of reddish-green rash and her lips were peeling from an obvious lack of moisturizer. Her fiery red hair was unusually frizzy and unkempt. Even in her dark grey power suit, she appeared disheveled and uneasy. Knowing looks bounced from one colleague to another as she timidly revealed the state's findings. Cleo was finding it very difficult not to marvel at Kennedy, especially after what took place at their spot. Instead, she fidgeted with her pen, going from dabbling on her legal pad to gnawing on the pen's lid for several minutes. The meeting (as most meetings go) dragged on and on. She and Kennedy stole longing looks throughout their time at the table. It seemed neither one of them was concerned about their obvious flirting even though Bernard's interruption changed the course of what was supposed to be that night.

Still, Cleo imagined their lovemaking, wishing their hot, burning bodies were entangled right then and there. Before she knew it, la la land took her for a ride filled with exhilarating ecstasy …

"Um, yes. Please don't stop. Oh, yeah, right there, right there, oh, yes, Kennedy." Kennedy's svelte hand squeezed and kneaded her left breast, her wet, burning tongue twirling and teasing Cleo's plump nipple.

"Ummm," Kennedy murmured, "tastes so good, can't get enough of you, Cleo, I swear, I can't."
Cleo arched her back. Her thick thighs gently fell open. Her entire body was on fire, rising and falling over and over again with each thrashing of Kennedy's tongue. Kennedy slid two fingers inside of Cleo's dripping wet pussy, pulsating riffs of pleasure and just the right amount of pain gripping her soul ...

"Cleo! Did you hear what I said?" Samantha said.

Her voice startled Cleo out of her erotic dream. She quickly sat up straight, rubbed her eyes and responded, "Um, no, Samantha, I didn't. Could you repeat it, please?"

Cleo's eyes darted around the large conference table. All eyes were staring in her direction, but she shook it off and waited for Samantha to repeat whatever it was she'd just said to her.

Irritated, Samantha shook her head from side to side and restated her directions to Cleo.

"Per the findings and recommendations of our audit, I'm going to need you to review a sampling of everyone's weekly summaries for the next three months to ensure that all case workers' notes are clear, concise, and updated regularly. I'm also going to need you to conduct the case management training for the two new case managers next Thursday. Any questions?"
Smugness was written all over her face as she somehow found her balls again after being chastised and threatened by the center's board president on the state's final report. Though Exodus fared well in comparison to similar agencies, the president expected and demanded *perfection*, which Mrs. Merriweather did not deliver. Little did she know the word had already gotten out about the tongue lashing she received, thanks to none other than the well-known office snitch, Katrina.

Cleo's chocolate brown eyes turned a few shades darker as anger smoldered inside, but she reminded herself that she was a 'professional', so she kept her cool. Her coworkers, on the other hand, were waiting with bated breath to see how she was going to respond. The two musketeers, Tuesday and Régine were huddled up along the back wall snickering together like a bunch of schoolgirls. It was obvious she wasn't going to get any moral support from them.

Cleo coyly rolled her eyes in their direction then turned her attention to Jim for moral support. He winked at her and that was enough to get her going. Second to Shelby, he was someone she knew she could count on in her workplace.

Leaning forward, Cleo squared her shoulders, plastered a wide, fake grin on her face and said, "Okay, Samantha, that's fine … and, no, I don't have any questions. Are we done here?"

A foreboding stillness echoed through the room; all eyes still glued on Cleo. Samantha must've noticed it, too; you could see it in her crippled demeanor. She rubbed an ugly rash that seemed to be spreading on her ruby-red cheeks as she spoke.

"Um, well, I suppose we are. That is if you're sure you don't have any questions for me." Her large, green eyes chiseled away at Cleo's outer armor, making her feel a little uneasy. Cleo chuckled to herself. *This bitch is really trying to get me started on her, but I ain't about to let this nothing-ass heifer mess with my money!*

"No, Samantha. I don't have any questions," Cleo repeated as she stood and nodded at everyone at the table, then exited the room.

She was glad Shelby had called in sick because she probably would've lost her job. Anyone with half a brain could see Samantha was desperately trying to annoy Cleo enough to get her started.

Truth be told, everyone at Exodus knew Cleo was more qualified, having earned a graduate degree in social work six months prior and had ten more years' experience with working with children and their families than Samantha. Rumors swirled around the office alleging racial discrimination and there were accusations of an affair with one of the board members, despite both of them having spouses, that sealed the deal for the promotion to be granted to Samantha instead of Cleo.

However, what Cleo had going for her over Samantha was respect from her colleagues. It didn't hurt that she was also well known and respected in the community, having recently been honored with the Indy Channel's Jefferson Award for outstanding community service. It was nothing for her to provide the daily needs such as toilet paper, toothpaste, toothbrushes, and underwear to her families, people living in Tent City, and anyone else she felt was in need. Cleo didn't do these things to be recognized, however. She later found out it was a group of current and previous clients that nominated her.

Her parents made a huge deal out of the nomination by hosting a wine and canvas soiree at the family's lake house in Brownsburg. Knowing how she dreaded being the center of attention, her siblings teased her to no end. She tried to be more understanding of her parents' insistence of having the party, thinking that perhaps if it was her child, she'd want to celebrate their achievements, as well.

After exiting the meeting, she stormed down to her office and closed the door, simultaneously shutting out everything in the world that was bothering her at that moment.

Unbeknownst to her, Kennedy was right on her trail.

Cleo heard a soft, but stern knock on the door right before she sat in her chair. Over the last few months, she had come to recognize that knock because Kennedy was the only one whose gentleness came through in her knock. It didn't hurt that Cleo had come to know this sweet gentleness from the encounters they shared both in and out of the office.

"Come in, Kennedy," she said as she plopped down in her chair.

Kennedy floated through the door, looking beautiful as always. In an instant, the warmth from her eyes melted away all that was wrong in Cleo's world.

How does she possess that kind of power over me? she wondered. It both scared her and pleased her all at the same time … but how was it possible for a woman (a gorgeous one, no doubt, but still a woman) to make her feel this way?

She walked over to Cleo and laid her delicate hand on her shoulder, reassuring all was going to be okay. "Are you okay?"

Cleo shrugged and nodded her head.

Kennedy cupped Cleo's face with both hands, leaned in and planted a velvety kiss on her lips.

She hungrily licked her lips, but somehow managed to pull away. "I wanna do you right here and right now, but, well, you know."

"My bad." Miss St. Martin backed away from her. "Sorry I wasn't able to get in contact with you sooner and for all that mess at Charade with Bernard showin' up like that." Kennedy threw her hands up in the air.

"Yeah, right. I still don't have any words for what happened. Also, there's nothing to be sorry about, Kennedy. You should know by now I want you so badly I can taste it." She stood up in an effort to quell her libido and directed her attention outside the window. In the distance, she could see several men from Brickman Landscaping Company pruning bushes, mowing the lawn, and getting debris out of the retention pond. She forced herself to watch the men do their landscaping work instead of having to face Kennedy.

Kennedy sighed and threw her hands up in the air once again. "Honestly, CeeCee, I wasn't sure what to say nor was I aware of how you really felt. I know we both were looking forward to being together and I was so ready to get into you, but, well, you know what happened."

Cleo turned her attention back to her. She could see guilt written all over her face. Setting aside her own feelings, she went to her.

"Okay now, stop it. It wasn't your fault that he followed you to our spot. Apparently, it just wasn't written in the stars that night," she said. "And it's not like we can't plan our next rendezvous, but we're obviously gonna have to choose a more discreet location, perhaps on the outskirts of Nap."

Kennedy's face lit up like a Christmas tree. Cleo relished in her smile. It continually warmed her from the inside out.

"Amazing!" she exclaimed as she grabbed her and gave her a big hug and planted another wet kiss on her lips. "Do you have a place in mind?"

"No, I don't yet, but I'll look into it."

"Okay, cool," Kennedy responded, bouncing up and down like a schoolgirl with her first crush. "Just keep me posted, boo."

"You know I will, sugar."

⚢ 34 ⚥

"How was the meeting?" Shelby asked.

Cleo had arrived home just in time to catch the six o'clock news on WRTV. Ericka Flye was talking about some kind of event going on at the convention center.

"Hey, Shell-Shell. Girl, be glad you missed it." Cleo loosened her belt and unbuttoned her slacks before stretching onto her sofa.

Shelby laughed, then asked, "What the hell happened? It was that damn Samantha bitch, wasn't it?"

"You know it was. She sure was trying to take me there, but I held my cool." A smug smile formed in the corners of Cleo's mouth. "You would've been proud of me."

"That heifer needs to be glad I wasn't there, shit, I'd probably be out of a job because I already want to knock her teeth down her throat," Shelby snorted.

Cleo shifted her body, then kicked her legs up onto her sofa. "Chill, boo. I keep telling you it ain't that deep." She shook her head in disbelief. It would seem they both possessed churlishness that lived deep down inside them and when provoked, that ugly green monster raised its head on command.

Shelby sighed. "I hear you girl, but she just bugs the hell out of me, and I just want to smack her one good time!"

"Hey, I just remembered something I meant to ask you on Saturday," Cleo said as she rose from her sofa and headed to her kitchen.

"Uh-oh, what did I do now?"

Automatically, irritation rose inside of Cleo, but she let it go. She forced herself to remember her BFF had been through more than anyone should ever have to endure.

"Girl, stop it. I just want to know if you heard from the asshole again or from Phredley." She opened her fridge and grabbed the Minute-Maid Cherry Limeade and sat it on the counter. She reached for the cupboard next to the sink, grabbed a glass and poured herself a drink.

Shelby got quiet on the other end of the phone—too quiet.

"Um, hello? Why'd you get quiet, Shell?" she demanded. "Spill it."

Cleo could hear her feet shuffling on the other end. She was biding time and she knew Cleo knew it.

"Shelby!" she shouted into the phone.

"Okay, okay, jeez! You can be so damn demanding sometimes, you know that?"

Cleo took a gulp of Cherry Limeade. "So, what else is new?"

Defeated, Shelby sighed again. "Well, if you really must know, no, I haven't heard from the asshole, but Phredley, haha, yes. He spent the night and, yes, I fucked him."

"Damn, I knew it," Cleo responded in disgust.

"See, that's why I don't like telling you everything! You can be so fuckin' condescending sometimes!" replied Shelby, her trembling voice filled with agitation.

Cleo decided to switch gears. She knew she could get up on her high horse and chide her BFF for doing crazy, misguided shit. But it wasn't like she'd never done anything off the wall, either. Besides, who was anyone to judge? After all, the *Good Book* says, "Judge not, that ye be not judged. For with what judgment ye judge, ye shall be judged: and with what measure ye mete, it shall be measured to you again." Cleo looked out her large bay window. The glowing, saffron-drenched sun was just beginning to set, and a few neighbors were out taking their evening walks, some with their beloved pets, while others pushed their bundles of joy in strollers.

Wow, Lord, my heart aches for me to be able to experience the same thing. I know I can provide all the love, attention, and support, along with a beautiful and nurturing home for Anya. Is the right man ever going to show up in my life so we can start building a life together? Or, could I have children in a lesbian relationship? Is that even possible?

She shuddered at the thought, then took another gulp of her Cherry-Limeade. "Look, Shelby, I'm sorry. You're right, my bad. You're a grown-ass woman and I have no right to look down on you 'cause you and I both know I'm in no way anyone's saint." She hoped her BFF could hear the sincerity in the words she just spoke because she meant them. First, there was more silence, which left Cleo breathless.

Then suddenly, she finally responded. "It's okay. I know you worry about me and are concerned about my well-being, but you know you sometimes act all high 'n' mighty and that's annoying as hell."

Cleo giggled softly. "Okay, yeah, I know … need to work on that. Now, let's get to the real shit. Was he any good?"

Shelby laughed. "Damn, girl, you are nosey! But then, again, I wouldn't expect anything less from my BFF."

Cleo relished hearing Shelby say 'BFF'. It was reassurance that their lifelong friendship was still intact. She didn't know what she'd do without her. Everything they'd shared and experienced since childhood was irreplaceable. No, she could not bear life without the closeness they shared. Though she didn't always show it, she loved and respected Shelby and hoped she realized it.

"Um, well, honestly, yes. For a young man, he wasn't too bad at all. In fact, he can eat the kittykat way better than that old punk-ass James." Cleo could sense the dimpled smile on Shelby's face through the phone. That's how in sync they were with each other. "Wow, he gave you head, too?"

Still laughing, Shelby continued, "Why, yes, of course. You know that has to come first. Stop playin' like you don't know. Remember, I asked him who taught him how to lick the pussy so good, and girl, I almost fell off the bed when he said it was his old babysitter."

Cleo about choked on her juice upon hearing what she just heard. She reached for the Kleenex box that was sitting on her coffee table and wiped off the spillage.

"Are you alright?"

Cleo regained her composure. "Oh yes. You did mention something about that the other day. So, he learned how to eat pussy from gettin' busy with his babysitter, huh? Damn. How old was he?"

"Oh, I think he said he was thirteen or fourteen. Funny thing is that the babysitter was-and still is one of his mother's closest friends. They carried on like that all through his junior and high school years and she never found out, believe it or not." Cleo shook her head in disbelief.

"Wow, ain't that somethin'? Just goes to show you it ain't just the men who are cradle robbers. There are some women out there that are just as nasty and trifling, straight up," Cleo said matter-of-factly.

"Yeah, you're right. It's also crazy that folks don't necessarily get all riled up when this kind of thing goes down between an older woman and a boy but it's a whole different story when an old ass man goes after a young girl. Everyone is up in arms, then," Shelby proclaimed.

The news ended and Cleo began surfing channels. "Hey, I know this off-topic, but do you know when Serena or Venus will be playing again? I always have a hard time finding out when they're going to play, and I hate that."

"Of all people, I'm keenly aware of how big of a fan you are of the Williams sisters, but, sorry, I don't have any idea when they're playing next. I just know that the U.S. Open starts in the next few weeks. Maybe you can check out the WTA website to find out." "Yeah, that's a good idea. I'll check it out tonight, thanks." Cleo had finished her drink and decided she wanted something a little stiffer. She headed to her kitchen and grabbed her special Gran Platinum Patrón, a birthday gift from Javon from a few years ago.

"Well, sis, I'ma get off here and settle in for the night. I'll see you at work tomorrow, okay?" After pouring herself a double shot, she settled back onto her sofa, lazily sipping her spirit and taking in a recorded episode of *Queen Sugar.*

"Yeah, that's a good idea. I'll check it out tonight, thanks." Cleo had finished her drink and decided she wanted something a little stiffer. She headed to her kitchen and grabbed her special Gran Platinum Patrón, a birthday gift from Javon from a few years ago. "Well, sis, I'ma get off here and settle in for the night. I'll see you at work tomorrow, okay?" After pouring herself a double shot, she settled back onto her sofa, lazily sipping her spirit and taking in a recorded episode of *Queen Sugar.*

After hearing about Shelby's rendezvous with Phredley, she was tempted to call Javon over, but only because he gave head better than either Reece or Craig. But she was not in the mood for his bullshit talk of marriage or his lies. Besides, the person that she really wanted to kick it with was undeniably unavailable to just pick up and come over on a whim.

"Alright, CeeCee. See you tomorrow, bright and early!"

"See ya then, bye-bye bestie! Love you lots!"

So, instead of calling Javon to satisfy her later on tonight, she settled on Orbit. He never let her down, unlike the men in her life. That is, as long as she had fresh AA batteries lying around.

⚢ 35 ⚥

"Yes, Kawhi. That's exactly how I want it done. That nigga James deserves a good ass-whoopin' just like that ignorant punk Joshua," Cleo said. She shook her head and reached for her lighter and third cherry-flavored cigarillo.

"Alrighty, beautiful," Kawhi replied. "I got you."

After taking a long drag, she relaxed into one of the emerald-green lawn chairs her dad dropped off a few days earlier. Even though he'd just bought the set last year, Mrs. Stinson had insisted he buy the stylish wicker set with deep seats upholstered in a soft blue fabric at Costco because she saw they were on sale. Cleo was grateful they decided to give it to her because her money was funny at that time and she really needed a decent patio set because the few mismatched pieces she owned had seen better days.

With no one to bother her for the rest of the evening, she delighted in the setting sun as she often did, dreaming about what could be, what used to be, and what was to become of her life. She also thought of the pending misfortune James Connor was soon to encounter but wasn't worried. In her mind, she was extremely adamant about no one fucking with the people she loved. Cleo was satisfied with her carefully laid out plan and with Kawhi at the helm, what could go wrong?

⚢ 36 ⚥

"CeeCee! CeeCee! Turn on the news, hurry, hurry! Channel six, channel six, now!"

"Slow down, Shelby, jeez! What's going on? Why are you acting all crazy?" Shelby's heavy breathing echoed on the other end of the phone.

"Oh, my Lord, Cleo! It's James, their saying he was attacked last night and is in the hospital!" Cleo's heart somersaulted. Kawhi and his boys got it done. Good.

But wait.

He was supposed to have texted her right after it was taken care of. Why didn't he do as he was instructed? The plan was meticulously orchestrated; every detail was laid out carefully—they had discussed it multiple times. *What the hell happened? Why didn't he do as he was told?* Cleo immediately got pissed off.

Well, I'ma have to call that nigga, see what the hell happened ...

"Cleo! CeeCee! Did you hear what I just said?" Shelby demanded.

"Yes, yes! I heard you! Give me a minute, damn, girl," she shouted into the phone. Cleo had fallen asleep after another rendezvous with Orbit. She had recently started watching old episodes of the *L Word* for research purposes.

She was still trying to figure this gay thing out and had heard some of her coworkers talking about it in the break room not too long ago. It didn't take long for her to become hooked, but she was sure disappointed that it lacked any kind of real diversity. *Damn, where's the sistahs at?!* She got turned on watching Dana and Alice fuck, then found herself reaching into her bedside drawer and pulled out Orbit.

She'd still be asleep if it wasn't for Shelby calling with the nonsense about that old punk-ass James. She looked for the remote but couldn't find it on the bed or bedside table. "Ah, shit! Hold on Shelby. I can't find the remote. It must've fallen on the floor." She flicked on the light and willed herself out of bed. As soon as her foot landed on the floor, she looked down and saw that it had landed in her house shoe. She picked it up and turned the TV on.

"A local man by the name of James Connor was badly beaten and found by his neighbor just a short distance from his apartment around ten-thirty this evening. He was reportedly attacked by a group of muggers who dislocated his right shoulder, blackened both eyes, broke his jawbone—causing him to lose several teeth—and then ran off with his wallet. They had already taken off by the time his neighbor heard him calling for help. The neighbor, who wishes to stay anonymous, stated that when he got to Mr. Connor, he was doubled over in pain, lying on the pavement and bleeding profusely from his mouth.

Unfortunately, neither he nor his neighbor was able to get a look at the alleged assailants who were dressed in black clothing and wore ski masks. If you have any information, please contact IMPD."

"Damn, that's fucked up," Cleo managed to say.

"Oh, I just can't believe it, Cleo." Shelby was sobbing on the other end. Cleo couldn't believe it, but then again, she could. She knew her friend very well.

Cleo permitted her body to relax, then settled under her bedspread, and clicked the TV off. She'd had enough of negative news for the night.

"Why in the hell are you sobbing, Shelby?" she blurted out. "That nigga ain't shit anyway and I have to say I'm a little shocked at your response, hell I would've thought you'd be gleeful." Shelby didn't say anything for several seconds. "Um, Cleo, is there something you need to tell me?"

Cleo was offended. "What are you talkin' about? No, I don't have nothing to tell you." She sniffled, then turned over on her left side. "What are you getting at, Shelby?"

Nervousness echoed through the receiver as she tried to find the right words.

"Well, it's just that you don't seem to be at all surprised about this news involving James, and, well, you know." Her voice trailed off.

"Well, if you're referring to that ass-whippin' your ex received years ago, well that nigga deserved it. But I really don't appreciate you insinuating I had anything to do with this James business. Hell, who knows how many enemies he's created. I'm sure you aren't the first woman he's laid his hands on."

Cleo was able to calm her rage, simmer down and play it cool. There was no way she was going to involve Shelby in her plot. As far as she was concerned, what Shelby did not know would forever keep her safe. Indeed, if her fail-safe plan did fall apart (dare she speak it into existence), and Shelby was ever alleged to be involved, she would immediately be off the hook because she wouldn't have a clue about what conspired between Cleo and her crew.

"Okay, okay, Jesus!" Shelby cried. "I just, well, I just wanted to be sure, is all."

Again, more dead silence.

"Go on and ask; I know there's something else you want to say, Shelby." She could hear the faint sound of Shelby's bunny house shoes shuffling on her wooden floor. "What are you doing? I can hear you dragging your big feet across the floor."

Shelby squealed, then replied, "I'm on my way to get a drink of water. Shit, I feel like I've been eatin' cotton, my throat is so doggone dry!"

Cleo turned over to her right side and remarked, "Oh, girl, that just made me remember how you used to say that all the time when we were teenagers, jeez."

She heard Shelby flick on the light switch, followed by a few faint *meows*.

"Oshun, get your ass down off that counter before I beat you to death!"

Cleo laughed. "What's going on?"

"Girl, Oshun was on my counter again and just jumped up and skidded off the counter, and her long-ass, bushy tail knocked over the fruit bowl. Shit, I don't know why you're laughing, that shit ain't funny. I've told her a gazillion times to stay off my counter!"

"You know what I'm laughing about, don't even try it," Cleo continued, relishing in her humor of the situation.

"Whatever, dammit. I swear, sometimes that cat gets on my last damn nerve. She may be finding herself another home soon if she don't quit that shit. She knows damn well not to be up on my kitchen counter!" Cleo listened as Shelby opened the fridge door and guzzled water on the other end of the line.

"Whoa! You better slow it down, girl, before you choke! Anyway, enough about that ol' crazy cat of yours. Now, what was it that you were going to ask me?"

Shelby finally stopped guzzling water. "Girl, I just got one last thing I'm gonna ask you and, yes, it's about James."

Cleo groaned.

"So, who do you think did it?"

"I'm going to answer this one last question about that nigga and after this, I don't want to hear his name coming from those lips of yours again, ya hear me?"

"Yes, I hear you," Shelby said.

She released a low sigh. "Honestly, I really can't say, Shell. Like I said earlier, it was probably in retaliation to him beatin' on some other woman. Hell, that wouldn't surprise me not one little bit. Or, like they said on the news, it really could've been just a random mugging. That woman beater was just in the wrong place at the wrong time, end of story, no matter how you slice it."

As soon as Cleo got off the phone with Shelby, her next move was going to be to text Kawhi and find out what the hell happened.

****

What the hell happened, Kawhi? You were supposed to text me when it was done. Get back at me ASAP.

After waiting more than an hour, he finally replied:

"Damn, sis, sorry. Been caught up in some otr biz. All went well. Did u catch the news? Yeah, serve that mf right. Get back at cha lata."

Cleo thought she would feel relief after getting Kawhi's message, but she didn't. Instead, she felt vexed. But there really wasn't anything else to do. Once again, she tried to calm down and get some rest. Lord knows she was going to need it to get through the workday tomorrow and being around that bitch-ass Samantha.

⚢ 37 ⚥

"Hey, sister, is Thema ready for her ballet class?" Cleo was en route to Symone's home, running late after an unexpected rendezvous with Javon's thick, wet tongue last night. He'd taken it upon himself to show up unannounced the night before with her favorite combo appetizer from O'Charley's and peach-flavored Smirnoff vodka. Several weeks had gone by since the last time they talked. All the messages he left detailed how he just couldn't see giving up on their love and how he was committed to fighting for her. She got a kick out of hearing him beg because she knew their relationship had come to an end long ago. But she was not one to turn down some good head.

"Yes, she's been ready. Where are you?" Symone inquired.

"On my way, sorry, running late. Just be at the door, I'll be rolling up in four minutes." The light at Grandview and Westlane had just turned green. She planted her foot on the gas and the Ridgeline's engine roared.

"Okay, hurry! You know them white folks don't like for the students to be late!"

Cleo shook her head, "I really don't give a fuck what they don't like, but I'll be there in a minute!" She ended the call on the car's Bluetooth.

Sure enough, she rounded the corner onto Rainbow Lane, then drove into the driveway. Thema, dressed and ready, was waiting on the front porch.

"Auntie! Auntie!" She ran up to the passenger side, swiftly opened the door and jumped in. "Come on, let's go so we won't be late!" she commanded. Symone stood at the door, arms folded, nodding her head. "Bye, Thema. Have fun and do what Miss Ackelberry tells you to do!" she yelled.

"I will, Mommy, promise!" Thema strapped the seatbelt across her chest and began bobbing her head to the CD Cleo was playing.

****

They arrived at Butler without a moment to spare. "Don't forget your backpack, Thema!" Cleo yelled. She had just jumped out of the truck and was just about to take off for the door.

"Oh, shoot!" she rattled as she did an about-turn, opened the truck door and yanked her pink and purple Doc McStuffins backpack from the cab floor. "Thanks for reminding me, Auntie." Cleo smiled. "You're welcome, sweetie." They both took off for the front door of the building, which was located on what used to be a hill that was used for sledding when Cleo was growing up.

Unfortunately, only her brother Devin was allowed to partake in this traditional winter voyage, along with their dad, one of his coworkers and his son.

"Girls are not allowed, it's only for the boys," her father insisted. It always pissed Cleo off when he presented her with that kind of bullshit. *Girls aren't allowed to do so and so and this and that.* Mr. Stinson lived and breathed traditional roles of *man* and *woman* and these values were often at the center of many arguments during her teenage years.

"Hey, Thema!

"Hi, Thema!"

Several of Thema's classmates ran towards her as soon as they rounded the corner into the medium-sized corridor area. Ever since the day Cleo first attended one of her niece's ballet practices, she quickly realized how popular she was among the other children. They all fawned over her as if she was some type of fairytale gazelle or something.

Cleo silently prayed that her popularity would carry on into the dreadful teen years, starting with junior high where the girls suddenly become strangers to one another, vying for the opposite gender's attention.

"Okay, okay, girls, settle down and line up for class. Miss Ackelberry has instructed me to start class on her behalf. She's running a little behind, but should be here any minute now," stated Ms. Snow, her uppity assistant.

Cleo rolled her eyes at her on the sly, then pranced over to an empty chair in front of the large viewing window.

A few other mothers and nannies settled into other empty chairs surrounding the window. Most were cordial in their greeting to Cleo except for a handful of upper-class women. She peered through the window only to see Thema smiling and waving back at her. Her niece's beautiful smile always warmed her from the inside out. A broad grin brightened her sullen face, reminding her of the reason she was there, and then decided to simply enjoy watching Thema and her fellow ballerinas perform a series of arabesques and passes.

⚢ 38 ⚥

Cleo hated to admit it, but she'd grown a bit nervous about the whole thing with Kawhi and his boys beating up James several weeks ago. Ever since they texted close to two weeks ago, she hadn't heard a peep out of him, despite numerous attempts to reach him. She was sure thankful that local news outlets had reported that the search was still on for James' alleged attackers and the police had no leads.

She planned to keep it that way. This was not the time for snitches to come forward with any information of the assault and she prayed Kawhi's fellow attackers wouldn't develop the itch to blab their big-ass mouths to others about their deed.

Lord knows how bitch-ass niggas can be sometimes.

****

Months had passed since Cleo and Kennedy first began their relationship. The sex was outstanding, and she found herself less and less interested in the opposite gender. This revelation kind of scared her because of her past. She'd been a boy-crazy girl since childhood. This sudden attraction towards women was utterly unexplainable and she yearned to learn more about what it meant to be gay, to actually be in love with a woman, or even if it were even possible for her. She just didn't know.

What made her current situation even more unfortunate was the fact that Kennedy's time was limited as she had other responsibilities to contend with. For example, she couldn't even spend the night with Cleo and that bothered her a lot. Truthfully, it wasn't like they were immersed in a 'real' or 'genuine' relationship. The only thing they had time to do whenever they could get together was have sex for the most part. But what was a girl to do? All this was new to her and there was no handbook, at least not that she was aware of. Besides, she was so into Kennedy, couldn't fathom the thought of not having her in her life.

⚢ 39 ⚥

“Yes, ma’am, I’m pulling into the parking lot now,” Cleo said to her mother. She hurriedly parked her ride, threw her purse over her shoulder, and made her way into La Cantina Mexican Restaurant. Upon entering the restaurant, she was taken aback by the brightly painted walls and Mexican-inspired décor.

"Hola, Señora. Welcome," said the miniature sandpaper-colored man. *Hector* was printed on his nametag, and he was sporting black trousers and a slightly wrinkled, solid black Oxford. His long, thick mane was slicked up into a single ponytail and his thin eyebrows connected over the bridge of his short, wide nose.

"Hola, Hector. I'm meeting my family here for dinner," Cleo said as she searched the large dining area for her clan.

"Sí, Sí," he responded and gestured toward the large open dining room.

After a few seconds of scanning, Cleo spotted Devin waving frantically in her direction. Cleo smiled and thanked Hector, then made her way to her family. Devin met her halfway from the small private dining room where the rest of the family sat in waiting. “Hey sis, you know you're late, right?”

"Don't start with me, brother. I almost got into it with someone on my way over here over some bullshit," Cleo responded, a frown plastered on her face.

Devin's sly grin turned to concern. "What happened?"

Cleo threw her hands up in the air. "Oh, I guess I wasn't going fast enough for this old hag who was all up in my bumper." Cleo adjusted her handbag on her left shoulder, then put her hands on her hips.

"So, she got all froggy with me, talkin' 'bout she gon' do this and that 'cause I was holdin' her up from something!"

As she went on and on about the incident, she stared into Devin's eyes as he listened intently, shaking his head in disgust at the audacity of it all

"Sis, you know some folk just ain't right, so don't let that bitch get to you like that." He draped his muscled arm around her shoulders as they began walking towards the rest of the Stinson family awaiting them in one of the restaurant's small private rooms.

Cleo sighed deeply. "You're right, brother. It's not that serious, but that heifer managed to get on my last half of a nerve."

"Auntie! Auntie!" Thema yelled when she saw them approaching. Today, she was dressed in a sky-blue short set with a matching tank top and flat, yellow sandals.

Instantly, Cleo's face brightened; she was elated to see her niece. "Hey, baby. How are you doing, sweetheart?" She reached her arms out and embraced her. "I see your big sis dolled up your hair. It looks beautiful."

"Yeah, she did Auntie. I love it! Look, look!" Thema twirled around. "Why are you so late? We already ordered our food, and the server already brought our drinks, and chips and—" She began tugging on Cleo's hair as she often did.

"Hey, hey, slow down, there, lil' mama." Cleo kissed her on her cheek, then set her down on the floor. "Come on, let's go eat."

They made their way into the room which was decorated in vivid colors of bright green, hot pink, and deep purple. A large terracotta vase was situated in the far-left corner of the room that also functioned as a water feature. The opposite side of the room had a full-length mural that featured a scene from daily life in early Mexico.

"Look who's here!" Thema yanked on Cleo's arm and pulled her along with her into the room.

Her father stood up from the table. "Hello daughter." Cleo went to him and kissed him on his cheek. "Hi Daddy." She turned and bent down and gently kissed her mother on her cheek. "Hello Mother."

It was obvious her mother wasn't happy that one of her children was late, but she was also happy to see her third born. "Hi CeeCee. Glad you could join us this evening."

"Glad to be here, too, Ma. It's been too long since we all dined together as a family." Down at the other end, Symone, David, Nahla, and Ava waved hello. She scanned the room for Sasha, but he was nowhere to be found. "Where's Sasha?" she asked as she made her way to the seat next to Thema who was already gorging herself on the chips and salsa.

"He's working overtime," Ava replied. "He sends his love to everybody and says he'll do his best to make it to the next family outing."

"Oh, okay." Cleo reached for a chip and dipped it into the molcajete salsa bowl. "Well, at least he's making some loot. Maybe he'll soon be able to pay me back that loan I gave him months ago." Everyone shook their heads in agreement and just then, their server approached her.

"Hola, Señora. Mi nombre es José, your server for the evening. Can I get you something to drink, perhaps water with lemon or maybe a margarita?"

He looked like a carbon copy of Hector, sans the buzz cut. "Hola José. I'll start with water with lemon, por favor." She began scanning the menu while Thema burned her ears up talking about something she did earlier. As the night dredged on, she knew her niece would insist on getting all her attention. This fact solidified her decision to order that margarita with an extra shot of tequila when José came back with her water.

"Nahla, how's school coming along?" Cleo asked.

Nahla swirled a chip into the salsa bowl. "Oh, classes are going great, but my parttime gig at the library not so much."

Cleo's eyebrows furled. "What's the problem? They working you too hard or something?"

José returned with her margarita. "Here you go Señora, enjoy." He handed Cleo her drink.

"Gracias, José."

"De nada." He replied. "Did you decide on an entrée?"

Cleo sipped her margarita. "Yummy, tastes good and yes, I did. I'll have the Pollo Monterrey, por favor."

"Maravilloso, Señora. I'll get your order right in. Everyone else, your entrées will be out momentarily. He surveyed the table. "Can I get anything for anyone right now?"

Everyone shook their heads. Mr. Stinson chimed in, "Looks like we're all good for now young man, thank you."

José nodded his head, turned on his heels, and headed out of the room.

Cleo returned her attention to Nahla. "Back to you, my dear."

"Well, it's nothing major." She sucked her teeth.

"Then what is it?" Cleo asked.

"Well, my hours got cut last month and I never really got a clear answer as to why, which has made me run short on funds, but—"

Cleo interjected. "Oh, you know you can call on your auntie anytime, no worries."

"Thanks Auntie, I appreciate it, but I think it's gonna get better soon. I heard some other workers are thinking about quitting, so that will free up more hours for me." Nahla smiled, then took a sip of her Coke.

Cleo dipped a tortilla into the cheese dip that José had brought to their table. "Okay, good to know and I'm glad your classes are going well."

Dang, I wonder how everyone would react if I told them about what's really going on in my life right now. Would they be accepting? Would they shame or disown me? Perhaps even embrace me? Cleo pondered these questions as she settled more into her seat and observed her family chatting and laughing together, something she cherished a lot. They were the one constant, outside of Shelby, that always gave her comfort. She prayed nothing would change the day she would decide to reveal her new and authentic self to them.

⚢ 40 ⚥

"What it do sugah?"

"Ah, nothing much, girl. Can I call you back later?"

Cleo was instantly curious as to why her BFF was rushing her off the phone. She could have sworn she heard a guy whispering in the background. She really wanted to talk to Shelby about James. She was in the middle of watching the news when they showed a follow-up story about the attack. One of his sisters had come forward stating she had been given a few names about who the attackers were, but Cleo didn't recognize any of them. She wanted to make sure none of them were truly connected to the beatdown. Needless to say, she was shaking on the inside.

If it ever got out that she was somehow involved, her world would come crumbling down around her. She was not ready for any such thing to happen. If only Kawhi would get back in touch with her. She'd grown very wary of him since the last time they communicated. Her gut was telling her something was amiss, she just didn't know what it was.

"Why? What are you doing? You got company, don't you?" She demanded.

"Shhhh!" Shelby said to the unknown male.

"Um, girl, yes, it's Phredley. He stopped by to say hello, is all."

Cleo was unmoved, but what could she say? Hell, Shelby had the right to get on for some, didn't she? After all, isn't it only natural for a lady to desire a little lovin' from time to time? Cleo took a sip of her cocktail before responding. "Well, alrighty, then. As long as it's not that asshole James, I suppose it's alright with me."

The sound of sheets ruffling could be heard through the receiver. "Well, okay, Cleo. I gotta go," and began giggling before hanging up the phone.

Realizing she'd been disregarded by her BFF, all Cleo could do was stare blankly at the phone. "Well damn," she commented to herself, then strode into the kitchen to get a refill of Crown.

After being ignored by Shelby, she thought she'd try to reach Kawhi, again. She ran into one of his baby's mommas at the Shell gas station at 71st and North Michigan Road after leaving the Mexican restaurant the night before. Come to find out, he'd gotten his number changed for the umpteenth time, so she gave her the most current one. Tentatively, she dialed his number and held her breath. He picked up on the fourth ring. *Whew. It's about damn time!*

"Kawhi, what's up? Don't you know I've been trying to reach you? What happened? The last time we texted, you said you'd get right back at me, but I ain't heard a peep out of you!"

"Slow down, sis," he responded in his deep, penetrating, baritone voice. "Everything's just fine. I've just been laying low, is all. Ya know, just keepin' the heat at a bare minimum, ya dig, sis?" He snorted.

Cleo wasn't sure of how to respond, but again, her intuition spoke to her, telling her that he was being honest and that she'd spent all that time worrying for nothing.

Damn, I need a smoke.

"You there, beautiful?"

"Yeah, yeah, I'm here, Kawhi. Man, you had a sistah freaking the fuck out, man," she said as she reached into her bedside table drawer and found the *Al Capone* cigar Jamaican Blaze case Kennedy had left there several weeks earlier. Her mind wanted to venture down memory lane of that particular afternoon rendezvous, but she refused to let it.

Instead, she held it in her hand for several moments, shook it off, and reached back in the drawer for her lighter.

"Eh, now, beautiful. I assure you, there was no malice on my part at all. I was protecting all of us," he pleaded. "Surely, you understand, don't you? Believe me when I say I was going to call you after things simmered down a bit."

Cleo took a drag off the cigar, sending up smoke-infused crop circles before her eyes. She stuffed a pillow behind her and leaned back. "I understand, Kawhi. I do, but damn, I was just worried especially when I didn't hear back from you."

"Kawhi Robert Leonard Abbott! Don't you hear me calling you, boy?"

Kawhi's mother was summoning him for something. Any time a black mother used your whole name, you know she means business, straight up, no chaser.

"No ma'am, I didn't hear you, I apologize, ma'am. I'll be right there," he clambered.

"Oh yeah, I just know you will, dammit," his mother swore in the background.

"Mother hen puttin' her foot, down, huh?" Cleo laughed.

"Shit, you already know. Mama Pearle Louise Betelle-Abbott don't play, ya heard? So, back to you, we good?"

Cleo took another long drag on her cigarillo. "Yeah, we good. Talk to you later," she replied, finally feeling like she could truly relax. No more worrying about the whole situation with James Connor. A few minutes after hanging up, she remembered learning about Robert S. Abbott, the founder of the *Chicago Defender*, an old African-American newspaper.

She'd been meaning to ask Kawhi if there was any relation because Abbott's story was so fascinating. It'd be cool if she actually knew one of his descendants. She made a mental note to remind herself to ask Kawhi about it the next time they spoke.

⚢ 41 ⚥

"So, how was it?" Cleo asked as she slid into the booth opposite a blushing Shelby.

"O.M.G., Cleo!" she screeched. "Girl, that lil' boy is rockin' this ol' body, I'm telling you, straight up."

Cleo couldn't help but notice the youthful glow encasing her BFF.

"Well, by the look of the grin plastered on your face, I would have to agree with you. Cleo felt a tinge of jealousy creeping through her bones. Thoughts of a young guy who tried to be her lover not-so-long-ago crept into her mind. She was beginning to think that perhaps she had missed out on something good.

"Hiya beautiful. Welcome to Applebee's, what can I get for you?"

Cleo was snapped back into reality after hearing the server's greeting. She looked up only to see the most dazzling cinnamon-hued eyes she'd ever seen. The server had a French accent that captured Cleo's interest very unexpectedly. The tall, slim, chocolate-coated sultana possessed the most exquisite, full black woman lips that made Cleo subconsciously lick her own lips.

Finally seeing the perturbed look on Shelby's face, she quickly made herself calm the fuck down. *Damn, girl! Snap out of it. You know you're not ready to come out to anybody, not even your BFF. You almost showed your ace. Better put it away before the 'real' you is revealed.*

"Madam, are you alright?" asked the beautiful creature standing before her. Her smile revealed a wide, sexy gap between her pearly-white front teeth.

"Yes, yes, I'm fine. I'll start with water with lemon, please. What's your name?"

"My name is Phina, Mademoiselle. Glad to be of service to you." She winked at Cleo and scribbled the order on her notepad. "I'll be right back."

Cleo nervously bit her thumbnail while looking at the perpetual perturbed look on Shelby's face.

"What the hell was that all about, Cleo? You were flirting with *her*!" Shelby leaned back and folded her arms.

A jolt shot through Cleo like a lightning bolt flickering in a dark, smoldering sky.

"Whoa, Shelby. What the fuck makes you think I was flirting with our server? What the hell's wrong with *you* to make such an accusation?" She was putting it all back on her. In no way was she ready to have *that* discussion with her BFF, no way, no how … not yet.

Cleo was trying really hard not to come off too defensive but also wanted to give the impression that she meant business and was in no way, shape or form into girls. And, honestly, it wasn't too hard for Cleo to get Shelby to second-guess herself. Over the span of their friendship, Cleo was undoubtedly the leader and Shelby regularly looked to her for guidance and assurance.

Weariness encircled Shelby as she tightened her grip around her shoulders. "Well, um …" She took a minute to clear her throat. "I, I, um, it just looked like—"

Cleo cut her off. "It looked like what?" she demanded, arching her back, quietly asserting her dominance.

Cleo's darkened eyes bore a hole into Shelby who appeared to be at a loss for words, once again clearing her throat. Before Shelby could say another word, Phina approached their table carrying a tall glass of water with lemon.

Phina smiled brightly at Cleo. "Here is your water with lemon, as requested, pretty lady." She purposely leaned in close to her, exposing her healthy, pillowy soft-looking breasts.

Ignoring Phina's obvious flirting, Cleo plastered a straight look on her face. "Thank you, Phina. Could I please have the chicken Caesar salad?"

Phina retrieved her notepad from the pocket stitched on the front side of her *Applebee's* apron and scribbled Cleo's order down. She slowly licked her lips, and then rubbed her perfectly symmetrical head, bringing attention to her lovely, closely cropped sandy-brown hair.

"Are you ready to order, Madam?"

"Um, yes, I suppose."

Phina gave her a perplexed look, then turned her Nefertiti-esque cinnamon-hued eyes in Cleo's direction.

Shelby cleared her throat loudly, "I'll have the roasted chicken salad." She thrusted the menu towards Phina, then refolded her arms.

Cleo thought Phina seemed oblivious to the shade Shelby was giving her.

Phina asked, "Can I get you anything else?"

"No, that will be all."

She finished writing down Shelby's order. "Alright ladies, thank you. Your entrées will be out in a short while." She began walking away, then, unexpectedly turned back towards Cleo, and winked.

Cleo blushed. If she were Caucasian, her skin would've been beet-red.

On the other side of the table, Shelby was steaming. "What was that all about, Cleo? What, are you gay now?" Shelby's words hung in the air like a pungent odor in a boys' locker room.

Cleo took a long gulp of her water laced with a few lemon wedges. She decided to go the cocky route and not let her BFF get to her. "Ah, come on, Shell. Like you've never been just a little turned on when a woman gave you 'the look' or winked at you before. Jeez, lighten up!"

She hoped the joke would brighten the mood that had quickly taken a nosedive when Phina came to their table.

"Humph! Girl, you know I don't roll like that. I love me some D-I-C-K, shit, there ain't nothing a woman can do for me. Real talk." Smugness was written all over her face as if she'd just been handed some type of morality award.

It had become obvious that Shelby's mood was not going to change as quickly as Cleo hoped. Not wanting the ugliness to continue, she changed the subject back to Shelby's playthang.

"So, anyway, back to your lil' man," lowering her voice when she said the last two words. "What is going on with him? Are you digging him like that or is the lovin' that damn good?"

And with that, Shelby was back to her old self again. She threw her hands into the air. "Oh, girl. Girl, girl, girl, girl, girl." She shook her head and began fanning herself.

Cleo leaned back against the worn brown leather backboard. "Damn, Shelby, it cannot be all that, I mean really. The boy is—how old is he again?"

Cleo really thought that she was exaggerating. She took another sip of her beverage, in complete disbelief as Shelby carried on about Phredley.

"Look, I'm not even playing with you, CeeCee! He really got some skills when it comes to licking the kitty." She giggled. "And his attachment ain't bad, either."

Cleo turned up her nose. "Girl, you crazy."

"Naw, CeeCee, for real, though. Let me—" Just then, one of their old high school teachers approached them. "Wow! Could it really be my two star pupils from psychology class?"

It was Jamie Martindale, their favorite teacher from high school. "Oh my God, Mr. Martindale, what are you doing here?" Shelby asked, eyeing the Applebee's apron and pen stuck behind his right ear.

He gave them both a hug and replied, "Oh, please call me Jamie. You haven't been my students for quite some time now." Cleo scooted over and he slid into the booth, next to her.

They both nodded their heads in agreement. Cleo noticed he pretty much looked the same as he did all those years ago, sans a little less hair. He wore a pair of starched black slacks and a taupe-colored I-zod short-sleeved shirt. "Well, we have one kid enrolled at Ball State and another to follow in a few months, so I picked up this server gig to help pay college fees." He shook his head and rubbed the back of his neck.

"Oh, I didn't know you got married and had kids," Cleo noted.

"Well, the oldest one, our son Jeremiah is technically my stepson, but, really, I don't believe in all that 'step' stuff. He's my son."

Again, they both shook their head in agreement.

"Which kid is off to college next?" Cleo asked.

A wide grin spread across his face. "That would be my little angel, Solani. She's decided to attend I.U. and we could not be more proud."

"Solani? That's an unusual name, but beautiful," Cleo said.

"Thank you. My wife's obsessed with Indian culture, so her name is Indian and it means *beautiful*."

"I love unique names, so I dig it. Which program is she interested in?"

"Ladies, here are your entrées, as promised." Balancing their plates, extra drinks, and a medium-sized serving bowl filled with breadsticks on the large tray, Phina handed Shelby's plate to her, and then grinned excessively at Cleo as she placed her plate in front of her. Granted, there had been times when women flirted with her, but not to this extent. It was beginning to make her feel uncomfortable, mainly because she felt she couldn't play it up like she wanted to with Shelby glaring down her neck. "Thanks again, Phina," Cleo murmured.

Still grinning, Phina replied, "Is there anything else I can get for you, Mademoiselle?"

Cleo stuck her fork into the salad bowl. "No, that will be all, thanks."

"Please don't hesitate to let me know if you need anything else, beautiful."

During the exchange, Jamie and Shelby looked on without uttering a word, but Shelby's body language was speaking volumes. A few seconds later, another frantic-looking server approached saying something about needing Jamie's help.

Jamie shook his head and stood up. "Sorry ladies, but I gotta get back to work. Make sure I get your contact info before you leave, okay? Maybe we can get together for lunch or something and get caught up."

"Most definitely, Jamie," Cleo said.

"Looking forward to it," Shelby chimed in.

Jamie walked off with the server, while Phina slowly walked in the other direction, her eyes still fixed on Cleo.

Shelby rolled her eyes again but stayed silent. Cleo was glad she didn't open her big mouth because she knew Shelby didn't want to be reminded of that little fling she had with Maxine, a.k.a. Max in high school. Their relationship was on the down-low, but with them being so close, there was no way she could keep it a secret from Cleo.

Cleo stabbed her fork into her food and ate a few bites. She looked up from her plate. "Are you okay? You seem to be in deep thought.

"Yeah, sure. I was just reminiscing about some stuff."

"Oh, yeah? Like what?" Her curiosity was piqued.

A grin appeared on Shelby's face. "Oh, you know, seeing Jamie made me think of our psychology class and all the fun we had." She took a bite of her salad. "Remember that time when Timmy and Colin got into it over Bronwyn and Jamie had to separate them before it got real ugly?"

"Damn, I'd forgotten about that incident. Then, the school security guard, what's his name, came and escorted Colin out of the room because he started acting like he was possessed by some demon or something!"

"Martin."

"Who?"

"The security guard, his name was Martin," Shelby said.

"Oh, my goodness, yes." She grinned at Shelby. "I remember somebody—I ain't gon' call no names, but *somebody* had a serious crush on Martin, ain't that right?"

"Why you gotta bring up old shit, huh?" Shelby hissed. Now, instead of rocking, she was squirming in her seat.

"Okay, okay, I'ma leave you alone about that one, but I was just sayin'."

Several minutes passed as they both remained quiet while chowing down on their food. They were supposed to be going down memory lane about the good times they had at North Central. Cleo finally broke the silence.

"So, Miss Cradle-robber, what's going to happen with Phredley? Are you trying to make this fling morph into a relationship or what?" She almost choked on the word 'relationship'.
Shelby looked at her, holding back laughter. "That's real funny, Cleo, damn, you alright?" She laid her folk down, after having eaten about half of her salad.

"Yes, I'm good."
Shelby shook her head. "Well, honestly, I don't know, CeeCee. After the first romp, I thought that was going to be it. But, well, shit, the boy put it on me so good, kept me coming back for more.
Now, you know, I still got a few tricks up my sleeve as well; had him blowing up my phone, trying to slide through almost nightly," she laughed. "We became magnets to each other, unable to pull away 'cause the fucking was just that good, know what I'm saying?"

Cleo was scrolling through her social media on her cell but was also paying attention to what Shelby was saying. Admittedly, she was curious about where Shelby's head was with Phredley. After all, he was her baby brother's best friend, and her family knew him and his mother since he and Sasha were in diapers. To her, he was just a little boy whose diapers she used to change; nowhere on her radar as a potential fuck buddy or, God forbid, love interest. "Yeah, I get it, Shelby."

She set her phone down and turned her focus on her. "But you do realize that he's fifteen years younger than you, right? I mean, it's not like you haven't known him almost as long as I have, hell, you and I used to babysit him and the twins back in the day. Since when did you begin lusting after him, anyway?" She felt herself getting riled up, trying desperately to remain level-headed.

"Damn girl, if you don't stop being so fucking self-righteous, jeez-louise!"

Shelby had a puzzled look on her face. "There you go, again. I thought this was going to be a no-judgment convo." She began rocking, something she only did when she was nervous, agitated, or in pain.

Cleo spoke up. "No, no, no, I'm not trying to be judgmental, Shell. I'm just trying to understand this sudden interest in someone so much younger than you."

Shelby narrowed her eyes, then cocked her head to the left. " Are you sure that's all this is about? Do I sense a tinge of jealousy coming from *the* Miss Cleo Stinson?" she demanded.

Cleo jerked in her seat and was about to say something that would've hurt Shelby's feelings. Instead, she bit her bottom lip. Just then, Phina and her Snow-White teeth showed up at their table.

"How are we doing, ladies? Food tasting good? Can I get you ladies anything else?" Her gaze rested on Cleo.

Instantaneously, Shelby found her 'tude again. "No, we don't need anything, now excuse us, please."

Both Phina and Cleo blankly glared at her. "Shelby! What's wrong with you?" Cleo exclaimed.

Shelby folded her arms. "Humph! Ain't nothin' wrong with me. You should be asking her," pointing her finger at Phina.

Before Phina could say a word, Cleo stepped up and said, "Phina, I am so sorry for my friend's rude behavior." Cleo began to gather her things. "Shelby, get your things and let's go."

Ignoring Shelby's incivility, Phina addressed Cleo, "Beautiful one, it has been a pleasure having you as my patron this afternoon." She reached for Cleo's hand, bowed, then gently kissed it, sending shivers down her spine. "Au revoir."

Obviously pissed off, Shelby snatched up her handbag and stormed toward the exit door.

"Thank you, Phina. It has been a pleasure." She dug into her purse and handed her a twenty-dollar tip. "And, again, I apologize for my friend's rudeness. I don't know what got into her," she said, shaking her head in disbelief.

Phina flashed those marvelous teeth again, full lips painted in a sexy hue of soft rose. And, for the first time, Cleo noticed the tiny diamond stud piercing on Phina's left nostril, adding another level of intrigue to the already alluring chocolate beauty.

"Much obliged, honey. Oh, I'm not worried about her. In fact, if you ask me, I sensed a bit of jealousy on her part because my attention was on you instead of her." She stuffed the bill into her apron. "Happens more times than you think, love." Again, she smiled brightly at Cleo.

Phina's last words felt like a sledgehammer on top of Cleo's head. *Damn, she could be onto something.*

By the time Cleo walked out, Shelby was gone. Well, it's good they drove separately because she was fuming on the inside and did not have anything nice to say to her BFF at that moment, anyway. Shelby's behavior made it even more difficult for Cleo to potentially come out to her. After watching her clown with Phina today, she wasn't so sure she ever would.

After all the discussion they had over lunch, she forgot to ask Shelby about James and where they were going later that night for drinks with the girls. She wondered if she'd heard from him or whether or not the police had tried talking to her again. Her mind was so discombobulated. She didn't feel like talking to her right at that moment, anyway. *Shit, I'll call that nutcase later on, after she calms down. I don't feel like cussing her the fuck out if she decides to come at me sideways.* And, just at that moment, Phina's comment crept into her mind.

Damn, could it really be jealousy on her part? Now that she was questioning her sexuality for the first time in her life, it made sense that perhaps Shelby could be battling demons of her own. Or could it be something more sinister or even more complex? Come to think of it, she had begun noticing how Shelby's mood swings had returned and that her drinking had increased again, sans that crazy-ass fiasco at Club Isis with Javon's stank ass.
Oh, dear God. We don't need a repeat of the craziness she went through after losing her baby boy, please Lord! I don't know if she'll be able to recover. Hell, I don't trust that I could, either, for that matter!

⚢ 42 ⚦

"Hey sis, how's it going?"

"Oh, it's going okay, Ava." She had just laid out five different outfits for their night out but was becoming more unnerved by the minute not only because she was struggling with what to wear, but also from the incident at the restaurant earlier with Shelby.

"Well, you don't sound that okay to me."

Cleo bit her lower lip. Not wanting to go into detail with Ava, she said, "Oh, Shell and I just had a disagreement earlier and she really kinda pissed me off." She picked up the royal purple pantsuit off the bed, strode over to the full-length mirror and sized herself up.

Ava giggled. "Ah, I see. The two BFF's had a lil' falling out, again, eh?"

She was oblivious to the details, so Cleo let the giggle slide. "Yeah, something like that," she muttered as she walked back to her bed, laid the pantsuit down and picked up the zebra print mini skirt and ivory-hued button-down blouse that still had the tag on it.

She'd forgotten all about it, despite having bought it at the Ann Klein store at the Edinburgh outlet several months ago during one of she and Shelby's shopping sprees.

"What are you watching? Your TV's a bit loud, ain't it?"

Irritated, Cleo shrugged. "A recording of last week's episode of *How to Get Away with Murder*. What's up? What do you need, Ava?" It was very rare for her to get a call from her little sister and when she did, it often involved something she wanted from her.

"Hey, hey, don't shoot the messenger. I don't want anything, jeez!" She shot back. "I'm at mom and dad's and she asked me to call and ask you if you're coming over for Sunday dinner," Ava said, sounding hurt. She was always the most sensitive of the Stinson sisters.

After debating between the two outfits, Cleo chose the purple ensemble. "Look, my bad, I'm just a little irritated right now. It's nothing against you, okay?" She almost felt guilty for taking her frustration towards Shelby out on her innocent sister. Almost.

"Tell them I'll be there and that I haven't forgotten to also bring the cabbage, okay?"

"Alrighty then, I'll tell'em. Talk to you later, Cleo."

"Yep, bye." As soon as she hung up from her sister, her cell buzzed. It was Shelby's assigned text ringtone,

Just letting you know I won't be joining y'all tonight. I already let the girls know.

Stunned, Cleo dropped her cell on top of her bedspread. *Well, I'll be damned, here she goes.* Cleo huffed and puffed, now she was no longer in the mood to hit the streets, either. Feeling totally dejected, she texted Donnieka and Crimson to let them know she was going to sit this one out, too. Immediately after sending the text, Donnieka called her, but she let it go to voicemail. Then she texted Cleo,

What the hell is going on with you and Shelby?"

Fuck it. Cleo tossed the outfits she was assessing for the night on top of the wicker laundry basket. *My ass ain't going nowhere, either 'cause I am no longer in the mood.* Cleo loosened the belt on her royal purple terry cloth robe, a birthday gift from Shelby several years ago, reached into her drawer and grabbed a pair of cotton boy underwear and a wife beater. On the right side of her bed, sat her laptop on the end table. She grabbed it and the remote control to her TV set and clicked the power button on. It was time to do some more window shopping, but instead of checking out clothing or furniture, she was going to be checking out new posts, praying that a good majority of them contained headshots and, more importantly, tits and ass shots.

Just looking for that one friend I can kick it with. We share the same goals when it comes to satisfying one another. We have a connection that includes daytime coffees and, perhaps brunch, then work our way into some flirting in public. What we do is our business. I require discretion, therefore, you must also. I'm not looking for a quick hook up. I want chemistry and attraction to whomever I'm laying my tongue on. I want consistency. This can be a regular thing, but only if you want to roll like that…I hope you do! As much as I love pussy and big breasts/nipples, your intelligence, maturity and character are what makes me hunger for more. Not your tits, flat midsection or round derriere. Don't get me wrong, I dig all that but, I need more, too. I'm a married (husband does not know) biracial cool femme, 41. I am aggressive and know what I want, what I need. You can be single, married, whatever. Just as long as you and I know what we got. I'm about as real as they come. Naturally, I expect the same from you. So, if you looking for that escape away from your world, venture into mine. On the real: please don't come at me sideways or respond with just "I'm interested" or one of those tired-ass one liners. Tell me about you in detail, what you're looking for, your interests/hobbies…more than anything, my goal is to get to know you on a whole other level than anyone else you've ever crossed paths with, so keep it real with me, sugar. No doubt, you'll get the same from me.

ABSOLUTELY NO MEN. NO COUPLES. NO DRAMA!

Make it do what it do baby

Experienced STUD here ISO horny experienced and curious females to play with. Let me kiss your entire body, suck and nibble on your nipples til they get hard and your pussi starts to throb and get moist, kissing your stomach making my way to your dripping wet pussi where I let my tongue run wild sucking and licking on your clit til your legs start shaking and you cum all in my mouth and while your begging me for more I slide deep inside you with my strap as a loud moan of pleasure escapes your lip and you dig your nails into my back.... Lol are you wet now? well let's talk I promise you won't be disappointed.... All females welcome ...Generous older women to the front.... Pls be DDD free.... Your pic gets mine serious inquiries only please put "Let's play" in the subject box to weed out the spam.... Can't wait to hear from you....

The stud's post included a photo of herself posing in front of a bathroom mirror, wearing a black wife-beater, no bra, and a large black strap-on with what looked like a 10-inch dildo. She obviously didn't want her face to be seen because she covered it up with a smiling emoji with its tongue wagging.

WHERE ARE THE NICE SEASONED LESBIAN WOMEN IN INDIANAPOLIS?

I'm a gorgeous 65 y/o active, single female in pretty good shape. I pride myself on not looking my age and I just moved back to town after being away for more than 29 yrs. I'm interested in gals to date first then, maybe down the line, we can entertain a LTR. Pls note that I'm not into just having sex. I really want to get to know you in every way before we can even think about hoppin into bed with one anotr. I got my own and I expect u to have ur own, 2. Are u a good woman with nice manners and knows how to conversate? I need a lady that likes to do fun things like going on hiking trips, making dinner at home, and going out for drinks every once and while. We got to establish a foundation first, then if the chemistry kicks in, we can go from there. I'm not worried about how you look so much as I need you to just be a good and nice woman. I only require you be at least 40 yrs old and have olive skin and on the feminine side, and enjoy wearing lipstick and blush on a daily basis.
I'm 5'8, hazel eyes, pale skin (mixed with Spanish and European). I consider myself a butch lesbian, so I like to wear masculine clothes, but am very much a lady. I like to wear my strap sometimes, but not all the time. I have some college and spent most of my life as an entrepreneur. I'm semi-retired now. My lover of over 15 yrs passed on about a year ago and I don't have any children, but if you do, it's cool.

I love the outdoors, including camping. I consider myself to be an atheist and have no particular political leanings. I come w/no baggage and no drama. U be the same, with a loving and joyful heart and be funny. I love funny women. If my post attracts you, pls contact me, tell me about yourself and how we might be good together. Your photo and contact info gets mine so we can get better acquainted. And, pls, pls, pls DO NOT send naked photos of yourself and I'm not into males or confused females, so don't bother me if that's what your into. I really hope to meet someone nice, so pls, be nice. Hope to hear from you soon.

Cum lick this fat-ass pussy now w-4-w, 33

I'm ready to get in between the sheets with the right freak. R U her? I'm a sho'nuff freak-a-deek, know what turns me on and always like to try something new, how abt U? I'm a single, bi, voluptuous Latina, 5"5, dark hair, seeking the same. Must be drama-free, have a funny bone, and pretty/sexi.

I like doing it all... that is if we click of course. Open to all body types, races and ages (must be at least 21). Must take pride in your appearance & hygiene, be open-minded with no over-the-top expectations, and willing & able to meet pronto. We can then take it from there.

Mutual attraction is an absolute, your photo gets mine & be ready to VV.

Cunning Scopophiliacs

Summer is here & so are the sexy/horny-ass Naptown females. So, we invite all the bisexual women to cum out N play w/ us—we've started a kik group dedicated to all things "bisexual" and the couples who enjoy them. We don't discriminate, but most of us are AA. If you're a single bi femme who wants to get together with couples and other femmes, send your kik name and stats. Let's make our own version of Freaknik, but on the DL!

Once again, Cleo's mind was blown. *Damn, there are some for real freaks all up in Nap, but who would've ever thunk it?* She got somewhat turned on with the pic of the Latina's brown sugar nipples on full display and began massaging her engorged clit until she fell into dreamland.

⚢ 43 ⚥

"But, Shelby, I'm your best friend! How could you keep something like this from me, after all these years?" Cleo exclaimed.

Cleo noticed Shelby's small frame retreated into a ball, much like a fetus, hiding her red-tinged eyes, tears cascading down her already wet cheeks. Miles Davis' trumpet bellowed in the background; seemingly a solemn reminder of what Shelby was feeling at that very moment. Before Cleo even realized it, she was on her feet, towering over Shelby, practically barking at her. Shelby froze, too scared to say another word.

Cleo had come over to Shelby's to try to find out what was up with her at Applebee's when out of nowhere Shelby made the revelation about her trifling-ass uncle. Cleo began rubbing her aching temples, she was so taken aback by the news. It reminded her of her own secret she was carrying around like the old baggage Erykah Badu sang about in her number one hit song from back in the day.

Cleo finally backed off. "I'm so, so sorry Shell." She reached to touch her, but Shelby recoiled as if trying to make herself shrink even smaller until she simply disappeared.

Guilt-ridden, Cleo removed herself from Shelby's presence, trotted into the tiny kitchen, reached into her liquor stash cupboard, and grabbed the bottle of Crown that Shelby always had in stock just for her. She bypassed the glasses, tilted the bottle straight to her lips.

Meow.

Cleo about jumped out of her skin. She hadn't realized Oshun had come into the kitchen, circling her as she sat slumped over at Shelby's counter which was teetering with what had to be weeks' worth of unopened mail.

How could this have gotten past me? Why didn't I notice all the telltale signs? Cleo's mind reverted to the past, trying to recall something, anything that she'd missed. *Well, there was that one time during one of their cookouts at Shelby's childhood home when her uncle Orson, her mother's youngest brother, kept teasing and pestering after her. He was so damn relentless*. She downed another swallow of Crown. *And that other time he was over visiting and wanted to take them to get ice cream and go play at Juan Solomon Park playground. She really wanted to go, but Shelby was damn near in tears, begging not to. Cleo couldn't remember the reason she gave as to why she didn't want to go—she thought she was just being a little spoiled brat.*

Just then, a cold shiver ran down her spine. The sound of Shelby sobbing was getting louder and louder, a sure-fire sign that there was no way in hell she was lying about this.

"Damn," she muttered under her breath. Having worked in social services for so many years, both Shelby and Cleo were no strangers to stories similar to Shelby's. But to now know Shelby had been a victim at such a young age was just too much for Cleo to handle.

Shit, did I just sit here and drink all that? She dangled the bottle in front of her and before she even realized she'd damn near drunk the whole bottle of Crown.

Meow.

Cleo took one last swallow, then looked down only to find Oshun's round body lying in a furry puddle at her feet. It's a good thing she looked before standing up 'cause Oshun probably would've lost a toe or two.

Alright, girl. Get yourself together before stepping back into that room. Shelby needs you and keep in mind that this AIN'T about you! Shell's hurting and has no one else to turn to, so snap the fuck out of it! Cleo told herself after picking up Oshun and rubbing on her. She had the most piercing blue-green eyes Cleo had ever seen on a feline; truly hypnotic.

After loving on Oshun for a few moments, then putting her back down on the floor where she immediately commenced to licking her long fur, Cleo reluctantly left the few drops of Crown in the bottle for the next time (which would likely be before she left), gathered her composure, then set off to see about her best friend in the living room.

As she rounded the corner, the deafening sound of uncontrollable sobbing could be heard coming from the living room area of Shelby's quaint apartment.

"Booo ohhh, booo oohhh, no, no, no dear God! Please make it stop, please, Lord, please, I'm begging you to make it stop. I just can't take the pain no more, God, I'm sorry, but I just can't! Make it stop, make it stop, please!"

Shame and embarrassment shook Cleo as her ears took in the piercing sound of Shelby's agony. *Here I was upset with her for keeping this from me all this time, but not once did I consider how she had to be feeling all these years. All the pent-up hurt and disappointment she must've been feeling, wearing her down, leaving her scarred for life. Now it all made sense. No wonder she developed a drinking problem at the age of twelve and succumbed to the lure of countless no-good-ass niggas all her life. Damn, Cleo, maybe you really are a bitch.*

Cleo picked up the pace and went to her. Shelby was now down on the floor, wrapped in the fetal position, rocking back and forth. A guilt-ridden Cleo crouched down next to her and embraced her tightly. "I am so, so sorry, Shelby, I really am." She squeezed her even tighter. "I promise you, everything's gonna be alright. We're gonna get through this together, whatever it takes, you hear me?" She cupped her face with both hands as Shelby's tidal wave of tears strode down her gloomy face.

"Now that I know what happened to you, I'm not going to allow what that fucking perv did to you to steal your joy any longer, comprende?"

Unable to speak, Shelby shook her head and held onto Cleo as if her life depended on it because, in a way, it did. "I'll be back," Shelby said as she stood up. "Gotta go to the bathroom."

"Okay," Cleo replied, her eyes following Shelby as she made her way to her bathroom down the hall. She turned her attention back to the television, then spotted Shelby's journal tucked behind one of the sofa pillows. Her curiosity got the best of her, so she decided to take a peek:

Friday, June 10, 2016
Lately my mind has been a total mess and I am often at a loss thinking about where my life is going. Joshua robbed me of the ability to ever bear children and I will never forgive him for that.

I also am experiencing nightmares again about all those times uncle molested me, causing me to have suicidal thoughts again just like that time I almost cut myself for real with one of dad's straight razors and I don't like having these kinds of thoughts. What's worse is that I have no one to talk to, not even Cleo cause she's just gonna overreact or even worse she'll probably say something fucked up like "oh, it's just all in your head Shelby. You just need to get over it." Sometimes the pain is so great that I just want to end it all to make it all stop, just stop. Maybe I should have just done it back then...instead of making superficial cuts on my wrist, I should've been strong enough to just do it like dude did in the Big Chill movie, hell I could have freed myself a long time ago and avoided so much of the pain I've been feeling since childhood.

If only.

Cleo heard the toilet flush and the water running before she could read the next entry. *What in the entire fuck is going on? Is that what my best friend really thinks of me, that I would dismiss her like that?* She was stunned beyond measure but knew she couldn't say anything because her Shelby was already in a bad headspace and bringing all this up and the fact that she read her private journal would be far too much for her to handle.

"You okay, Shell? Is there anything else I can do? I'm so, so sorry for what happened to you, I really am, and if your uncle was still alive, I'd have Kawhi and his boys—"

Shelby threw her hands up in the air, catching Cleo off-guard. "Please stop Cleo, no more violence, okay?"

Cleo looked on as Shelby rubbed her forehead after sitting down on the sofa next to her.

"But I'm just saying—"

Shelby focused her blood-shot eyes on Cleo's face once again and no other words were needed.

Cleo hung her head in defeat. "Okay, I'm sorry." Cleo looked at her again as if seeing her for the first time, just as she had when she learned about her fling with an underage Phredley back-in-the-day. *Damn, I guess the saying is true. You can know a person for a lifetime and still not really know them.*

⚢ 44 ⚥

"Are you on your way?" Jim asked Cleo who was knee-deep in compiling reports and making follow-up phone calls all morning.

"Are you telling me it's noon already?"

"Um, yes, my dear. Kennedy and I are waiting on you, so hurry on down, please."

Hearing Kennedy's name made Cleo shiver. They hadn't spoken since their last

rendezvous. But, with this meeting, there would be no more avoiding the inevitable and she was scared shitless.

"I'm so sorry Jim, I was up to my eyeballs in paperwork and lost track of time, but I'll be right down," she assured him.

"Okay. See you in a few minutes, then," he replied.

Cleo hurriedly gathered up several files and her weekly calendar and headed down to Jim's office. Before entering, she practiced her breathing techniques and then opened his office door.

"Hello everybody. Please excuse my tardiness." Kennedy and Jim were talking quietly at the small table located in the right corner of his sparsely filled office. Cleo promptly sat in the empty chair next to Jim and placed the files she brought from her office on the table, all the while avoiding Kennedy's gaze.

"Not a problem, Cleo," Jim replied with a smile. "Kennedy and I are very aware of how easy it is to lose time when you're swamped with phone calls, reports, et cetera. Now, back to our meeting. We were just discussing the changes in our form—again—and the reduction in our already reduced staff."

Cleo observed him rubbing the back of his neck and shaking his head. It was obvious he was not having a good day.

"And now we as managers must restructure our teams for the fifth time this year," Kennedy added, never lifting her gaze from Cleo. "So, Cleo, have you given these issues any thought?"

Cleo stirred in her chair, realizing she could not avoid Kennedy's eyes any longer. Perspiration trickled down her brow and she reached up with her trembling hand to wipe the droplets away.

"Well," she began. "Actually, yes, I have thought about both issues and came up with some strategies on how to make the best of this difficult situation." She opened the top folder that laid on the table and withdrew several pieces of paper, handing one to each of them to peruse.

"As you can see from my notes, I would like to enact these various strategies. Luckily, we now have that new caseworker who replaced Tamika," she smiled, something she hadn't done in a while and it felt nice, reigniting her work mojo.

"His name is Mahlon Smith. He has over ten years of experience and was educated at my alma mater, I.U. He received his graduate degree in social work earlier this year and comes with outstanding recommendations. I'm very excited to have him at Exodus."

"Great to hear, Cleo," Jim quipped.

Kennedy added, "Yeah, for sure, can't wait to meet him! When does he start, today?"

Everyone laughed. "No, not today, tomorrow will be his first day and in fact, I will be training him. I have an appointment scheduled with Miss Dunbar and he'll be accompanying me. "Now, back to my list."

****

"CeeCee, can I talk to you for a minute?"

During the meeting that lasted a little over an hour, they put their heads together and came up with a very workable plan that everyone was satisfied with. Now all she had to do was type it up and get it emailed to Samantha within the next couple of days.

"Oh, hey Kennedy, of course. Come on in and close the door," she replied. Instantaneously, anxiety kicked in. She tried her best not to let it show. "What can I help you with today?"

Kennedy sat in one of the seats in front of Cleo's desk. As always, Cleo was finding it impossible to not be taken away with her stunning beauty. Today, her body was wrapped in a lovely animal-print wrap dress with matching five-inch heels, gracing her slender neck was a handsomely handcrafted black beaded necklace, while her silky mane was also wrapped up in an identical print headscarf, with a few ringlets peeking through.

"How are you doing, Cleo?"

"I'm okay, and you?"

Now Kennedy's nerves were beginning to show. Cleo took note of her trembling voice when she spoke.

"Well, I know we haven't talked since the last time, well, you know ..."

Cleo grimaced. "I try not to think of the last time so much."

Kennedy coughed, then shifted from her right hip to the left in her seat. "I can understand why you're upset with me, Cleo, but please believe that I never meant to hurt you," she pleaded. "I don't want to go into a lot of detail here at work because of the lack of privacy, but I was wondering if you'd be available to talk after work today?"

Cleo stirred in her chair, took a deep breath, then focused on the photos she had on her desk of her, Nahla, and Thema at the Artsgarden's Art & Soul event back in February. She was stalling and after 'dating' for the last several months, Kennedy knew it.

"Well?" Kennedy probed. "And, stop stalling, CeeCee."

Again, Cleo forced her eyes back to her. "Okay, okay. That's fine. Where do you want to meet?"

"The weather's nice, so how about we go down to the circle?" She smiled, her lovely white teeth gleaming as they always did. "We can chill together, maybe get some iced coffee from your favorite spot on the Circle, um, what's the name of that place, again?" She teased.

Cleo wanted to still be mad at her for everything that wasn't kosher with their situationship. But, she just couldn't. Her heart simply melted whenever she was close to Kennedy and all she could think about—at least the majority of the time—were the good times they had shared since starting their, for lack of a better word, romantic entanglement. Cleo ached for those good times to become even more prevalent in her life … in both their lives—together.

"It's called Starbucks," Cleo deadpanned, knowing full well she already knew the answer.

"Oh, yes, now I remember. They have pretty tasty, iced coffees. She smiled. "So, what do you say?"

"I suppose that would be okay." Apprehension echoed in her voice. It was obvious she was feeling some type of way.

On the other hand, Kennedy tried to keep things light, upbeat. She stood up to leave. "I'm looking forward to talking to you later, CeeCee. In the meantime, don't work too hard."

Cleo leaned forward in her chair. "You know, despite everything that is not so rosy between us, I have come to appreciate your sense of humor, Kennedy."

She began walking to the door, then with a wicked smirk on her face, murmured, "I know you do."

⚢ 45 ⚥

"I'll have a Caffè Vanilla Light Frappuccino." Kennedy turned to Cleo, giving her that irresistible, I-wanna-fuck-you look in her eyes, seductively licking her lips.

"And you?"

Cleo unconsciously licked her lips and winked at her before turning her gaze to the barista. "I'll have what she's having, please."

"No problem," Keegan, the barista said. "Can I interest either of you in any of our delectable pastries? Our Cuban pastry is our bestseller."

Both Cleo and Kennedy's mouths began to salivate. "Does it have cream cheese on the inside?" Kennedy asked.

Keegan's thin lips spread into a broad smile.

"Yes, indeed, it does, Miss. Should I get another one or are you going to share this one?"

"We'll share," they said in unison.

He reached into the refrigerator unit with his stubby hand, retrieved the pastry and placed it on a small plastic plate. "Will that be all?"

"Yes, thank you," she replied. "How much?" she asked as she dug into her purse.

"Are you paying for everything, ma'am?" Keegan asked.

"Yes," Cleo replied.

He looked at them both quizzically. "Okay, your order comes to $15.26, ma'am."

She pulled out a twenty-dollar bill and placed it in his hand. "Man, you're an expensive date," she teased, turning her attention back on Kennedy.
Looking yummy as always, she batted her eyes at her. "Well, what did you expect? This is Starbucks and we're in downtown Indy where every damn thing is expensive!"

"No argument there," she said, breathlessly.

"Here's your change back and thanks for coming. Enjoy," Keegan stated.

"Thanks, Keegan," they said in unison, again.

"Let's head outside and enjoy the fresh air, what do you say?"

"Sure, why not. I just hope this time there won't be any interruptions like before," Cleo responded.

"Do I detect some irritation in your voice, young lady?" Kennedy was walking in front of her or more like sashaying.

"Boy, you've never been one to hide your true feelings, huh?"
Kennedy batted her eyes and smacked her lips.

"Naw, I never did to tell the truth." They chose a small table facing in the direction of the Soldiers and Sailors monument. Several people were milling about, some taking in the free-flowing waterfalls surrounding the monument, while others sat on the steps, looking gleeful as they took photos, laughing and chatting among themselves.

Before responding, Cleo took a sip of her Frappuccino as she took in the scene unfolding around them.

Kennedy chose the seat right next to her. "Cat got your tongue?"

Cleo managed a smile. "No, no, just checking out all these folks doin' their thang, is all."

"Um, I see," replied Kennedy. She nibbled on a piece of the pastry. "Oh, my God, this is delicious!" she exclaimed. "I can see why, or should I say *taste* why this is their number one seller, but I'm still waiting on an answer, CeeCee."

"Oh, just being here at this coffee shop reminded me of that time when we ran into your sister-in-law or should I say, she ran into us just before we were about to launch into a deep conversation, you remember that time, don't you?" she quizzed.

"Now it all makes sense," Kennedy said.

Cleo glared at her. "What are you talking about?" She watched as Kennedy readjusted her bosom in her wrap dress, obviously teasing Cleo.

"Ever since we first began seeing each other, I quickly caught on to how your attitude can suddenly change and how you stare off into space sometimes, like you're deep in thought. I didn't get it at first, but after spending as much time as we have together, I've gotten pretty good at picking up the different hints and clues about my sexy-ass lover."

More like stolen moments, Cleo thought, folding her arms and holding onto her anger. "Oh, so you really think you know somebody now, huh?" She could be so stubborn at times, just like her mother.

Kennedy, not wanting their time together to be tainted by something neither had control over, began tickling Cleo, knowing she'd give in.

"Okay, okay, stop it," she giggled.

"Oh, naw, don't stop. I'm enjoying this."

Cleo and Kennedy both looked at each other, then at the suited-up Caucasian man seated a few tables over.

"I've been watching you two ever since y'all walked into the coffee shop," he revealed. "And, if I may be so bold, I would love to see even more, that is, if I can get an invite."

"Excuse me? Who do you think you're talking to, you per—"

Kennedy cut her off, not wanting to draw any more attention to the situation than necessary. "No thank you. We're not interested."

He stood up and walked over to them, full white-man brazenness on display. "Ladies, ladies, please don't misunderstand me. I merely want to watch and I'm willing to pay." Standing at least six-foot-seven, square jaw and square shoulders and sporting a fresh cut, he looked like one of those models on the cover of a seedy romance novel.

His crooked smile revealed gleaming straight, white teeth and a tiny Medusa lip piercing.

Hmmm, that piercing sure seems out of place, Cleo thought, but it goes to show you to never judge a book by its cover.

"Pay? What do you mean, *pay*?" asked an incensed Kennedy. Meanwhile, Cleo sat there, too stunned to move or speak another word.
Did this dude just say he was willing to pay us? His unusual request had her floored as that kind of question had never been hurled in her direction before.

Uninvited, he took the liberty of sitting down at their table. "Look, I'm not trying to offend, please, believe me, it's just that I noticed the two of you when you walked in." He flashed that crooked smile, again. It was obvious he thought he had a way with the ladies. "You see, as someone very familiar with women who love women, I could tell the two of you share more than just a platonic friendship, so I was just thinking, you know, we all could have a little fun, is all and like I said, I am willing to pay handsomely to watch, say five hundred each." Again, he flashed that damn crooked smile of his, along with dragging his long, thick, pasty-looking fingers through his thinning blond hair.

Kennedy was not having it. "Look here mister, we're not interested, so you can get to steppin' right now."

"But, but, wait a—" he clamored, looking offended.

"No, there's nothing else to be said, dude." Cleo had come out of her frozen state. "Get the fuck outta here before I call the cops on your ass!"

"Cops? You'd really do that, call the cops on me, but we're just having a—" he stuttered, eyes bulging.

"Damn right, fucker, now go!" she demanded, standing up in defiance.

After seeing Cleo stand up, he stood up, almost knocking the chair down to the ground as he high-tailed it out of there.

"Ugh! The nerve of these mofos!" Cleo sat back down and took a swig of her beverage. "But, for real, did he really say he was willing to pay us a thousand dollars, though?"

Kennedy did the same. "I know right? That was some bold-ass shit right there, damn!"

"I tell ya, you just never know about these creepy males walking on planet Earth, especially the ones who believe they're white."

"You know, I've heard you say that a few times now, 'those who think they're white', what do you mean by that?"

Cleo took another sip of her beverage. "Great question, love. I learned it from reading Ta-Nehisi Coates, and it basically refers to the made-up concept that Europeans conjured up eons ago in the meek attempt of setting themselves apart from us and others whose skin is rich in melanin."

Kennedy looked perplexed, but also intrigued. "Oh, wow. I've never heard that before. Interesting. I've heard of that Coates guy, but don't know much about him or his work except his book, *Between the World and Me.*"

Cleo finished off her beverage. "Oh, yeah? Did you read it? He's a cool cat, very intelligent and a great writer. You should look him up sometimes," Cleo suggested.

"Okay, I'll add that to my to-do list," she said, winking at Cleo. "And no, I haven't read it, just heard people talking about it." Just then her cell buzzed.

Cleo starred in the opposite direction, looking wounded.

"Oh, it's him," Kennedy said, nervousness echoing in her voice. "Hi babe, what's going on?"

Cleo huffed and folded her arms. The realization that she was never going to have her all to herself hit her like a ton of bricks.

"Yes, I remember. No, silly I didn't forget about that. Okay, I'll see you later. What was that? Yeah, remember I told you I was gonna hang out with Cleo for a little while this evening? Yes, yes, I did tell you, honey, don't you remember? Okay, okay, I won't be out long. Okay, bye."

Cleo noticed exasperation etching in the corners of her delicate mouth. "Checking up on you, huh? After the shenanigans at Charade, he ain't trippin' on you being with me, the one who got his wife eating pussy, as he put it?" She watched as Kennedy glared at her as she put her cell phone back into her handbag.

"Look, you don't have to be like that CeeCee, damn."

"He said it, not me. I was just repeating what your husband said to us that day," Cleo replied, her voice filled with defiance. Feeling like her world was coming to an end, she got straight to the point. "You don't wanna do this anymore, do you?"

"Huh?" Kennedy stuttered, taken off guard.

"I can see it in your eyes. You don't want me anymore. You don't love me, anymore," she responded in an accusatory type of way. Like a thunderous storm, tears puddled in her eyes that had suddenly become red and swollen.

"Well, I, um, well—" Kennedy's skin lost all its color, making her look like a ghost. Her beautiful eyes darted around, unable to look at Cleo—a tell-tale sign she was deliberately being evasive. The silence was scorching, despite people buzzing around, laughing and talking all around them.

"Can I get you two ladies anything else?"

Upon hearing the barista's high-pitched voice, they both jumped, startled by the piercing sound of the woman's child-like voice, reminding Cleo of the old school vocalist Michel'le.

"No thanks," Cleo managed to get out, turning her head in the opposite direction. She did not want a stranger seeing her cry.

"Okay, well if you need anything just holler," said the barista, turning on her heels back towards the entrance.

Again, silence enveloped them for what seemed like an eternity to Cleo, who was still unable to say anything else.

"Well, um, CeeCee, I, um …" Kennedy's voice trailed off, unable to complete a sentence, either.

Cleo looked on as Kennedy's eyes began welling up with tears as well. *Oh, damn, this is the end. We're done, it's really over. I can't fucking believe it.*

"Okay, okay, I was hoping this wasn't going to be this difficult, but, well …"

"Well, what Kennedy? Just go on and say it." Cleo shifted in her seat, looking on as Kennedy seemed to find the right words.

"Please CeeCee, don't hate me. Please don't hate me. I don't know what I'm gonna do if you say you hate me. I … I … ever since that craziness went down at Charade, Bernard and I been goin' at it and after almost eighteen years of marriage, well, I really had to do some soul searching. I mean, I've known him since childhood, he was my high school sweetheart and now we have children together, and, well … I had to get real with myself, Cleo."

"Damn, I can't believe this shit," Cleo muttered under her breath. "I mean I figured one day this was gonna happen, but, fuck, I just didn't think it would be so … so soon." She covered her face with trembling hands, then dropped her shoulders, completely and utterly thwarted.

Kennedy reached into her handbag again, only this time she retrieved a small traveling Kleenex container and wiped away her tears.

"Believe me when I say I've given this a lot of thought, Cleo, I really have, but I just can't leave my family," she stammered. "I'm so sorry, I really am, but at the same time, I don't want our friendship to end, please. I mean I understand if you need some time … well, come to think of it, and this has been on my mind too. All this hasn't been fair to you, what with me having family obligations and I knew it always bothered you that I could never stay the night and cuddle … as much as I always wanted to, but, well, you know …" Kennedy stopped mid-sentence and stared at Cleo, seemingly looking for a sign of something, anything.

"Cleo, are you alright?" Kennedy asked, waving her delicate hand in front of Cleo's face. "You have grown so quiet, something I didn't expect, but …"

"Well, I guess there's nothing left to say, Kennedy. I mean, really in the back of my mind I always knew this was just going to be temporary, I was just your experiment—"

"Whoa!" Kennedy interrupted. "Experiment, really Cleo? Damn."

Cleo rubbed the back of her perspiring neck, then readjusted herself in her seat. "Well, okay, in lookin' back on things, I can see why you'd think that, my bad, but damn, this ain't easy you know."

She looked on as Kennedy relaxed her spine and laid back into her chair, sipping on her beverage.

"Yes, I get it," Kennedy replied, giving her a sympathetic look.

"I suppose the word 'experiment' was a bit harsh, especially being that you and I were each other's first as far as female lovers go. It's just I so wanted to explore with you, be with you all the time, but, yeah, deep down I knew it really couldn't go anywhere." She downed the last of her beverage.

They both stewed over their feelings, looking on as people continued milling around, taking in an older couple boarding one of the horse-drawn carriages, the spunky wife looking like she was so full of life and love, it reminded Cleo of what she lacked, a genuine loving relationship, causing her even more heartache than she was already feeling at the very moment.

Cleo rose abruptly from her seat, "Okay, I gotta get going, Kennedy." She watched as Kennedy's eyes grew wider, seemingly teeming with hurt and regret.

"Wait a sec, CeeCee," she pleaded. "You never answered my question, can we remain friends, please?"

Cleo glared at her. "I'm going to need some time." And with that, she grabbed her backpack and began walking towards her Ridgeline, leaving Kennedy with her mouth hanging open.

⚢ 46 ⚥

"Hey girl, whatcha up to? How ya feeling?" Cleo implored. Cleo reached out to Shelby for a few reasons, one, to see how she'd been doing since she paid her a visit, and two, she no longer wanted to dwell on what just happened with Kennedy. *Better to focus my energy on someone else's issues rather than my own.*

"Oh, hey, CeeCee. I'm feeling much better actually, thanks for asking and I did finally schedule a counseling session as you suggested many times. I know it's high time I got control of my demons, so thanks for pushing me. I was in the middle of changing my sheets, Phredley's on his way over."

"Ah, so y'all still kickin' it, huh?"

Shelby laughed, "Yeah, I mean, ya know, he's been good to me, CeeCee, and honestly, I need the distraction."

But, damn, don't you think you need to take some time to yourself? You were just balling your eyes out the other day and not only that, you obviously got a lot going on mentally judging from what you wrote in your journal.

Cleo knew she could not say what was really on her mind so instead, she responded with, "A distraction you say? Alrighty then. I'll let you go, and I'll chat with you later."

"Okay, later alligator," Shelby replied.

****

Cleo drove home in a daze after the conversation she just had with Kennedy … a conversation that she was still grappling with. Once inside her home, she peeled off her clothes, flicked on the TV and grabbed her laptop. Okay, it's time for me to move on for real. A few minutes after logging into the dating site her cell jingled right next to her. *Who the hell is this bothering me?* She looked at her screen. It was a text from Craig, the negro who, at times, played the part of *Mr.* Suave-Super Lover,

WYD?

No, this nigga didn't. He got some fuckin' nerve, shit; ain't heard a peep out of him for weeks, but then again he was always good with pulling them disappearing acts. Damn bastard. I ain't got nothing to say to him!

She didn't respond and swiftly put his number on her block list. *I ain't got time for his bullshit, for real.* She continued scrolling through the site and stopped cold when she saw:

If you're curious about what lesbianism & bisexuality is all about, come join us, the Naptown Sistahs for our bi-weekly powwow. We'll engage in this intriguing topic over dinner, answer any questions you may have and we have resources at your disposal. It's time to build and lift our community, so come join us. Send us a message at 'naptownsistahs@networklist.com' to get details and location. We look forward to meeting you and feel free to bring a dish to pass!

The wee hairs on the back of her neck rose. *Damn, can it really be true? There's an actual social club for gay women? Well, it must be serendipity after what just transpired with Kennedy ... a sign that it really is time for me to move on.*

Cleo nervously opened up her email, clicked on the new message link, copied and pasted the address in the email address box, then slowly, methodically, typed her message. After penning the message, she sat and stared at it for several moments, contemplating on whether or not to send it. *Well, this is something I've been thinking about for a long time, anyway, and here's an opportunity for me to really dig in, see what being with other like-minded women is all about, sharing, learning ... playing.* "Fuck it," she muttered to herself, then clicked 'send,' instantly feeling waves of exhilaration.

She continued scrolling through the personal ads while listening to Trevor Noah go in on that orange thing for the umpteenth time on *The Daily Show*. After a half an hour passed, she heard her email notification. It was a Naptown Sistahs rep thanking her for contacting them, along with a few more tidbits about their newly established group and the address, date and time of their next get-together: this Sunday at six o'clock. *Whoa, this Sunday?* Cleo rubbed her chin. *Damn, I don't know if I'm ready; seems so soon after Kennedy. But shit, then again, she was really never mine to begin with, so...Guess I will be going...*

⚢ 47 ⚥

Perspiration soaked Cleo's shirt. She was about to embark on something she'd never experienced before: a potluck for women who love women, and she was nervous as hell. And, to top it all off, she didn't have anyone to confide in since she and Kennedy went their separate ways. Her BFF was still in the dark about her budding lesbianism, too. Cleo recognized the time was near as she was feeling more and more comfortable each day with the changes she was experiencing inside herself.

Her sexual feelings had gone through a complete metamorphosis right before her eyes. But she never saw it coming, which, of course, was a bit unnerving, but nonetheless, she knew it was happening. It made her wonder if other women—or even men, for that matter—had experienced the very same thing, going from one hundred percent heterosexual to the opposite end of the spectrum or somewhere in-between. After experiencing such a metamorphosis, she also reflected on the infamous Kinsey study done back in the '50s that revealed many people were neither all the way straight, nor totally gay.

According to what the researchers discovered, sexuality is *fluid* and can change at any point in a person's life. There was only one way to get past her jitters: get out of her truck and walk to the door. Cleo glanced in her rearview mirror one last time, then grabbed her purse and a bag of Doritos she'd picked up from Kroger on her way to her destination.

Well, here goes nothing ...

"Hola!" the short light-skinned cutie said upon opening the door. "Bienvenida. Mi casa es su casa. I'll take those chips if you'd like."

Cleo was a little taken aback upon being greeted in English and Spanish, but she was sure glad she remembered the little Spanish that she'd taken back in her high school days.

Cleo handed her the bag. "Gracias."

"My name is Zarita, and you are?"

"Hello, my name is Cleo."

"Hola, Cleo. This is your first time, isn't it Señora?"

Cleo rubbed the back of her neck, then shifted from her right leg to her left. "Um, yeah. How did you know?" she asked.

Zarita giggled a little. "Oh, honey, I have a photographic memory," she replied, then took the black hairband off of her left wrist and proceeded to thrust her thick mane up into a ponytail.

"I remember every single face that steps through our door." She was wearing very short shorts and a thin, white tank top that clung to her body, her small, firm breasts stand at attention could easily be noticed. A pea-sized dark brown mole appeared below her tiny button nose and her large, round almond eyes danced under the foyer's soft chandelier's light. Her skin glistened like pure honey.

A lump had developed in Cleo's throat. She was beginning to wonder if she'd made a mistake, but there was no turning back now.

Cleo laughed nervously as she tried desperately to keep her eyes from focusing on Zarita's sexy chest. Instead, she turned her attention to the heavenly black angel painting hanging on the wall. She homed in on the artist's name, *Leanna Conway*.

"That is a beautiful painting. Do you know the artist?"

A wide grin appeared on her pudgy face. "Why, yes, I do. Leanna is my wusband."

Cleo had a blank stare on her face. "Your what?"

Once again, Zarita giggled, took her hand and guided her to the living room. *"Tienes mucho que aprender, Muchacha."*

Okay, Cleo's memory wasn't that good. Outside of *muchacha,* she had no idea what she had just said to her, so she just nodded her head. As they headed towards the living room area, a Salsa-inspired number could be heard coming from the surround sound speakers. Upon entering the spacious room, Cleo was immediately taken aback by the scene unfolding before her very eyes. Could there really be that many black lesbians in Nap? Her lil' mind was blown. So much chocolate; she was beside herself with the variety of women staring back at her.

"Hey, everybody, meet Cleo. It's her first time, so all you vultures in the room, please don't scare her off!" Zarita said, then walked over and set the chips Cleo had given her on the table, along with all the other snacks.

"Hello, Cleo," everyone said in unison.

"Ah, damn, Zarita. Why would you say that to us? Ain't no vultures in this room. At least not yet." Cleo saw the tall, slim boyish-looking, ebony-complected woman standing by the ornate ivory-colored fireplace. A few moments later, the woman headed toward her.

"Greetings Cleo. I'm Ceason." She stretched her right hand out. "Nice to meet you—and welcome." Cleo was struck by her height. She had to be close to seven feet tall—like Brittney Griner tall, at least. "Hi, did you say your name was Season as in it's about to be fall season?" Cleo asked as she returned the friendly handshake.

Ceason let out a low grunt. A kind of a chuckle. She was dressed in a dapper ensemble, deeply pressed and cuffed black jeans, a checkered Oxford shirt and a purple bowtie. Her hair styled in short, neat twists and black-rimmed eyeglasses finished her look. Very attractive, indeed.

"Um, no. It's spelled with a 'C' instead of an 'S', but don't fret. People get it wrong all the time, so I'm used to it."

"Hmmm. Ceason," Cleo repeated, then sat down in a chair by the table with the snacks. "I kind of like it. Where did it come from?" she asked.

Ceason sat down across from her and crossed her legs. "Well, my mom claims she got it from some old romance novel she read as a teenager and from that moment on, she said if she ever had a girl child, her name was going to be Ceason." She shook her head.

Cleo reached for the chips and dip on the table. Nervousness howled deep inside her belly. She desperately tried to squelch it with food.

"Hey, she's not bothering you, is she?" asked the pretty and petite milk chocolate lady.

Cleo laughed. "No, she's not, but thanks for asking."

"Of course not, Chemine." Ceason folded her arms and pretended to pout. "How dare you insinuate that I would ever do such a thing."

Chemine extended her hand in Cleo's direction.

"Hello. I'm Chemine Goldnyk. We're so glad you decided to come join us this evening." Then, she turned her attention back to Ceason. "And, you, Miss, everybody saw you make a beeline to Cleo, so quit playin' like we don't know." She reached in and rubbed the top of Ceason's head who in turn blushed like a little schoolgirl.

Good. At least these women have a sense of humor. She was glad to see they were not all stuck up and mean. In her experience, far too many black women tended to be very standoffish, especially when they didn't already know you.

A short time later, two more women walked through the door holding brown bags, undoubtedly filled with liquor. One of them she recognized immediately: the cutie in the green Mustang.

Cleo's eyes widened, but she stayed frozen in her seat. Miss Green Mustang recognized her immediately, too, but said nothing. However, her mesmerizing eyes were telling another story.

"Whaddup, whaddup, my peeps," said the short, mocha-colored stud. "Did y'all decide on our topic for the evening, yet?" She set the two bags she had down on the counter that bridged the kitchen to the open living room.

Zarita approached her and landed a big, wet kiss on her lips, indicating that she had to be her 'wusband' Leanna. "I think we finally settled on *bisexuality*, sweetheart, just as we said already. How does that sound to you?"

Leanna wrapped her arm around Zarita's waist, then replied "Oh, that's fine with me, babe."

"Come, *Mi Amor*. There's someone I want you to meet." Hand in hand, they walked over to Cleo. "Cleo, this is my boo Leanna, Leanna, meet our new guest of the night, Cleo." Zarita's cute, pudgy face was beaming, and her eyes danced as they had earlier. She was clearly enjoying herself.

"Nice meeting you, Cleo. I hope you're having a good time, thus far." The two engaged in a cordial handshake. Cleo was quickly taken by Leanna's smoldering teal eyes. She had always been a sucker for pretty-eyed men, but now it would seem the same could be said for her budding taste in women, as well. Leanna's eyes alone would be reason enough to get close to her; they were absolutely captivating.

"Thank you, Leanna. I'm having a pretty good time getting to know everyone. Also, I wanted to say that you are a very skilled artist. The first time I saw your work was at StarWing's grand opening." She glanced over in Miss Green Mustang's direction who was looking good enough to eat dressed in all black attire.

A wide grin appeared on her face, revealing a large gap in between her two front teeth. The bejeweled tongue ring twinkled every time she opened her mouth.

"Oh, thanks. I'm glad to you're enjoying yourself. If you need anything, just ask. Again, we're so glad you came."

Cleo smiled at her, then turned her direction back towards Miss Green Mustang who still had her eyes locked on her but kept her distance. Cleo was beginning to wonder why. She was positive she recognized her. So, why not just approach and say hello?

Damn.

"Um, Cleo, did you hear what I said?" asked Ceason, who was waving her hand in front of Cleo's face. She was so enthralled with looking at Miss Green Mustang that she forgot all about her.

"Oh, sorry, Ceason. I didn't hear you, what did you ask me?" Cleo adjusted herself in the chair and made herself stop the staring match that was going on between herself and Miss Green Mustang.

If Miss Green Mustang wants to talk to me, then she's just gonna have to make the first move. I don't know anything about being in the life, so it's up to her to make the first move.

"I asked if you were from around here," Ceason asked for the third time.

"Well, yes and no. I was actually born in Toledo, but my family relocated to Indy when I was about ten." She bit into the finger sandwich that Chemine gave her. "So, I consider Naptown my home. How about you?"

"I'm an army brat. My parents were both in the service. The Air Force to be exact. So, as you can imagine, we moved around a lot."

"Oh, yeah, I bet you did. You probably didn't attend the same school for too long, either, huh?"

Ceason became visibly upset, tears welled up in her eyes. Cleo was dumbfounded. *Was it something I said?*

Automatically, Cleo reached over and touched her on her thigh. "Are you alright?" she asked, her voice filled with concern.

Right at that moment, Cleo looked over Ceason's shoulder and saw Miss Green Mustang staring intently at their interaction with a puzzled look on her face. Some freckle-faced redbone chick was trying to chat her up, but it was clear all her attention was on the exchange unfolding between Ceason and Cleo.

"Um, yeah, yeah, I'm fine. I'm fine," she insisted. "It's just that, well, your question stirred up some old feelings inside me that I hadn't felt in a very long time, but, hey, really. I'm okay." Ceason's eyes darted back and forth between Cleo and Miss Green Mustang. She apparently noticed the muted synergy between the two and wasn't liking it at all.

Uh, oh. What have I done now? Cleo had to force herself to focus on Ceason instead of Miss Green Mustang. It was not her intention to disrespect Ceason who, over the last hour had managed to settle her nerves. Besides, she was paying her attention and what woman doesn't invite that into her space?

Cleo readjusted her chair once again so that she would no longer be facing her potential wooer. "So, how long have you been attending these meet-n-greets?" she asked.

Ceason's contorted face turned to stone in a matter of seconds, making Cleo flinch.

"Do you know her?" she demanded.

"Huh? Who?"

You know who." She gestured her head toward Miss Green Mustang. "You've been staring at her ever since she walked through the door."

Cleo shuddered. *Damn, had it been that obvious?* She immediately became self-conscious. Her jittery eyes surveyed the room as she nervously began twirling her hair. Had anyone else noticed her staring at Miss Green Mustang? Cleo's throat developed an incessant scratch that would not go away. She grabbed her half-empty bottle of Dasani and took a long gulp. "Um, no, I don't think so."

Ceason's unending glare ripped right through her, deflating her very being. Could she tell she wasn't being *totally* honest with her? Cleo took another drink of water.

"Well, I, um—"

"Are you alright Cleo?"

She turned around and looked up into the eyes of none other than Miss Green Mustang.

Before she could give a reply, Ceason jumped up and went in on her. "Excuse me, Taj, but no one called you over here." She pointed her long, thin finger in her face. "See, that's your problem. You always tryna play Captain-Save-A-Ho, but nobody needs you to come rescue them."

Did she just refer to me as a 'ho'? Cleo said to herself.

An eerie quietness settled across the room. Cleo nervously blinked as she backed away, watching the shocking scene unfold before her very eyes. *Oh, so that's her name. Taj. I wonder if it is her given name ... nah, no way. No sensible mother would actually name her child that. It's got to be short for something or maybe even just a nickname.*

Taj balled up her fists. Her glare was stone-cold as they stood toe-to-toe. "Girl, I'm telling you right now, don't make me whip your ass like I did a few months ago. I know you don't want to revisit that unfortunate encounter."

Anger smoldered in Ceason's emerald-green eyes. "Fuck you Taj. You just got lucky that day 'cause I was a lil' drunk, but don't think for one minute you can take me like that again."

"Alright, alright, gentlewomen." Leanna stepped in and took control of the ugly situation.

"There ain't gonna be no fighting up in our house tonight, so either drop it now or get the fuck out." Though she was short in stature, confidence exuded from her as she gave both of them the *look*.

Taj stepped back and smiled. "Ain't no thang, cuz. You're right. It's not that deep." She gave Ceason one last hard glare, then walked over to Cleo. "Sorry about that, sweetie. You shouldn't have had to be exposed to that type of ugliness, especially with this being your first time coming to one of our meet-n-greets."

Cleo's body trembled with fear. Suddenly, she wished again that she had not come. It would seem that her presence was the cause of the ugly encounter. The thought made her stomach gurgle. She began feeling like she would be overcome with the collywobbles at any moment. She stared deeply into Taj's amber eyes, searching for something, though she wasn't sure what that was.

"Hey, you don't look so good. Let's get you outside for some fresh air." Taj grabbed her hand and escorted her through the thick crowd.

It took all her might to keep her shaking legs from buckling. Hushed tones and piercing eyes dotted the room as they passed through.

"Lee, I'm gonna take her outside for a lil' while to get some air." She looked down at her with concern, then returned her attention to Leanna. We'll be back shortly."

"No problem, Taj," she tipped her Corona bottle and nodded her head.

Taj grabbed her jacket off the coat rack by the front door. "Did you bring a jacket or sweater? The temp has dropped down big-time, sweetheart."

"No, I meant to grab it before I left home, but forgot."

"Well, let me know if you get too chilly and I'll let you wear my jacket, all right?"

Cleo nodded *yes* as Taj led her out the door.

⚢ 48 ⚥

It was mid-September in Indy, meaning that it could be sixty-five degrees outside, sun shining brightly and not a cloud in the sky, but by nightfall, the temp could plunge as much as ten degrees or more.

Still holding hands, they strode along in silence down the canal heading towards New York Street. Periodically, they glanced at each other and smiled as they treaded along the cement walkway punctuated by vintage streetlamps, lush green trees and the murky canal water.

"So, where are you from?"

"I'm from a town not too far from here, Terre Haute. Have you heard of it?"

"Of course, silly. It's only about an hour from here," Cleo responded.

Taj laughed. "Well, eh, not everybody's heard of my lil' hometown, despite the fact that ISU is located there."

Why was she feeling like she already knew this woman? Perhaps they were long-lost lovers in a past life? Could it be?

"Yes, you're right. It's not like Terre Haute is another Chicago," Cleo teased.

"How about you? Were you born a Hoosier?"

Cleo smirked and ran her fingers through her hair. "Well, that would be a *yes* and *no*. I was born in Toledo, but my family moved here when I was little. So, because I have lived here most of my life, I do consider myself a Hoosier."

Taj stole a look at her. "My God, you are so fine."

Cleo blushed. "Thank you, Taj. You're a very sexy thang, too, ya know." She reached over and touched her cheek. "By the way, what is your full name?"

"You first," she deflected.

Cleo took a mental note of that but didn't question her. "My name is Cleo Saraphene Stinson." Pride shined in her eyes as a wide smile spread across her face. "I'm named after my dad, Cleofus."

"And, what about Saraphene? That's really different, er, I mean unique," Taj commented.

Laughter rolled through her body. She was used to this kind of response to her middle name. "Well, my mother came up with that one. Sara is her favorite aunt's name, and she adores Josephine Baker, so she decided to combine the two."

Taj nodded her head. "Oh, that's cool. Lynn Whitfield rocked in that leading role! I loved watching that movie and learning about Miss Josephine and the fabulous life she led over in Europe, complete with lions and shit! Hell, I even heard that she liked to dip and dab, too. I would have been a willing participant, fo' sho'!"

Cleo poked her in the stomach. "Alright, now, you need to quit it, lady! And, what do you mean by 'dip and dab' … in what?"
Just then, their conversation was interrupted by out-of-control teenagers screaming, jumping, and pretending like they were going to push each other into the canal's dark water. They looked at one another knowingly, both recalling their crazy, topsy-turvy teen years and somewhat impatiently waited for them to pass by.

"Oh, I heard she liked to get down with women just as much as she did all them men that lusted after her," she responded matter-of-factly.

Cleo doubled over in laughter. "Please tell me you're not one of those people who believe everything they're told or read," she pleaded.

Offended, Taj folded her arms. "Of course not, woman. I'm just sayin', shit … it wouldn't surprise me at all if she indulged from time to time back in the day. Lord knows she wasn't the only popular star who was gettin' their groove on back in the day."

"Touché, touché. So, back to you. What's your full name?"
Taj winced.

"What's the problem?"

"Well, it's just that I really don't like my name, 'cause it's so … so dopey."
Cleo wasn't buying it. "Spill it."

Taj shifted in her seat and scratched the back of her neck. "Oh, alright, alright, jeez! "She redirected her eyes to Indy's cityscape. The pyramidal cap on Chase Tower glowed under the piercing moonlight. "Tajohnna Prudence Mildred Campbell," she whispered.

"What? I couldn't hear you."

"Tajohnna Prudence Mildred Campbell," she repeated a little louder.

Disbelief blanketed Cleo's face. "You got two middles names … why and who are you named after?"

Relief seemed to flood Taj's face. She apparently expected a different response from her. "Both my maternal and paternal grandmothers."

"Oh, okay. That's cool."

"Hey, guess what?"

Cleo knew she was changing the subject but didn't let on. Instead, she looked into her beaming eyes.

"What, Taj?"

They had just approached the softly lit glass war memorial. "My great uncle's name is etched into the memorial, believe it or not." A broad smile appeared on her face, revealing a set of upper braces. Cleo had not noticed she was wearing braces until that very moment.

"Oh, that's way cool. Show me where it is then!"

Taj led her to the opposite side of the ship-inspired memorial and pointed out his name,

"Abraham Cornell Jenson." She stroked the etching with her long slender fingers, obviously reminiscing.

"Wow, that's pretty sweet, Taj. I take it you had the chance to get to know him before he passed on?"

"Yes, indeed, I did. He was like a father to me. My whole family just loved him. He told us so many fascinating stories about his time in the service, things you would not believe, Cleo." Tears welled up in her soft eyes as she spoke of her great uncle. "He was one of a kind, ol' Abraham."

They strolled over to a wrought iron bench close by and sat down. "Oh, I'm sure he was, I'm sure he was," Cleo replied. Several minutes passed by as they sat in silence, each focusing on their own thoughts. Shortly thereafter, a young family walked by heading towards the memorial. The family patriarch stood about six feet tall with cocoa skin and a military-buzz haircut, while his short, round wife with long flowing soft curls walked with an infant strapped to her chest. A pudgy toddler who looked like a little chocolate morsel tightly held onto his mother's leg. They nodded their heads at Taj and Cleo. "Hello," Cleo smiled. "You have a beautiful family."

"Thank you," the smiling couple said in unison. Though she was happy to witness such a lovely black family, she couldn't help but feel that incessant aching in her heart. Seeing them reminded her of what she was missing in her life.

"Hey, you okay?"

Cleo jumped. Taj's voice startled her. She immediately felt stupid and did her best to play it off. "Oh, yes, yes. I'm fine, really." She re-adjusted her body on the bench.

"You're right, Cleo," Taj rose off the bench and watched the patriarch point to a name on the memorial just as she had done moments ago. "They really are a beautiful family."

"Um, yeah, they sure are," she managed to say.

"Anyway, enough about the beautiful family, let's talk about you."

Taj rubbed the back of her neck and let go a low grunt. "How about you start first? I've been wanting to know more about you since the first time our eyes met in that parking lot at Culver's so long ago."

Cleo grinned ear to ear. "Oh, so you do recognize me?"

She walked back to the bench and sat down next to her. "Of course, I do. How could I forget?" She reached over and gently stroked her rosy cheek.

"I've been thinking about you ever since that day, but never thought I'd get the opportunity to talk to you face-to-face."

Her confession made Cleo blush. The grinning on her face intensified. "Okay, well, dang, where should I begin?"

Taj reached for her hand. "Wherever you want. I've got all night, baby girl."

"Wow, um, okay," she replied.

Cleo took Taj on a journey about her life beginning with her parents, siblings, and nieces. During their exchange, she did not interrupt but simply listened, really listened intently to what Cleo openly shared with her.

Cleo would later learn Taj would not be as forthcoming about her life story.

****

"Well, well, well. Y'all decided to join us again, cool," Leanna observed as the two walked through the door. She then took a quick swallow of some kind of mixed drink she was holding in her hand.

Taj smiled. "Real funny, Lee. I told you we'd be back, didn't I?"

Leanna looked back and forth between them and broke out into a loud, piercing cackle, affirming she was drunk as a skunk.

"Vamos, baby, leave the two lovebirds alone, now." Zarita approached them, and then swiftly yanked Leanna down the hallway.

Taj shook her head, then reached down and grabbed Cleo's hand as they walked back into the living room. The crowd had gotten a little smaller, but that didn't stop a few of the remaining ones who were going back and forth about the night's chosen subject.

"I just think it's disgusting and there ain't nothing you can say to make me change my mind, for real!" exclaimed the redbone chick that was trying to mack Taj earlier. She became visibly upset upon seeing Taj reenter with Cleo.

"Well, I'm telling you that it's not nasty. Why do so many lesbians, especially black ones think that about bisexual women? I just don't get it," said another young stud dressed in hood attire. "Shit, I used to think like you, Naylena. I dated a bisexual woman once and she schooled me on the real deal."

Oblivious, Cleo smiled at Redbone, who in turn rolled her eyes and folded her thick, hairy arms. Taj ignored her and led Cleo to the sleek black leather loveseat on the opposite side of the room.

"Oh, really? Must've been a white heifer. Everybody knows you like them pink toes, Jumanne," Naylena retorted.

"Would you like another Dasani or something stronger?"

Cleo sank into the loveseat. "You know, I think something stronger would be great. Surprise me," she replied. The perpetual feeling of fluttering butterflies made her feel very gleeful. She'd finally met the one woman that caught her attention on that fateful day back in February. Quiet as it was kept, a lot of fluttering was going on in her pants as well, but she fought hard to keep it on the down-low.

No words could explain what I'm suddenly feeling inside. I'm beginning to understand what I was feeling for Kennedy was not 'love' ... I mean I did care for her, enjoyed our fleeting moments together, making me believe it was love, but now that I'm here with Taj, Miss Green Mustang, I now see we were destined to be together. But, damn, it's so hard for me to comprehend the astronomical somersaults going on ever since I first laid eyes on Taj when she and Leanna walked through the door. How could a WOMAN make me feel like this? It's just mind-boggling, but I'm already feeling a connection to her and even to this lesbian thang. Fuck! My mind is inundated with questions ... I can't even deny it. But I know one thing, it's time to learn more about this LGBT culture I'm slowly, but surely becoming a part of ...

Jumanne gawked. "Whatever, hater."

Naylena stood up and stretched her ill-built frame. Cleo could not believe how hairy she was. A shadow of a beard could be seen on her narrow face, along with those dark, ugly hair bumps. No wonder Taj rejected her, Cleo thought.

"Naw, seriously, Jumanne. Tell us what pink toes shared with you. You done stirred up my curiosity now, shit." Empty beer bottle in hand, she shuffled over toward the liquor table, tossed the empty bottle in the trash, then grabbed another Bud Light.

Another woman chimed in. "Yeah, Jumanne. Tell us what your ex shared with you."

Jumanne reached for her red cup on the coffee table. "Alright, people. First of all, I know some of you folks believe bisexuals are promiscuous. That's totally not true." Excitement beamed in her huge, bubble-like sapphire eyes as she continued speaking truths about bisexuality. "Some folk believe that it's not natural; that no animals are bisexual. Truth is that most animal species are bisexual in much higher percentages than us homo sapiens."

Naylena laughed out loud. "For crying out loud, are you fucking kidding me right now, Jumanne? Do you really think we're that *stupid* as to believe this bullshit you spittin'?"

Jumanne brushed the waves on top of her head, then leaned forward in her chair. "I really don't give two shits if you believe me or not. It's called *research*. If you don't believe me, then go on and conduct your own and see what you come up with, that is, if you even know what the word *research* means and *how* to do it."

Naylena rolled her eyes at Jumanne. "Umph! Yes, I know what research means and how to do it, thank you very much, smartass."

Jumanne gave her a wicked smile, then leaned back into her seat, sipping her drink. "One last thing I'll say about bisexuals and then I'ma leave it alone. Far too many feel like they are a big reason why HIV/AIDS have spread like it has, especially among black women and men, for that matter. But the truth is unprotected sex is the culprit, period. Mofos need to wrap that shit up and sistahs need to do a better job of protecting themselves out here in these streets." She looked over at the woman who had asked her to explain herself earlier. "So, what do you think of them apples, Cillian?"

Cillian sat across from Jumanne by the snack table. Tall and slim with high cheekbones and a short blond pixie cut, she reminded Cleo of a supermodel. "Well, I have heard some of the stuff you just said, but I suppose if I really want to know more about it, I need to do as you suggested—conduct my own research."

Jumanne nodded her head in agreement.

"How are you doing?" Chemine asked as she sat down next to Cleo.

"Oh, I'm good, Chemine. Thanks for asking." Cleo gave her an assuring look. She then found her eyes searching the room for Taj but she didn't see her.

"She went to the bathroom. She asked me to tell you that."

Once again, Cleo found herself blushing. "Oh, okay."

"You really diggin' Taj, aren't you?" She gave her a perplexed look while sipping the mixed cocktail she held in her right hand, staring deep into Cleo's eyes. "Did you two already know one another? Inquiring minds want to know."

"Um, well, in a way, yes."

"What do you mean?"

"Well, you see, we first laid eyes on each other at a Culver's parking lot way back in February but didn't get the chance to talk until now."

Chemine nodded her head. "I see. Well, there must've been some kind of spark at that parking lot 'cause folk already talking."

Cleo looked at her, anxiety etched in her face. "What do you mean by *talking*?"

Just then, Taj returned. "Hey, what are you two talking about?"

"Nothing, silly. I was just chattin' up our new friend here while waiting for you to return," Chemine replied.

Taj handed Cleo a red cup filled to the brim with what looked like sangria. Cleo accepted the cup, then stuck her nose in it to get a whiff. Taj giggled and confirmed that it was indeed sangria.

Cleo took a long sip of the magenta-hued beverage while pondering Chemine's unsettling words. Chemine rose from Taj's spot on the loveseat and gave Cleo a reassuring look as she pressed a piece of paper into her hand.

"Don't forget to call me, okay?" She winked at her and then headed over to talk to a few women standing by the opened balcony doorway.

Taj settled down next to her and took a swig from her Corona bottle. "Hey, babe, what was that all about, did she upset you or something?"

Babe. She called me babe. Wow.

Cleo downed another gulp of sangria. It burned just enough to let her know it had a fair amount of rum in it. "No, no. Everything's fine," she lied. "We were just shootin' the shit, is all."

Taj seemed to pick up on Cleo's discomfort and switched tactics, "So, have you been listening to these chicks while I was gone? I could hear Naylena's big mouth while I was in the bathroom. That E.D. always got something negative or dumb to say," she stated.

"E.D.?" Cleo repeated.

Taj gripped her firm abs, letting jolly laughter fill the room. A few heads turned in their direction, obviously wondering what was so funny.

"Oh, I'm sorry babe. I forget sometimes not everyone has heard that term before and to be honest, I can't for the life of me remember where I heard it, either. The real word is 'earth disturber' and, basically it refers to someone who is always startin' some shit—like a troublemaker or a drama queen," she explained. "She and Ceason have earth disturber syndrome in common, but they certainly aren't the only ones in Indy's LGBT community."

"Oh, okay. That is an interesting term and no, I'd never heard it before." She smiled and made a mental note to add it to her vocabulary. "As a newbie to this kind of get-together and this topic, I can honestly say what Jumanne shared about bisexuality was very enlightening. I mean, I really never gave it much thought before. It's never been on my radar." She fingered her cup, then took another swallow. "It has certainly been a spirited powwow. I've learned a lot tonight!"

Delight danced in Taj's eyes. "Well, I'm glad to hear it, babe."

For the remainder of the night, they mostly talked among themselves, and only threw in their two cents from time to time on the subject. For Cleo, the conversation revealed how little she knew about bisexuality and secretly wondered if she was bisexual. She made yet another mental note to conduct research on the subject in the near future.

****

"You ready to go, sweetheart?"

Cleo's eyes popped open. She'd drifted off to sleep on Taj's shoulder. She sleepily rose and stretched her arms into the air. "What time is it?"

Taj glanced at her diamond-encrusted wristwatch.

"It's a little after 2 a.m."

She blinked her eyes several times. "What? Are you kidding me, it's really two in the morning?!"

Taj smiled, shook her head, and reached for Cleo's hand. Yes, beautiful. It is 2:12 a.m., to be exact. Why, is there somewhere you need to be?" Taj looked into her eyes, searching.

Cleo had no intentions of being out so late. But, then again, she had no idea she was going to run into the one woman who caught her attention months earlier, either.

"No, Taj. It's just that I really hadn't planned to be out so late." Taj's hand felt warm and smooth to the touch. She gripped it a little tighter and was overcome with raw emotion.

Damn, I just met this woman and already feel like she has a stronghold on me. What the hell?

Taj stood up, then reached out for Cleo's hand.

"Okay, good. I think it is time to call it a night. I gotta be at work at seven."

"Are you serious? You should've told me, Taj!" Cleo exclaimed as they bid farewell to the few stragglers that were still hanging around. Just before exiting, Zarita approached them.

"Señora, I hope despite what happened with Ceason, you'll decide to come back. We'd love to have you." She smiled and gave her a warm hug.

"I will, I promise." She returned the embrace.

Taj chimed in. "Of course, she'll be back. She's with me now." She possessively wrapped her arm around Cleo's waist.

Zarita and Cleo looked at her disbelievingly and shook their heads. "Oh, so even though you just had the pleasure of meeting Miss Cleo, you're already staking your claim, eh?"

Smugness appeared on Taj's face as she tightened her grip around Cleo's waist. "Damn, right. She's the one. This I know for sure."

Cleo's heart skipped several beats. She searched Taj's twinkling eyes and could see she was dead serious. Uneasiness settled inside Cleo, though she wasn't sure why because she was definitely feeling Taj and truly felt they had a connection. She was anxious to see where this new journey would lead them.

"Wow," she managed to say.

Zarita stepped back and put her hands on her hips. "Well, I hear you, Taj." She winked at Cleo. "Taj is a good woman, that much I know." She looked them both over. "I think you two may have something, but I will need to consult my crystal ball to learn more, though," she said, half-jokingly.

"Oh, boy. Time to go, for real. Good night, Z. Tell my girl I'll holla at her tomorrow sometime." She opened the door, stood to the side so that Cleo could walk out first. "Good night, Zarita. I appreciated the hospitality and look forward to the next time."

In response, she smiled. "Great to hear. We enjoyed having you, too."

⚢ 49 ⚥

The night's brisk air encircled them as they slowly walked to Cleo's vehicle, hand in hand.

"Nice ride," Taj said.

Cleo grinned. "Thank you. I absolutely love my Ridgeline." Cleo clicked the alarm button on her keychain.

Taj stepped in close and wrapped her arms around Cleo's waist. "I've truly enjoyed our time together and can't wait until the next time."

She returned the warm embrace. "I enjoyed myself, too. It was nice meeting so many cool women. My mind is still blown by the sheer number of black lesbians living here."

"Oh baby, you ain't seen nothing yet," Taj commented. "There are a whole lot of women who love women, not to mention the married ones creeping around, along with the ones who claim to be bisexual. Just you wait and see!"

She shook her head in disbelief, giggled, and laid her head on Taj's chest. *Damn, she smells so good, what is that she's wearing?* Cleo inhaled deeply, the fresh and fruity blend of delectable spice and bosk teasing the teeny hairs in her nose.

"Sweetie, what is that wonderful fragrance you're wearing?" Cleo looked up at her, their bodies still wrapped in a tight embrace, neither wanting to be the first to let go.

"Oh, you like that, huh?"

Cleo stuck her nose into her shirt and inhaled deeply again. "Mmmmmm, yes I do. What is it?"

Taj ran her fingers through Cleo's mane, sending a welcomed chill down her spine. "It's called *Black* by Kenneth Cole. You've never heard of it?"

"Yes, I have, actually, but I don't recall smelling it before. The scent is so captivating, I love it!"

Taj pulled her into her chest, so close that not even a credit card, as thin as it was, would fit in between them.

Several more minutes passed by, both relishing in the peacefulness of the moment, neither wanting it to come to an end. Suddenly, Cleo jumped. "Hey, you gotta be at work in a few hours, Missy! I so don't want this night to end, but I want you to get some rest. By the way, where do you work and what time do you clock in?"

Taj reluctantly let her go, and then fumbled for her car keys in her back pocket. "Right now I'm holding down three jobs. My main gig is Coca-Cola. I started working there almost fifteen years ago. I also work for FedEx on the weekends and clock in time is at seven. The last one is seasonal and it's at McGraw-Hill."

"Whoa!" Cleo exclaimed. "Why are you working three jobs and do you mean that place off North Michigan Road?"

A grin spread across Taj's face as the glowing light from the streetlamp bounced off her steel braces. "Well, pretty lady, there are things one wants in this life, starting with building a home and, yes, it is located on Michigan." She stared up into the twinkling stars in the sky, then redirected her eyes back to Cleo.

"Oh, so you wanna build a new home, huh?"

"Yes, I do. It's something I've been wanting to do for a long time," she revealed.

Cleo reluctantly slid into her Ridgeline. "Well, I think that is just fantastic! I have long wondered what goes on in the old Target building. So, what exactly do you do there?"

"We score standardized tests, like the ISTEP. You said that the building used to be a Target?" she asked.

"Yes, madam. In fact, I can take you way back about those buildings. Cleo was beaming with memories of yesteryear. "Target used to be Airway and next to it was Super X Pharmacy and on the far left was a Kroger!"

Taj's jaw dropped. "I had no idea. Interesting, very interesting."

"On the opposite side, there used to be a Linder ice cream parlor, a Fayva shoe store, and the list goes on and on, but we can get into all that some other time. You need to get home and get some sleep, young lady," Cleo said, with weak sternness in her voice because she wasn't ready to depart, either. "Again, it's been a wonderful night getting to know you and I look forward to the next time, Taj." She slid the key into the ignition and reached her hand out to Taj.

In turn, Taj gently kissed the back of her hand.

"My dear, it indeed has been a phenomenal night I won't soon forget. Thank you for finally coming into my life..."

She paused for a moment, searching for the right words to say next.

Emotions bombarded both women, then Cleo spoke up. "I know, sweetheart. No need to say anything except see you later."

Once again, Taj smiled, her braces twinkling in the moonlight. "See you later."

****

Cleo had no idea how she got home. She felt like she was in a very delightful dream that she did not want to wake from. On autopilot, she parked her truck in her garage, somehow managed to insert the correct key into the door lock, turned the key, and unlocked the door. She floated down the hall into her bedroom, her feet barely touching the ground.

Somehow, she undressed, slipped on her nightgown, then crawled into bed, all with a huge smile plastered on her face. She was on cloud nine. *Wow, I cannot believe that I only met Miss Green Mustang tonight. We made an undeniable connection. Ain't no telling where this road will lead us, but I am anxious to go on this ride and ride it till the wheels fall off!*

Suddenly, her cell phone began ringing, interrupting her thoughts.

'Taj' flashed on the screen, once again making everything alright in Cleo's world.

"Hello?" She was purring on the inside.

"Hey babe. You made it home safely?"

Cleo turned onto her back and clenched her legs closed, already feeling things down there.

"Yes, I did. Not sure how, but I did," she replied softly. "You're home?"

"Yes, I'm home. Just wanted to make sure my future wife made it home safe and sound. Now I can get some Z's so I can get up in a few hours and go to work. Sleep well, babe and I'll check in with you later today. Night, night."

Cleo was overcome with her emotions, relishing in the memories they made together earlier; she didn't even hear what Taj said to her.

"Hey, babe? You there?"

Finally, she snapped out of it. "Oh, yes, yes, I'm fine." She sat up and pulled the sheet closer to her neck.

"Okay. You almost had me worried when you didn't respond right away."

"Sorry," she murmured.

"Okay, babe. Sleep well."

"You, too, and have a good day at work. Goodnight."

"Thanks, nighty-night.

***Song Lyric Credits

More Bounce to the Ounce
Songwriters: Roger Troutman
Performers: Roger Troutman and Zapp Band
More Bounce to the Ounce lyrics © BMG Rights Management, Songtrust Ave, A Side Music LLC D/B/A Modern Works Music Publishing

Don't Be Afraid
Performer: Aaron Hall
Songwriters: Gideon Oakley Black / Nicholas Michael Black / Colton Fisher / Aaron Hall
Lyrics © Universal Music Publishing Group, Kobalt Music Publishing Ltd.

Rumors
Performer: Timex Social Club
Songwriters: Michael Marshall / Alex Hill / Marcus Thompson
Rumors lyrics © Emi April Music Inc., Universal Music Corp., Cicada Music Publishing, Electric Feel Music, Tracks Of Heavenly Music, Kmr Music Royalties Ii Scsp, Songs Of Universal Inc., One77 Songs, Jackie Boy Inc.
Just Be Good to Me
Performer: S.O.S. Band
Songwriters: James Samuel Iii Harris / Terry Lewis

Made in the USA
Monee, IL
08 November 2023

45952789R00224